HEART OF THE MATTER

Back in Affrica's room, the would-be couple argued.

"How could you say yes to him?" Alex asked.

"Alex, I had all the press in my face and people were taking pictures of me. I had to say yes."

"Why, Affrica? Why did you have to say yes? To . . . to Delroy?"

"Because he asked me in front of about a hundred people, most of whom had a camera aimed at my face."

"You lied to them all. You don't want to marry Delroy."

"It wouldn't be bad. We're so busy that we would never see each other."

Alex couldn't believe his ears. "You're actually considering it?"

"Alex, I have to go through with this."

"No! No, you don't have to go through with it."

"I'm doing it, Alex." She folded her arms across her chest and looked at the floor. When she looked back up at him, his beautiful face was contorted in disbelief. He kept shaking his head as if he didn't believe what he was hearing.

"And what about us?" he asked slowly.

"What *about* us?"

HEART OF THE MATTER

Raynetta Mañees

BET Publications, LLC
http://www.bet.com
http://www.arabesquebooks.com

ARABESQUE BOOKS are published by

BET Publications, LLC
c/o BET BOOKS
One BET Plaza
1900 W Place NE
Washington, DC 20018-1211

All Kensington Titles, Imprints, and Distributed Lines are available at special quantity discounts for bulk purchases for sales promotions, premiums, fund-raising, and educational or institutional use. Special book excerpts or customized printings can also be created to fit specific needs. For details, write or phone the office of the Kensington special sales manager: Kensington Publishing Corp., 850 Third Avenue, New York, NY 10022, attn: Special Sales Department, Phone: 1-800-221-2647.

First Printing: January 2002
10 9 8 7 6 5 4 3 2 1

Printed in the United States of America

Prologue

"Are you sure you could talk her into this?" the gray-headed gentleman asked his younger counterpart. "She's not some stupid girl."

"I've got her," replied Delroy Roberts in an attempt to reassure the old man.

The older man, August Watson, had for the last eight years been the Mayor of Passion, a small city in Michigan. He resembled Sean Connery, minus the accent, distinguished and respected in Passion. His gray hair was always brushed neatly back. His eyes were a warm blue kind. He had a strong handshake and looked people in their eyes when he spoke. The people of Passion loved and trusted him. He made great speeches and people overlooked his many faults.

The two sat in a dark blue Lincoln Town Car, government issued. They were in an abandoned parking lot behind a condemned plastic factory. The streetlight had been purposely knocked out. No one could see them, and they would see anyone approaching from a great distance. Mayor Watson turned to look at Delroy finally. The younger man stared straight ahead at the darkness ahead of them.

"I need someone in office that will continue

where I've left off. How are you going to talk her into this?"

"Affrica respects my opinions. She feels secure in our relationship," the young man whispered.

"I need certainty, Delroy. How can you be sure?" August did not usually put his confidence in anyone, especially one who would not look him in his eyes. August had no choice but to trust Delroy. He was desperate at this point. Affrica Bryant had to become the new mayor. He would have asked Delroy to run for office, but he felt the people would not vote for him, even with Watson's backing.

"Trust me, Mayor Watson, she's going to buy it. With both of us putting pressure on her, she's going to succumb. What about Ramona, will she talk?"

"I don't think so. We're safe. She's so scared of, uh, losing her job, and she won't tell anyone. Plus, I have some dirt on her that will keep her quiet as a mouse." Delroy nodded approvingly, his pinkie ring glinting in the moon's light.

Delroy was a graduate of Columbia University with a master's in social and political design. He always had high aspirations about becoming a politician. But New York held no opportunity for him politically. The closest he came to politics in New York was being an intern to a popular senator. He came back to Michigan and proceeded to work his way up the ladder at Michigan's Department of Business and Professional Regulation. For whatever reason, he could not get into any position of real power.

He was a good-looking man, with an obviously high-maintenance appearance. His rich dark skin glowed from the monthly cucumber facials he received. His mustache, beard, and fingernails were all meticulously groomed. He had what some people considered sexy bedroom eyes; the heavy eyelids made him look suspicious to others. They were beady little eyes.

His suits were all custom made. His body was chiseled. He worked out often in the gym, but his routine was for toning, not building bulk. He always thought that overly muscular men were not taken seriously intellectually. He drove a BMW with a shiny high-gloss, bone-color finish.

After serving the governor of Michigan for two years he returned to Passion, his home town. The mayor's then chief of staff had just resigned and moved out of state. Delroy got the position almost immediately. He supervised all of the mayor's department, attended city council meetings, and analyzed policies for accuracy.

The older man scrutinized Delroy. "Delroy, this has to happen; you have to get her to say yes."

For this operation to proceed, the mayor needed someone smart and greedy. He also knew he needed someone who would make love to a woman, then betray her for financial gain. August Watson knew Delroy pretty well. Though August could have easily won the election, Delroy was still an asset.

The mayor had watched Delroy closely before he asked him to join his team. Later Delroy became a part of the underground team that stole money from the mayor's own budget. That team included the city's treasurer, the police commissioner, and five other staff members.

The current budget was a mess, but seemed flawless. Maxwell Townsend was the treasurer. A graduate of Yale with a genius IQ, he was paid very nicely to be quiet. He doctored the books and used a lot of creativity to make it look as if things added up. For example, he told the office of emergency management that they had $1,900,000 in the budget in case of any disaster in Passion. In actuality there was only about $85,000 currently in the budget. The greedy mayor and his cohorts had stolen the rest.

There were two men in the police department who worked with August and the police commissioner. They were the middle men between a petty drug dealer named Jay Blow and an anonymous high-ranking official who was a distributor for a small-time Italian drug dealer.

The police chief was up in arms about the current state of affairs. The police department was crumbling, and crooked cops were being allowed to return to their regular beats. The police commissioner kept overriding the police chief's objections to certain people being on the force. The commissioner defended his overrides by citing statistics of rising crime and not enough police. The press didn't have any newsworthy events, so they drew attention to the increase in crime, causing the citizens to get in an uproar. Their homes were getting broken into and there wasn't enough money in the budget to hire more police. This led the police to get harsher and pick out potential criminals, and the newspapers began questioning the fact that the police department was being too harsh.

Though Mayor Watson knew he was a contributor to the crime and was involving the poor citizens of Passion, he quickly appointed his Deputy Mayor Affrica Bryant to investigate Michigan's finest.

The deputy mayor then, who would soon become the mayor now. The investigation produced nothing conclusive. Everything seemed stacked against her. No leads were found and sometimes entire file cabinets came up missing. She could not get any clear answers from the police departments. The police chief seemed more lost than she, and his secretary seemed unwilling to share any information she had. That was a lonely time in her life. She went to work with everyone glaring at her. The investigation ended when Affrica was redirected to new assignments. She couldn't have been higher.

Delroy and the mayor were still in the dark vehicle.

"Seriously, I've got her tied around my finger," Delroy said. The window was frosted from the cold.

The mayor looked him over in the dark. "Are you sure it's not the other way around?"

"I'm positive. I actually flew to see Evelyn and her folks. I'm going to go back to see her next week for five days. Affrica thinks it's a seminar. She trusts me. She believes whatever I tell her."

"Look, Delroy, you must not understand the gravity of this situation. I cannot run for mayor again. We need someone who knows everything and nothing. Someone who is secure in a position of power. Someone those people out there will vote for. I need someone who will listen to me—I can be her 'adviser.' "

"I understand, sir."

Mayor Watson turned around, his blood boiling. He did not feel that Delroy understood how serious this was.

"Listen, young man, there's millions of dollars invested in this . . . millions. Everything is really hanging by a very thin thread. If that thread gets shaken even a little, it's over and both of us will be going to prison for a long, long time." He held his hands to his face.

"I'm telling you this because we are friends." August did not believe they were friends. "We cannot fail. There's too much riding on this."

Delroy started feeling a sinking in his stomach, and his palms were sweating. *What the hell am I doing here?* he thought. He could not believe he had lowered himself to this level of dishonesty. But with the money he was going to make, he and Evelyn would never have to work again if they didn't want to. If his investments went well, his children would never have to work or worry about money. *Who would turn down two and a half million dollars?* It wouldn't all be in cash, but in a combination of mutual funds, certificates of deposits, bonds, and offshore accounts.

His only job was to persuade his "girlfriend" Affrica to run for mayor of a small city.

He had already convinced her that he loved her, and he had already fooled her into thinking he cared about her. They made love like normal people, they argued and went out to dinner like a regular couple. But Delroy was not really there. Affrica was making love to a shadow of a man. A figment of her imagination. The relationship she thought she had did not exist. Delroy defended his decision to use her and hurt her in the long run by pointing to the money, to the fact that he would be set for life, forever. *Who wouldn't do it for this kind of money? The only thing getting hurt is some feelings. Two and a half million dollars for some feelings!*

"I'm going to advise her to keep on everyone that's already in office. I'll tell her it will make her transition easier. Even when she reads the budget, everything will seem fine. Maxwell will deal with that part."

"Trust me, sir, we got her."

"All right, all right, good, good. Just take care of

her. I'm doing my part." The mayor sat up and placed his hand on the ignition.

"I think I've got her eating out of my hands, sir," Delroy said confidently.

The old man dismissed the young man with a shake of his hands and started the Town Car. He drove Delroy to his own car, which was not parked far away.

Twenty minutes later, Delroy pulled up to Africa's two-story brick town house. He spent a few nights there each week, going back to his house to collect clothes and call Evelyn.

She had left the front light on for him, a welcome beacon.

He tried to shake the guilt and wave off the fear that threatened to engulf him. He knew what he had gotten into was a big deal. But he had forgotten how big. He hadn't realized his life could actually be at stake and that he could disappear off the face of the earth or have a fatal "accident" because of this charade. He knew that the $2.5 million was pennies compared to the amount of money that was being risked. Delroy took a deep breath and rubbed his hands over his brown hair. He was ready.

One

Affrica Bryant woke up to a cold dreary morning. It was a little after six o'clock and it was the second time she heard her phone ring.

Today would be her first full day as mayor of Passion, Michigan. Without getting out of bed she turned toward the window. Her drapes were open and a faint, dingy light was entering the room. *Great,* she thought, *this is his how my first day is going to be. Dreary and sad.* She did not want to get out of bed. She stared at a picture of her grandmother for strength. Affrica's pretty dark brown eyes grew misty thinking about her. She had died two years ago.

The ringing phone snapped her back to the present. She wasn't getting it. Months ago she had removed the phone from her bedroom when she found herself in bed at two o'clock in the morning discussing electoral strategies with her boss, Mayor Watson. He liked to call late at night to talk about the election. He tried to school her on the ways of a political candidate. She accepted some of his suggestions, but others she didn't. She didn't like manipulating people for gain. She didn't care what she was running for. Affrica had started having bad dreams about the election, so in turn she had made the bedroom a "no business zone."

Affrica knew the person calling was either her mother or Ramona, her deputy mayor. Where was Delroy?

She rubbed her sleepy eyes like a child and stretched her arms gracefully over her head. She pulled off the lovely pumpkin-colored silk scarf that she tied to her head at night.

Last night Affrica kept dreaming about jumping out of airplanes. She would startle awake when she hit the ground.

Mayor, she thought, *I'm the damn mayor,* swinging her toned legs out of bed.

She did some stretches and deep breathing. She had on silk boxer shorts and a soft baby-blue tank top. She stood very straight, trying to center herself. Affrica eyed the smart wool suit hanging in the clear dress bag.

She surveyed her bedroom. Three large cardboard boxes were packed waiting for the movers. *I can't believe I have to move,* Affrica thought. She pouted softly. Affrica would be moving to the Mayoral Mansion, like all the previous mayors. The place was so stuffy and old. It was decorated like a museum. A large change for Affrica, who had her house designed with a warm, feminine touch. She had vases of dried eucalyptus in every room. Pictures of her heroes, Malcolm X and Harriet Tubman, adorned her living room, paintings by African-American artists were hanging up in rich frames. She even had one hanging in the bathroom.

This had been her grandmother's house. It was left to Affrica after she died. Most of her grandmother's furniture was still there. Beautiful antique dressers and tables. Her grandmother never went to antique stores though. She was a notorious flea market shopper. She would drive out of state sometimes if a really large bazaar or big antique convention was happening. Mostly she went to Chicago. For fifty or sixty dollars, she picked up a lot of nice pieces worth thousands of dollars. Her grandmother had had a great eye for antiques. Affrica kept all the furniture, changing only the couch, and had a large bed put in the master bedroom. After her granddad died, she had opted for a twin-size bed.

Affrica wanted to bring all her things. She would miss her own smells and comforts. She had packed all her favorite books, her Toni Morrison and Zora Neal Hurston books. She also packed her Bible, *Acts of Faith*, her video copies of *Soul Food*, and *Do the Right Thing*. Most of her clothing was already moved, and she insisted that she bring her own bed with her own pillows. She wasn't looking forward to living in that drafty mansion.

She couldn't understand the rule of having to live at that Mayoral Mansion. It wasn't even a real mansion. It was a very large colonial house with round-the-clock patrols and concierge. Past mayors would live there in the fall and winter, and when spring came they would alternate between homes. Affrica could not wait until spring. She touched the boxes as she left the bedroom. She was only taking two pieces of art and decided to take one painting and a three-foot-tall mahogany sculpture. Her mother had given it to her when she had come back from Ghana, West Africa.

She slowly made her way to the kitchen. Her brown skin got goose pimples as she left the warmth of the bedroom. She rubbed her face and turned on the coffeemaker. Habitually she reached up into the cabinet for her Blue Mountain Coffee, but realized she had already packed away most of the day-to-day food. *Damn.* She needed coffee. Affrica felt slightly panicked and sat abruptly on the wooden chair in her kitchen. Her kitchen window faced a beautiful backyard framed by a row of trees that gave the impression of the edge of a forest. She saw the morning sun peeking through them. It made her smile, even without the coffee.

Affrica had enjoyed being the deputy mayor. Before August had offered her the possibility of running for office, she was considering breaking up with Delroy and finally taking her bar exam. She even thought about leaving Michigan after Watson's term. Maybe go back to New York. So initially Affrica had resisted August's suggestion that she run for mayor. She thought is was a foolish idea and, having some experience of politics, she knew how difficult it was for people under thirty-five years old to win office. But August was persuasive, if not honest. He was very complimenting though. As time progressed she had started to think more about it. Mayor Watson had even offered her full control on the Irving Housing problem. She almost did it then, but she finally committed when Delroy started questioning her "loft principles."

"You would be in a position to do the most good. Why would you shrink from this opportunity?" he had said when she went to him with her reservations.

Delroy knew Affrica liked being challenged. He used reverse psychology on her. "I don't think you should listen to Watson. He's an old man."

"What do you mean by that?" Affrica had looked at him suspiciously.

"I'm just saying he might not know what he's

talking about. I mean you have no experience and you are young."

"Delroy, are you kidding me? I have so much experience working with August, and the people know me and like me. Me being young and a woman has nothing to do with this."

"I'm just saying . . ." He looked at her calculating and said the final thing he knew would put her over the top. "And you're black."

She had accepted the candidacy.

The living-room answering machine displayed four messages.

The first one was received at 5:45 A.M.

"Affrica . . . Affrica, wake up. It's past five o'clock . . ." It was Ramona, who sounded calm and ready to work. "You need to get your big ass out of bed . . . Okay, listen, I finished the speech. I added to some of the parts you wrote so you need to get up . . . now . . . Affrica? You have to be in the conference room before eight. You have to tell me how you're going to answer to the press about your inexperience. I wrote something on that too, okay? Call me as soon as you wake up . . . okay, bye."

How can Ramona sound so chipper at five-thirty in the morning?

Affrica yawned again, the sense of dread staying with her. She took a deep breath. The next message was her mother wishing her luck. Affrica smiled at the machine. Her mother was currently staying in New Jersey. A prisoner in Stone Brook Prison, who felt he was wrongly accused of murder, was telling her his story. She was going to find counsel for him and maybe a new trial if she could find enough evidence. She was also helping him write a book.

The third message was Ramona again and the

final message was from her best friend Holly Toreau, who was now in London with the Alvin Ailey Dance Troupe. When Affrica heard the voice she stopped the machine; she wanted Holly's voice to be the last one she heard before she left the house for her first day on the job.

She debated whether she should call Ramona back or take a shower. She knew she had more than enough time to practice her speech and get to the press conference on time. Affrica called Ramona.

"Finally, Ms. *Mayor.*" Ramona was already showered and dressed. She was applying a coat of mascara to her already long eyelashes. She had been up since 4:30.

"Girl, remind me why I said yes to be the mayor, again. I am not feeling good."

Ramona was one of the few people Affrica could speak frankly to. Even though Delroy was her boyfriend, Affrica's relationship with him was somewhat formal. "Please, no second-guessing." Ramona went straight to business. "Do you have a copy of the speech in front of you?"

"Ramona, wait. I haven't even brushed my teeth yet."

"It'll take two minutes. I know you know the speech by heart already. But the improvements I've made will make the speech a little more balanced. It's only a few things. I thought what you wrote was brilliant, I must say. But even brilliance can be improved upon." Ramona blotted her lips and smoothed her bun. She was done. Her round face was accentuated with a light touch of blush. Her lips were painted a muted red. She wore a dark blue Ann Taylor suit that held her form deliciously. The full girdle she wore modestly restrained her soft belly.

Wearily, Affrica went back to her bedroom and retrieved the ten-page speech from her nightstand. She had spent the whole night practicing and memorizing. She had a superb memory—she had it down pat. It was exactly fourteen and a half minutes long and outlined her radical plans for an overhaul of all the city's departments. She knew it could possibly cause some friction among the people she would have to work with for the next four years. But she thought they would understand; after all, most of them were underbudgeted anyway. They should welcome the change. The press would be able to ask her questions. The heads of the myriad city departments would be there, as would Delroy and that thorn in her side, Police Chief Bartholomew.

"Okay, I've got it." Affrica held the speech in her hand.

"So you see on page six, paragraph one; add the Department of Cable and Radio. We need to add at least one paragraph about cable and radio. You don't want them to feel ostracized."

"I thought we had something about that department somewhere in there."

"I know, me too. But in going over it, we didn't put in anything."

Affrica paced her shiny parquet floor, scribbling notes onto the paper. She started up her laptop and printer. "Got it. It's added. What else?" When Affrica's computer had finished loading, she entered all the changes and printed it up, leaving the printouts on the antique table.

A little while later she entered her peach-colored bathroom, with a towel over her shoulder. She turned on the bathroom light and stared at her reflection.

In college one of her boyfriends used to call her "ginger snaps," because her skin was such a rich dark color. Affrica had dismissed the cute term of endearment as being too childish. But that was the best way to describe her. Her natural hair was braided into elegant cornrows. She looked regal when her hair was braided. She rebraided them herself twice a week. One of the things her departed grandmother had taught her was how to braid, and braid well. Growing up, the young girls always asked Affrica to braid their hair. Her grandmother knew that someone who had hair that thick had better learn to braid it herself.

She touched the tight braids and smiled, satisfied with herself.

Affrica was a beautiful woman without being arrogant. Her warm eyes were delicately shaped, and she had a strong nose and a full, stubborn mouth.

She smiled and squinted at her image. She had inherited her dad's thick jet-black hair *and* his tendency to be a control freak and overachiever. She had inherited her mother's compassion and flawless skin.

Affrica began reciting her speech to the mirror audience. She imagined the facial expressions she would probably make and shook her head in disbelief.

Ramona was right. It all just happened too fast. Are they going to tell me it was an error? I didn't think I had a chance. People of the city loved Watson, but I did not think they would vote for me. Her thoughts were racing, going a mile a minute. Too many thoughts. She didn't want to be doubtful of herself. She felt a small sense of brooding. Affrica couldn't explain the feeling. She felt she had the necessary ability and drive to make a good mayor. But she knew for a fact there were others in Passion much more qualified than she. Delroy, for instance. He was older than she and had contact with every department in the mayor's cabinet. Why didn't Watson ask him?

When she had questioned Delroy about his feelings toward her possibly being the future mayor, he had challenged her. Delroy knew Affrica could not resist a challenge. Especially if someone told her she couldn't do something.

Affrica thought about Delroy and made a sour face. *He's so weird.* Sometimes he gave her the impression that he didn't think she could do it, that she couldn't be the mayor. Then he would turn around and act as if she were the smartest and most qualified woman on the planet.

She was still trying to figure out how to break up with him, but things were too hectic. *Once I get settled in office and I have a handle on things, I'm going to sit him down. I'll just have to deal with him for now.*

She couldn't put her finger on it. She just did not want to spend much intimate time with him anymore. He wasn't ugly, nor was he stupid. He could carry on a decent conversation, he was neat, and she did like challenges. Their business relationship was great. She rolled her eyes at the thought of having to work with him so closely for the next few years. *What if we broke up and had to work together?*

Affrica picked up her living-room cordless phone and dialed her mother's number in New Jersey. She answered immediately. Affrica felt instant nostalgia hearing her mother say, "My daughter the mayor."

"Oh, so you finally got that caller ID."

"No, I did not get it. Indinka got it." He was her mother's boyfriend. She called him her life partner; they refused to get married after having been together so many years. Together they sailed out to save the poor oppressed people of the world.

"How was the inaugural ball?" her mother asked brightly.

Affrica knew it was artificial; her mother cared nothing about balls. But she was trying to be supportive.

"It was fun, Mom. I wore red and talked business the entire night."

Affrica loved her mom dearly. She did not always understand her, but her mother had a huge heart and a giving spirit.

"So you ready? Don't let the press get you down, just because they challenge you. Challenges are good."

"I know. I'm as ready as I'll ever be."

"Good, you can do it. Black women are natural leaders. Look at who raises the children."

Affrica couldn't believe how encouraging her mother sounded. "Wait, who am I speaking to? Is this the same woman who told me I would get corrupted if I became mayor? The same woman who told me change was impossible once you became part of the evil ruling system?"

"I should not have said those things."

"Don't tell me you don't believe that anymore."

"No, it's not that I stopped believing that . . . it's just . . ." She was silent for a moment. "I believe in you."

Affrica felt her throat close and tears welled up in her eyes. "Oh, Mom."

The entire time Affrica was campaigning, her mother had been unusually silent, and when Affrica had asked her outright what she thought of Affrica's plan to become the mayor, she told Affrica she was selling out. She had not supported Affrica's campaign or her run for mayor.

"Affrica, I think sometimes I let my politics get in the way of my being a supportive person. I am sorry and I have all trust and faith that *you* will be that positive beacon of possibility that Passion needs." Her voice wavered but she did not cry.

"Thank you, Mom, I needed that. I was feeling so overwhelmed. Jerimia would be so proud of you." Affrica was sniffling lightly.

"All right, call me if you need *anything*. Don't worry about me, concentrate on what you are doing and call me when you get settled. Indinka says—I'll quote him, 'Peace, beautiful Nubian mayor.'"

This made Affrica laugh. Even as she hung up the phone and wiped her eyes, she felt refreshed.

Affrica had always been interested in politics. After graduating from Chicago University with a B.A. in political science, she had attended New York University's law school and returned to Passion ready to change things. She wanted to improve the lives of the poor, underprivileged in Passion.

She had spent most of her life in Michigan living with her grandmother.

Her mother had been heavily into the plight of the poor people of the world, but not really interested in staying home to play with her daughter. She was always going off to save somebody somewhere. Gwen Bryant had walked with Martin Luther King and gone to Woodstock to protest the war in Vietnam.

She was a very slim, light brown woman with dreadlocks to her waist and deep, penetrating eyes.

Passion was never big enough for her. So she

moved to Detroit, where she felt her skills could better be utilized. Even after the sixties Affrica's mother was still trying to organize people and motivate them to change their situations.

Affrica wanted to change too, but from the inside. Not doing rallies like her mother but going into politics, learning about the laws and the system. She wanted to work within the system to make dramatic positive changes in the life of people.

As her mother was radical, she was practical.

Her father and her mother did not get along. They were never married. He was an accountant and wore a suit and tie every day. He was a very strict man, who went to college late in life, but once he entered he was on the dean's list the three years he was there. He became a CPA six months after he graduated from school. He got his master's quickly after that.

When he had time he would pick Affrica up on weekends sometimes. They would sit watching movies mostly, sometimes they'd work on his yard, cleaning up leaves and debris. He continued to take her on weekends even after he married and had more children. Although Affrica was always grateful for his continuing presence in her life, she always wondered if there was more to him. She did not feel as though she really knew him. They were as different as day and night. Affrica still did not know how they had ever gotten together.

Affrica ran the hot water in the shower. She wanted to be mayor for the ability to really make some major positive changes in some people's lives. *Even if it's only a few hundred people.* She poured the rich almond soap onto a washcloth and scrubbed her skin. *People need to feel as if where they rest their heads is theirs. Restless children need a place to be besides school.*

She soaped and scrubbed her body, the water trailing down her flat stomach to her prettily painted toes. As she let the shower remove the tension she felt, she closed her eyes for a long time, going over the speech in her head. She turned the water off after she felt she knew it inside and out.

She stepped gingerly out of the steamy shower and wrapped herself in her favorite fuzzy white robe. She loved the robe, as it made her feel pampered. She only wore the bathrobe on special occasions like when she was going to a wedding, or going out to a party. She would keep the robe on while she combed her hair, painted her toenails. In the winter she would get nice and toasty, then change into her formal clothing. She knew Delroy hated the robe. He thought it made her look like a marshmallow, and a marshmallow was not sexy.

Oh, Delroy. He was getting on her last nerve. She wasn't really sure how to end the relationship. *I'm just not feeling him the way I used to. Even the sex last night; it was fun, but it was missing something.* Affrica could not place her finger on what exactly was missing. But she knew something was not right.

After her shower she rubbed her skin vigorously. She was still freezing by the time she got to her bedroom, two doors from the bathroom.

Affrica thought about the intensity her day was going to be. Her stomach jumped like a dolphin. Flipped around a little. She dressed slowly, making extra sure she didn't get a run in her stockings. She slipped the knee-length skirt up her nice legs and zipped the back. Glad she didn't have to hold in her stomach. She stood in her hot-pink bra. *Not bad.*

She slipped on her crisp white poplin shirt and held her jacket in her arms. She looked great.

She called Ramona. "I'm dressed and ready to go." She popped in the cell phone earpiece and attached the phone to her belt. She needed her hands free. Ramona gave her the updated itinerary of the day. Most of the day would be spent in meetings.

"The city movers are coming by at one o'clock. Leave the key with City Hall security and they'll pass it on. We are having lunch with the Environmental Control Agency about the river, three-thirty your meeting with the cabinet to discuss the city's four-year objective . . . Did you get all that?"

"I'm getting it, girl. Sounds familiar though."

"Good; then we have to . . ." Ramona said, her phone getting static. "Can you hear me? . . ."

Affrica could no longer hear Ramona. She pulled out the earpiece and took a deep breath. August Watson had told her that being mayor was almost the same as what she was doing before, but it would be less focused on one department. Affrica did not believe him though. He said she would have to be a little broader in her understanding of the workings of all the different departments that made the city. Some departments were very obscure and fast changing. She studied for office as if it were a college course or final examination. She even went back to her government law books.

"But you don't really have to worry about all that," Mayor Watson had told her. "That's why you have department heads. They will summarize and fill you in on all the goings-on." But Affrica learned on her own, asking questions and reading. Sadly, even with Affrica being the deputy mayor, a lot of people didn't want to talk to her. They thought August had sent her to be a spy. But eventually she disarmed them with her good graces and confidence. So she learned a lot.

Affrica noticed though that August Watson left a lot of the departments on their own. He went to a lot of expensive lunches and trips to Aspen for conferences.

Conferences. Is that what they're calling skiing these days? she had thought. Affrica kept most of her radical ideas to herself and allowed August to teach her about being the mayor of a city. She learned a lot by watching and by going to meetings and planning committees. When Affrica was the deputy mayor she filled in for Mayor Watson at different forums. The public then started associating her with the mayor and a position of power.

Today at the meeting, the press would get to ask her a few questions after her speech, and all the department chiefs and heads would summarize their problems and update everyone on what was going on. It was going to be a long busy day. The meeting alone was scheduled for three hours.

She collected her briefcase, laptop, and file folder filled with technical contracts and formal agreements she had to read and sign. She surveyed the boxes, double-checked all the labels, and felt a little sad about leaving her house after four years. She made sure the oven was off and there were no irons left on. She loved the house, redbrick with two stories and a very large front yard, obscured by the large number of trees.

When Affrica was a little girl it was the best house for kids to play hide-and-go-seek. Her grandmother used to give the kids in the neighborhood cookies and juice. She invited them over, trying to make Affrica more social; she tended to be a bookworm if she wasn't inspired to make friends. Her grandmother liked to keep the house open for kids to hang out, having barbecues and small parties.

Before moving in with her grandmother, Affrica lived with her mother at Irving Housing Projects.

Her mother had her enrolled in a Freedom School. A school with an all-African-American curriculum. Her grandmother allowed her to continue there and helped to maintain Affrica's studies. She did make Affrica go to church with her and would teach her to cook and braid, of course. Tell Affrica real stories in history. The amazing things her grandmother had seen in her lifetime. Kids liked Affrica growing up; she never had trouble making friends. The girls liked Affrica because she knew over a hundred hand games with clapping and jumping, she could cornrow anyone's hair, no matter how short it was, and she never got tired of turning in double Dutch. She was a skinny girl with two long braids down her back. Always thoughtful and ready to share, but stubborn as a mule.

As she grew up, her body rounded out, with what were once long giraffe legs turning into toned and shapely legs. She remained stubborn and gave men a hard time reading her. She wasn't really into guys until college; before that she was busy studying and didn't pay the boys any mind.

Affrica really got involved with men in college. She went away to school and quickly learned the ways of the undergraduate and lost focus on studying. She made friends, partied, played spades in the cafeteria for hours, drank her first beer, and had sex for the first time.

Her mother and grandmother had to call her father to set her straight. After a week living with him, she changed and started studying again.

For Affrica, college was the first time away from any parental supervision. Though she was a very intelligent girl she just had to let loose. Had to get the rebellion out of her system. Once she was over it and her father talked with her, she was able to balance the studying with social gatherings.

By her junior year she was back on the dean's list and an applicant for a scholarship to New York University. She received a full scholarship to NYU and moved to New York, where she lived with her best friend Holly.

Holly grew up in Passion too. Her mother was heavily into the black movement, and the two girls would often find themselves in long meetings with their mothers. The girls used to find themselves the only young children there and they would go off and play, leaving the political worlds to the adults. They would play in each other's large Afros, exchange books, and play with dolls and other toys.

She met Delroy in New York by sheer coincidence. She didn't know that he was from Passion. It was at an African-American political action seminar, a nonprofit organization that groomed intelligent blacks in politics. Delroy was an active participant in the seminar. She thought he was very arrogant at the meeting, but next thing she knew she was having a one-night stand. When she moved back home, he was already part of the mayor's staff and did not seem interested in her. But then after some time passed he started to make goo-goo eyes at her. They worked relatively close to each other and were kept very busy with their jobs. It was only a matter of time before they started dating. Delroy had seen to that and August had made him.

* * *

Affrica stood in her living room in front of the answering machine, her coat on and her briefcase in hand. She rewound the tape a bit and pressed PLAY. Holly's deep voice filled the room. She said simply, "Dear sister dreamer, you've been voted into a great gift. You now have extraordinary power, and I know you will be fair and use it wisely. Be well and I'll speak to you soon."

Affrica took a last deep breath before closing the door of her house. She called Ramona again.

"Okay, girl, what's going on now?"

"Where are you? The press is outside and nobody else is here yet." Outside Affrica's house, Morgan Stephanie, one of Passion's *Daily* reporters, followed her, asking questions about her becoming mayor.

"I have press behind me," Affrica said into the telephone. The wind was blowing profusely and her coat whipped around her long legs and business suit.

The reporter stood in Affrica's way. With a graceful step Affrica sidestepped her and kept walking. "Do you feel favoritism played a large part in your winning the mayoral race?" the red-headed reporter asked her. This same woman had called Affrica an inexperienced child in her newspaper column.

Affrica remained calm and faced the woman and her trigger-happy photographer.

Before Affrica could answer, the reporter asked, "Do you think there should be an age limitation on who holds office?"

Affrica placed her belongings on her car. She was not going to let this woman make her late for her meeting.

"I don't think age has anything to do with being a capable mayor. It has to do with knowledge of the position," she said smoothly and gave the cameraman a great smile. She answered a few more questions and entered her car. Affrica's charm and dignity impressed the cameraman, but not the reporter.

Affrica checked her sterling silver watch. She was still early for her first day of work, a little shaken up by the persistent reporter.

She stopped at her favorite diner, Peach Grove Diner. When she entered she saw a huge banner saying CONGRATULATIONS. She was touched that they would go through such trouble for her.

Olivia Jacobson was the head waitress at the diner. She was always there, no matter what time Affrica came by. Olivia had known Affrica's grandmother very well. Olivia was a good friend to Affrica. Though they hardly talked on the phone, the two often spoke for long periods when Affrica came in to eat. She was one of Olivia's favorite customers.

The morning crew sang and put a candle on a muffin, and after the short festivities they gave her her regular morning order already waiting for her. Coffee with cream, dark, two sugars, buttered cinnamon raisin bagel with a little jelly, and a piece of fruit.

Everyone congratulated her on winning the election. The other customers joined in and congratulated the beautiful mayor. They thought she was going to be a great mayor. Olivia was sad that Affrica would not be coming out their way much anymore, unless she was going home for something. The chef of the Mayoral Mansion would now be preparing her breakfasts.

Affrica left with her bag of food. Sipping the coffee at red lights and nibbling quickly on the bagel, she turned a left into the parking garage of City

Hall. She checked her makeup, smoothed her eyebrows, and reapplied her lipstick. She stretched her pretty legs out of the vehicle calmly. Retrieving her laptop, briefcase, and file folder in one graceful sweep, she made her way toward the imposing building. Workers and department heads greeted her at every turn. Affrica realized she was now under close scrutiny. The whole world was looking at her.

She called Ramona again. "I'm here," Affrica said breathlessly, the cold air knocking out her voice.

"Good. We have time to meet before it all gets started. See you inside."

As she entered her new job, security greeted her pleasantly and opened the door and she stepped inside the building.

Two

Passion, Michigan, was a midsize city. It had large buildings and thousands of businesses. It was a middle-class city all around, except a few scattered places where the poor citizens tried hard to make ends meet. These areas were often sadly crime-ridden. The poor people did not get much protection from the criminals. They had to fend for themselves.

Chicago, Illinois, was directly across Lake Michigan, and if you stood by the waterfront, you could see the marvelous skyline. Detroit was on the other side of the state, facing another large lake. It was a good five hours' drive from Passion.

The story goes, the people who founded Passion said the breathtaking sunsets arose passion in all who saw them, inspiring the name of the city.

Passion, Michigan, had never had a black mayor, though most of the people in the city were evolved enough not to care what color the new mayor was. A few cared and based their voting decision strictly on that fact. They would be proven wrong when she proved her capacity and talent as an elected official. The press did not help matters, as they asked Affrica inappropriate personal questions about her past, about her own involvement in the Black Panther movement, though she was only a little baby when her mother was in the organization. They said she was inexperienced in positions of leadership even though as deputy mayor she had implemented new laws and had strategy meetings with all the department heads in Mayor Watson's cabinet. And the press did not back down.

But surprisingly with Mayor Watson's backing and her confidence and impeccable speech-making skills she won over the one opposing candidate, Mark Tennenbaum. The press seemed obsessed with Affrica's age. But Affrica was a young, intelligent woman. She knew she would have twenty-five different city departments to look after, and she knew what every single one of them did, what their operating budgets were, and what their current state was. She knew a lot of them were either over-budgeted, or underbudgeted; her job as mayor would be to sit in long meetings and vote on budgets and new laws, which excited her. She might even change the things she did not like passed during August Watson's rule. She had a lot of new ideas.

Affrica confided only in Ramona about all the changes she wanted to make. Ramona had been Mayor Watson's secretary, but she was so much more than that. Ramona was the one who had told her to keep all the changes to herself.

"Don't disclose all the changes you want to make, till you are in there and mayor. People don't like change that much, even when it's good for them," she had told Affrica. "So do it after the inaugural party."

Ramona arranged interviews with the press, kept files and notes on everything. She knew more about the departments than August himself. So instead of just keeping her on as a secretary, Affrica promoted her to deputy mayor and gave her a part-time secretary, though knowing Ramona, she wouldn't give her much work.

Most of the city offices were located in the Guy P. Lawson Municipal Building. City Hall, some of the other offices were located in the City Center Building. The Mayoral Mansion was a three-minute walk to City Hall. This was where Affrica would be spending most of her time.

She knew the police department needed a complete budgetary overhaul. The Community Development Office was nonexistent; Watson didn't feel it was a necessary department. The surplus from the budget went to the purchase of a boat. The city's finance and treasury department had a super person in charge, who was almost impossible to schedule a meeting with. But in Affrica's studying of the budget, she realized she would have to sit down with him to go over the preliminary numbers, which did not add up. But Affrica had to find time in her schedule to meet with him for hours. The fire department was fine; the parks department was a shambles.

Affrica had a ten-page outline on the reorganization she wanted to make on all of the city departments. She would get the $93 million city operating budget to balance somehow.

Having worked close enough with August the past four years, she knew he really was not about making changes. Affrica worked with him to gain the experience and learn more. She was tolerant of his forgetfulness and manipulation of people, though she hated that about him. She had thought, though, that she would be able to take whatever she had learned as deputy mayor and use it to excel as a lawyer. But now he had talked Affrica into being the mayor. She had to be ready for anything.

Passion needed someone like Affrica, someone who cared and was honest. Someone who finally had the people's interests at heart.

Affrica was bored and hungry. The meeting was going on its fourth hour. She maintained a calm composure. This was her first day as mayor and she was already weary. On the outside she appeared very interested, but she had already spent the entire morning in the conference room in meetings.

Earlier she had been pretty excited. She had had her speech ready and been very interested in what the department heads had to say after they heard it. She knew she would make a considerable impact on the press and citizen groups.

Her speech had gone well, she thought. She had taken Ramona's suggestion and been very empathetic to all the departments. She offered to meet with them and allow them to tell her what changes really did need to be made and what their budgetary concerns were. Ramona had smiled from ear to ear as she stood at the podium, looking like the president of the United States. Her confidence had been unshaken even with cameras trained on her, capturing her every breath. Her braided hair shone with health, and her suit was enhanced with a silken scarf tied around her shirt collar.

Most of the press was already gone and her speech had already been made. The conference room was packed with myriad city officials and department heads. She had addressed all their concerns on her ability to be mayor. Most of the staff of Mayor Watson's was still there, with very few changes. The old mayor had asked her to keep most of them on. They were all very qualified so she felt obliged to keep them in place as the old mayor had requested. She found it surprising though, after the press had gone, that most of the department heads voiced disappointed in August Watson's performance as mayor. Though they did not come out and say anything negative against him.

"Our sewage treatment plant is not operating efficiently. It's been operating only at eighty-five percent these past seven years. Even though the EPA said it's perfectly fine for it to operate at anything above eighty percent, I still think we need to revamp the system," Morris Spitfeld said to Affrica.

Morris Spitfeld was a short, very pale man, moderately tall with thick glasses.

Delroy interrupted him. He looked down at his folder. "Don't you think, Mr. Spitfeld, if there was any danger the sewage filter would have been changed a long time ago? Budgetary demands don't allow for cosmetic changes," Delroy almost spat at him.

"I . . . I . . . understand, Mr. Roberts, but this is not a 'cosmetic' change." He pushed up his glasses, his light skin blushing profusely. But he stood his ground. "This . . . this is a change that would benefit all of Passion. The treatment plant will operate more effectively. If we installed a new water-pressure provider, we could process and manage much more." He exhaled, looking triumphant.

Delroy shot him down once more. "But, Mr. Spitfeld, aren't you asking for this new filter only because you saw Pleasantville received their filter last month and you just want to—how do you say?—keep up with the Joneses?"

Affrica ignored Delroy. She felt that if she paid

him any attention she would have to reprimand him for being a jerk. That wouldn't be good for their relationship.

She whispered with Ramona as they had their heads buried in a sewage budget folder. It seemed to make sense, but something was not adding up. They were slightly perplexed, but did not want to show it. They nodded at each other as if they had come up with a plan. Delroy attempted to eavesdrop, moving his chair closer to theirs, but he was locked out.

Maxwell Townsend, the city's treasurer, raised his hand to speak. The overhead lamp caught his platinum watch. He was a light-brown-skinned man, with a slight gap in his teeth and curly salt-and-pepper hair. He had been scribbling notes while Mr. Spitfeld was making his speech. Maxwell was a true genius in every sense of the word. He had graduated from Yale with a degree in accounting, and had become a CPA. He went back to school and received a master's degree in computer science and decided a year later he wanted a Ph.D in computer development. Everyone expected him to go and work at a large corporation or teach. Maxwell did teach, but he also made heaps of money working for Watson. Not only did he make a lot of money, but he was able to polish his hacking skills. He could make any budget look good, even if it was a mess. On the outside the numbers added up and it all seemed to make sense.

He stood up and buttoned his dark suit, which fitted him perfectly. He had a broad, flaring nose and dark brown eyes. In his early forties, he had been married for fifteen years and divorced two years ago. He flirted tremendously and slept around a bit.

He looked around the room. Everyone was waiting for him to speak. He cleared his throat and tightened his tie a bit.

"I would implore Mr. Spitfeld to begin looking for ways within his department to use what reserves he has, instead of trying to debauch the system. Our budget does not—"

Affrica stood up, interrupting him. "I understand what the budget says. I think the sewage system should be a primary consideration." She wanted to end this discussion. She knew she would have to meet with Maxwell privately and discuss the budget again. Maxwell gave her a dazzling smile. He loved beautiful ladies, even when they told him what to do.

The task of being the city's mayor all of a sudden seemed monumental. She already had her own concerns on her ability to be mayor, but then August had gently persuaded her to run. He had even supported her through the campaign, making speeches with her, introducing her as the new mayor even before the election results. Delroy also had put the pressure on her.

Personally Delroy had initially been reluctant to the idea of Affrica being mayor, but August had upped the ante and offered him more money if they were successful in the manipulation of the woman.

The press was pretty ruthless. There had even been a poll taken by the press stating that 54 percent of people thought she might be too young to do a good job. Not to mention the fact that she was a woman and African-American—of course they did not print that. But they questioned everything else.

August had prepared her extensively on what to tell the press about her age and experience. They prepared her for all the questions that would be thrown at her. The possible questions: would she be able to interpret laws fairly? Would she be able to enact policies for the betterment of the people of Passion, Michigan? Would she be able to deal with governmental corruption if she had never dealt with anything like that before?

During the meeting the department heads had voiced their own concerns on things never getting done. Budgetary limitations. They each had their own agenda. But after Affrica did some research she discovered there really was enough money in the budget to help each department fully. She would have to sit with the department heads alone and go through files and lawyers and contracts in order to deal with them. She took pristine notes. After the initial outbursts, Mr. Spitfeld continued to discuss the sewage system. He had diagrams and graphs to show them the extent of the need for the new parts. Affrica thought they were done talking about the sewage department.

But now she couldn't do anything but scribble into her notepad and pray it would all be over soon and she could get some food, go to the bathroom.

Ramona was to her left taking notes, marking file folders, and writing into a palm pilot. She actually looked interested in all the talk of sewage system treatment information. *That's why I hired her. Ramona works well and takes it all very seriously.*

Ramona Jones was one of the most organized people Affrica knew. She was a pretty thirty-eight-year-old woman. Her hair was usually pushed back and tied into a tight bun. She had a light sprinkling of brown freckles on her nose. She was slightly over-weight, with a large round behind with flaring hips. She was a divorcee that dated only men who were neat like her. She found to her chagrin that even though they seemed neat on the outside, they usually were pretty messed up on the inside. Ramona had a good sense of humor, which was surprising since she took everything so seriously. Everything in her life was on a schedule, even her clothing.

She had schedules on when she would wear which suits. She owned twenty business suits and rotated them through the month. The first suit in the rotation was always the dark blue Ann Taylor with the ruffled white shirt underneath. She usually wore them with black pumps. The last suit of the rotation was always the light brown wool pantsuit. When she bought new outfits she would add them to the end of the rotation line.

She had a slight crush on Maxwell, who in turn thought Ramona was a foxy lady, but then he thought most women were foxy.

Affrica and Ramona had slowly become friends. Affrica was a little reluctant, because she knew just how anal Ramona could be. They had worked together in the mayor's cabinet. After meeting for drinks one Wednesday evening and speaking to each other personally as opposed to business, Affrica had found Ramona to be funny and likable.

Tuesday night was the night that the girlfriends would get together and gossip. At work, when they did speak, it was work related. Tuesday was *their* time. The maître d' always sat them in a place where they could speak comfortably and not be overheard or eavesdropped on. They never used anyone's real name when they talked about them. They used childish codes, and really juicy gossip was reserved for the car.

* * *

The meeting was rolling along. Affrica stifled a yawn. Ramona looked at Affrica and smiled at her, before turning back to Mr. Spitfeld. Out of the corner of her eye Affrica noticed someone entering the room quietly. She did not turn her head, but could see the door pretty clearly. Ramona did not turn her head either; she stayed focused on Spitfeld, but under the table she kicked her friend.

Alex Bartholomew, Passion, Michigan's, chief of police. *Handsome* Chief of Police Bartholomew. Affrica's stomach did a back flip. She knew he was scheduled to address the board last, but when she didn't see him she thought he wouldn't come. They knew each other well from the investigation of the police department by Mayor Watson. They were always at odds, talking over each other, but trying to remain civil and professional at the same time.

Alex was thirty-seven years old and an incredibly attractive man. With expressive dancing eyes and a smile so charming, most people gave up any information they had. Women were drawn to him.

He noticed the new mayor immediately when he entered the conference room. He also noted that the vile police commissioner was there too.

Alex was late because one of the young men he was counseling had beaten up his girlfriend and was in jail. Alex had to deal with that situation first, even though he hated being late. Initially he did not want to be part of the meeting. He thought he was going to get the same runaround that old Mayor Watson had given him. Alex's gut told him something shady was going on and he wanted the police commissioner gone. He felt the commissioner was unfair and was trying to corrupt the police department. The corruption was deep and entrenched. Alex resisted it every way he could.

Somehow old Mayor Watson was involved, he felt, but he could not put his finger on the trouble.

He looked around the room and back to Affrica. She was a stunning woman, he had to give her that. She was facing him slightly and her profile was regal. Her dark lips were full and were slightly pursed. He could tell she was not interested in what the speaker was saying, by her hands. They were busy, moving around too much. It was something subtle, but he noticed it.

But why is she such a pain? Alex did not realize he was staring at Affrica so intently, until his name was called and the conference room was clapping and waiting for him to address them.

Affrica and Ramona exchanged subtle glances. They passed notes to each other.

Hungry, Affrica's note said.

Hungry for what? Ramona replied. She had drawn a happy face next to it.

Hungry for food! Affrica wrote back. They were like schoolgirls trying hard not to giggle. The women were relieved the meeting had gone well thus far and they were slightly giddy.

Alex stood at the wooden podium. He pulled the microphone up higher. He was a little over six feet tall; the speaker before him had been short. Alex flashed the room a winning smile and everyone relaxed. Affrica was no longer bored. She crossed her legs and looked at Delroy. *What garbage is he going to tell us now? I swear he thinks just because he's cute he could get whatever he wants.* She moved closer to Delroy, whispering something meaningless to him, while Alex began his speech. In midwhisper Affrica suddenly realized that what she was saying to Delroy was truly irrelevant. She was merely buffing Delroy's ego as an unconscious reaction to the fact that an

attractive man was in the vicinity. She knew Delroy
needed assurances of her affection. But she wasn't
going to do this, make him feel better by acknowl-
edging him when a fine man was around. She scrutinized Alex with cold, unimpressed eyes. She tried
anyway, would not succumb to his manipulation.
His disarming smile. She straightened up, listening
intently to Alex's speech. She took a lot notes. She
was professional about the situation and was actually interested in what Alex had to say on the police
department.

"The police department is working diligently to
overcome the rising crime."

Delroy sucked his teeth slightly. He didn't raise
his hand. "Yes, but the crime rate of Passion is going through the roof."

Alex looked at Delroy calmly and continued,
"Rising crime has a lot more to do with the eco-
nomic stability and moral fabric of a community
than law enforcement. We can put more patrols on
the street, arrest more people, and create stiffer
penalties, but that does not deal with the conditions
that create criminal tendencies. We all have heard
the proverb 'It takes a village to raise a child.' Well,
the rising crime is perpetrated primarily by the children of this village. Are you asking yourselves what
you are doing wrong?"

The room straightened up, ready to object. Africa agreed with him wholeheartedly.

Alex wanted them to see that these so-called
criminals were the same kids that were taught by
their schools, and parented by Passion's citizens.
Why weren't these kids being taken care of? Why
were so many of them lost? Most of the heavy crime
that was happening in Passion was—and Alex hated
to admit this—from Irving Housing Projects. In

most of the neighborhoods in Passion, crimes were done by the young people of Passion. They were starting gangs, and hurting each other. Their influence was starting to be felt in other parts of Passion.

"Listen, these kids come from your school system. What happened there, why aren't they being taught the survival skills needed to be successful out there?"

"I don't think you should blame the failure of the police department to properly handle crime on the people of Irving Housing," Affrica retorted. She was livid. She had been very calm and collected, though the entire time Alex had been talking she wanted to stand up and yell at him. He was blaming all the crime in the entire city of Passion on a small group of people, just because they were poor.

"The police force is not failing to handle crime. We attempt to suppress it before it springs up, and we deal with it as soon as it happens. But, as I said before, Mayor Bryant, the cause of crime is not the police department. We are not blaming the people of Irving Housing for all the crime, but most of the arrests in Passion are made from the people who live in Irving Housing. I am stating a simple fact. If I may continue . . ." Alex looked at Affrica, also with a calm look on his face. He was even smiling slightly.

The room looked at her.

"Go on." She waved her hand at him.

"All I am saying is, we need to get together. All the heads of departments, Councilwoman, Senator, Mayor." He looked boldly at Affrica. "I propose a motion to call a meeting to deal specifically with the issues at the Irving Housing Projects, as it relates to community relations and law enforcement."

Everyone in the room began whispering and nodding their heads.

"Can I get a second?" Alex asked the assemblage. However, he glanced at Mayor Bryant.

Delroy almost got whiplash as he turned his head to face Affrica.

Affrica raised a hand and said, "I second the motion." She faced a stupefied Delroy. "Well . . ." she whispered.

Delroy straightened, shuffling through his papers, and finally found a calendar. "Um, Uh, the motion has passed. We will schedule a meeting. Tentative date is two weeks from today. Everyone concerned will receive a memo by tomorrow."

Affrica sat back. She had helped to pass the motion, her first real action as mayor. She acted as if she were getting her papers together but she was actually thinking about the police chief and how stupid he had made her feel.

I don't think I misunderstood what he said. She shook her head gently.

Ramona was in front of her. "January twenty-fifth is your next open day . . . Yes?" Ramona had already written it in.

Affrica nodded. "Good." She conferred with Delroy on the specific day and time.

Later on a few more people were left over from the meeting. Maxwell Townsend, John Perry, Affrica. While the gentlemen prepared to leave, the police chief returned. Affrica and he hadn't spoken a word after the meeting. The men left noisily and Affrica began fixing her papers. Alex was on the other side of the room, retrieving his date book.

He had gotten out of the parking lot before he

remembered that after leaving the men's room he had not returned to the conference room to get his book. He turned back to City Hall and as he entered saw that a few people were left. He saw the men getting ready to exit and attempted to make a mad dash for his date book. He did not want to be in the room alone with the mayor. But as he approached her, she did not notice his entrance. She was staring down at something with a look of serenity on her face. Alex was moved. The official mask was gone and in her face was gentleness and compassion. His heart shuddered. He started to walk past her, but she looked up, startled.

"Oh, I thought I was the only one here." Her hand was on her chest. Alex had a smile on his face. Affrica frowned slightly. "Hello, Mr. Bartholomew." She smiled cordially and shook his hand forcefully. All business.

What is he, sneaking up on me? There was nobody here and all of a sudden he's standing in front of me. What was I doing? She turned and started placing her papers in a folder.

Motioning to the table, Alex said, "I just forgot my date book."

"That's responsible. Do you forget your gun sometimes too?" she said sarcastically.

Alex looked at her incredulously, taken aback. The sweet face was gone. "I was about to say congratulations on your becoming mayor—"

"Thank you, but I really don't need your vote of confidence."

"No, you don't, because you have August Watson's vote and that means a lot in this city," he shot back.

Affrica was fuming as she turned to face him. "Why don't you just come out with it, Mr. Bartholomew?" Her hands were on her hips and she waited.

Alex moved in a little closer. "You won't be able to pull it off."

Affrica was so upset she could barely see. "Listen, Mr. Bartholomew, let's just drop this mess that we do. You just take care of what you need to take care of on your end. And I'll do my job as mayor."

Affrica turned on her heels and left the room.

Three

"I don't understand women, bro. It's like they don't know what they want. They say they want you, but when they get you, they don't want you anymore. Then they want you back. . . ." Patrick shook his head.

Patrick Gomez was one of Alex's good friends outside of the police force. Patrick was a landscaper for a large construction company. They both had a commitment to their jobs.

Patrick was an attractive Puerto Rican man. He had short black hair, his body solidly built from all the lifting he did. His skin was a permanent caramel color from working with the soil in the sun daily. These days he didn't work outside, as he was now drawing up landscapes for the company.

Patrick shook his head again. "Women don't make no sense," he repeated. "Now she wants me to act as if I don't like her. Why? Why would she ask me to act as if I don't like her? Make me beg, she tells me." He shook his head.

Women who were walking in passed by the two friends' table on purpose, shaking their hips a little more, lingering by them longer than necessary. They sat at O'Neal's, a smoky bar where cops and

firemen hung out. O'Neal's was where cops went
to unwind. It tended to get very loud there. A Ja-
maican man was the true owner of O'Neal's. A Scot-
tish man stood behind the bar.

Alex munched on the oily fries in a basket in
front of him. "Patrick, you're making it difficult.
Just do what she wants." A pretty redheaded woman
was scoping Alex from the bar. "I'm not claiming
to be a know-it-all of women, because as you can
see I have managed to keep myself single, but . . ."

The redheaded woman walked by their table and
looked at the two men, giving Alex a blinding smile.
He smiled back and continued to speak to Patrick
without missing a beat.

"I *do* know that if a woman asks you to do something—kinky or whatever—you *have* to do it. She
needs it. Women don't like asking for things. When
they do, they mean it." Alex looked at Patrick seriously, then shrugged his shoulders. "Or, they want
you to do the opposite of what they asked, in which
case you messed up by doing what she asked."

Alex sat back in his chair, the bottle of beer dis-
guising his smile. The beer was warm. "I'm done
with this one."

The waitress came immediately with a refill when
Alex put the bottle down.

"Here you go," she said shyly. She handed him
a bottle of ice-cold beer. She had even opened the
bottle. She gave Alex a funny look.

"You see, that's what I'm talking about!" Patrick
hit Alex's shoulder.

"You are the Mack!"

"No, I'm not macking, man!"

"Honey brought you a brand-new bottle of beer
without you lifting a finger. I bet you she was watching you since you got here."

"Anyway, so work is not getting easier." Alex changed the subject abruptly. He hated when the conversation turned into a discussion about how attractive he was. He like the fact that he had good looks, but he didn't think that aspect of himself was so important.

When Alex was younger some of his female teachers gave him high marks for no reason but that he graced their classes with his beauty every day. All his life he'd been an attractive man. As he got older, he grew a slight beard to hide the dimples, but the beard only accentuated the gorgeous parts of his face. His body was long and sculpted. He had a very firm butt and a toned stomach. He swam fifteen laps every day at the YMCA, his body cutting through the water with Olympic speed. He was currently enrolled in Capoeria, a martial arts style whose techniques came from Brazil via Africa and which was developed by slaves who needed to hide the lethal martial art in something harmless, dancing and music. The moves in Capoeria included standing on your hands, spinning while crouching.

Alex liked to be busy.

His father was a strict military man and wanted his son to join one of the regiments. He was a marine and very proud of his service to the country. But Alex had tried the marines and the army. He excelled in both and served his time, but they weren't for him. His father did not hide his disappointment in his son. Alex was a good son by all definitions. He did not visit much. Every time he went to his parents' home, his father would bad-mouth cops and compare cops to the military. He said they were prissy and had easy jobs.

"Most cops don't never see any action. You could spend your entire life as an officer and never fire a gun," his father would say.

"That's a good thing, Dad." Alex had gone through this with his father before.

"Dad, we are here to protect, not kill citizens."

Sadly this frustration kept Alex away from his parents. His hand would touch the phone, but his mind would tell him not to call. He loved them dearly and knew they were not getting younger. But it was hard being comfortable while having to justify his very existence. So he went by twice a month, most of the time hoping his father wasn't there. His mom was much more accepting. She just wanted him to get married and have some pretty babies. He could talk to her.

Along with being the chief of police, Alex was also a counselor to two young men, who were losing their way.

Alex lived in a comfortable home in Linden Hills. He had trees surrounding his property on all sides. He spent weekends shirtless in his front- and backyard. Mowing the lawn, fixing things, washing the car. The new owner of Luscious Nails thought she and he were dating. She had come into town five months ago and they had gone to dinner a few times. They kissed once, but it was a quick peck on the lips good night. She called him a few times that week to see how he was doing. But he only returned her calls once. She talked about her car and New York City too much.

Alex finished the beer. Within seconds, the waitress was back at the table.

"Can I have a soda, please? By the way, what's your name? I've never seen you here before."

The waitress stuttered. She couldn't believe he was asking her her name. "Joanie. My, my name is Joanie. It's my third day." The waitress left their table smiling broadly.

Patrick shook his head at Alex and the waitress and burst into laughter. "What's up with work, man?"

"I thought I had a handle on it but when these boys are running around this city like they ain't got sense, I worry about us and I worry about them."

A rowdy pool game was getting started. Four men were throwing twenty-dollar bills on the felt table. Patrick and Alex watched for a little while, enjoying a moment of silence between them. Patrick tried to order another beer. The waitress passed him by twice without noticing his hand up.

Alex began, "What's bothering me is the fact that the *mayor* was blaming us cops for the high crime rate."

"Oh yeah, that meeting with the new mayor, old nemesis."

"She was saying why aren't the police doing more? And, and where are they getting lost and whose fault is it? I wish I could sit her down. Yeah, you know, even when I tried to make peace with her, she threw it in my face. She's so arrogant, full of herself. I know she's just like Watson."

"Corrupt."

"Very corrupt. She's too mean to be innocent. She's just so . . . and what kind of name is *Affrica* anyway?"

While Alex was talking, Patrick noticed how animated he was. He was gesturing, and his voice was up. It dawned on him. "Ah, you like her! Oh, man, you like her."

Alex felt his heart thud in his chest. "No, no." But he felt a smile creeping into his face. He tried to stifle it.

"Oh, man, you like her. Your wicked witch of the west." Patrick laughed so hard tears came to his eyes.

"No . . . no!" But an image flashed in Alex's mind. An image of a different Affrica from the one he had argued with today. He shook it out of his head.

"Hell no, especially knowing she's affiliated with old Mayor Watson. I wonder how much she's getting to keep up this charade. I'm going to find out what she is into."

"She sure is fine though."

"I didn't notice."

"What's up with what's her name, Miss New Yorker? Don't tell me she's already kicked to the curb. She was beautiful," Patrick said vehemently.

"Yeah, but she hates jazz." A dull throb had started at the base of Alex's head.

"You're crazy, man. Don't worry, Miss New Yorker is not half as fine as the mayor. But she ain't mean." Patrick left the table to start a game of darts with a friend.

Alex sat back smiling to himself. The image flashed in his head again, again, and again. He stood up, grabbed the last of the french fries, ready to challenge anyone to a game of pool. He refused to give Affrica another thought.

Four

The next morning Alex woke to find himself staring at Affrica. She was very close and he could smell her. In fact, there seemed to be the taste of her in his mouth. She was wearing some kind of purple fabric. It was loosely wrapped around her. No, it was wrapped around them both. It felt like a semi-wet, very large towel. She leaned close and began to flick his earlobe with her tongue when he realized that his eyes were closed. He popped his eyes open to the bright glare of the morning sun beaming through the parted curtains of his bedroom. He was alone.

"I'm going to kill Patrick," Alex said and shook his head.

Alex's house was neat for a bachelor pad. It wasn't overly neat, his bed usually staying undone. But he washed his dishes and picked up after himself. His two-story town house was done in a simple style. Alex enjoyed space, so it was not clogged up with a lot of furniture. He had one large comfortable couch in the living room, with a nice-sized TV with a DVD player. On one large wall Alex kept his enormous record collection. He also had a turntable that he kept dust free and oiled.

The house was decorated with all that he collected on his travels, when he was stationed in the military. Brazilian and African art decorated his walls. He had a handmade rug from Indonesia. His living room was the most comfortable room in the house. Large throw pillows dotted the floor. It was a warm, masculine room. The colors he chose were rich reds and muted yellows. His "toys" were masculine also; comfortable couches, complicated televisions, records and turntables and karate movies.

Alex also had many books. He loved to read. He read the classics, *To Kill a Mocking Bird, The Invisible Man.* He also read philosophy and books about religion and the martial arts. He wondered what Africa read.

No. I'm not going there. She's a fine woman, but it's too complicated. My life is complicated enough. She seems like the intellectual type, maybe Toni Morrison. But she liked Missy Elliot. Maybe Sistah Souljah, Terry McMillan, with a little Essence *magazine. Yeah, that's probably exactly right too.*

Alex, clad in only in gray cotton sweatpants, made his way to the bathroom, shaking his head at his woman foolishness. He laughed to himself. He frowned at himself in the mirror, scratching his light beard like an old man.

The bathroom was a simple room, a $1.99 shower curtain the only decoration. There was always enough toilet paper and toothpaste. Besides scrubbing it and the tile every other week, he did not think much about his bathroom.

He brushed his teeth vigorously. They were straight and white. One was slightly chipped from a vicious football game. They were pretty but not too perfect.

His eyes were his best features, though he was

perfectly handsome everywhere. His eyes were as dark as a new moon sky. So dark and deep, you thought you might just fall in. A lot of women fell in. Headfirst.

Alex was starting to feel a little restless. It seemed there were so many hurdles. Every time he thought he had a name or something tangible to back up the horrible nagging feeling, something would stop him or a wall would be put in front of him somehow. In a lot of ways, being a cop in Passion was a lot easier than being a cop in a large city. But smaller-city cops had their share of problems. Alex had been assigned to so many violent cases, so many deadly cases in recent years, he sometimes felt as if there were some type of war going on. His father didn't know how much he really went through.

His last case didn't really have to do with being a cop. He was playing Big Brother to a young man from Irving Housing. The young man, Melly, was beating on his wife. The Housing Project was such a small place. Everybody knew everybody else's business. Some people had been whispering about the man's wife, Anastasia, walking around with black eyes and bruises. Without making a fuss about confronting Melly violently or arresting him, Alex had taken the young man to his home. He had sat the angry Melly down and wailed on him, for two and a half hours, about violence and women, telling him about women being the guardians of the world.

"Would you hit your mother, Melly?"

Melly had just shrugged his shoulders, acting as if what Alex was saying meant nothing.

"Melly, I asked you a question; would you hit your mother?"

"No!"

"So why the hell are you not treating Anastasia

like that? Why is she so different from your mother? What if I beat you down? Just because I could, because I had force? I'm bigger than you." Alex had looked at Melly so harshly that Melly began to shake.

Melly had looked at his hands. "Yo, man, she just talks so much mess."

Alex exhaled. He had broken through to Melly. They could now seriously talk about the situation. At the end, they invited an upset Anastasia to join their dialogue. They decided with Alex's probing that they would have to separate and live apart. Melly would be moving down South to live with his grandmother.

It was such a sensitive case. He didn't know how to convince this young man, who had seen so much violence in his short life, not to inflict violence on others. He felt like a hypocrite sometimes, because he carried a gun.

Alex cooked a quick breakfast. Eggs and a bagel. He wore his shoulder holster over a plain white shirt. His pants fitted him well. He had a casual jacket, which was currently on the back of a chair. He wore spit-shined comfortable black leather boots. He couldn't believe how durable the boots were. He eyed a few folders as he ate, with the mornings world news on the kitchen radio. He put the folders down and he telephoned the graveyard-shift crew at the department, to ask them how the night went. He did graveyard once a week. Since he was the chief of police he didn't really have to do any, but to keep morale up, he did it anyway.

"Hey, Jackson," Alex said into the phone. He heard a lot of voices in the background. He didn't hear any cursing, which was usually the case when someone stayed at the precinct jail.

"Yo, Chief, we had only two loiterings last night. No arrests. We was scared at the station. It was too quiet."

"I hope the men went home then. Don't tell me ya'll sat in your cars drinking beer all night again." Alex held his head in his palms.

"No, boss, nothing like that at all, sir."

"Has relief come in yet?"

"Yes, sir, we will be exiting the premise at 0700 hours."

Alex hated when they spoke police jive. But he went along with Jackson. "Jackson, tell Sarge I need some men dispatched to Forty-four Irving Housing to check on Jay Blow."

"Possible drug dealer, right, sir?" Jackson knew that already. In fact he knew Jay very well.

"Yeah, Jackson. I put the case on his desk last night. Call me if there's any trouble." Alex hung up the telephone. He took a thoughtful bite of his bagel.

Most of the cops were hardworking dedicated men. *But to get caught selling marijuana to some kids at Irving Projects. That had to be the dumbest thing I'd ever seen a cop do.*

Alex was brutal with his officers who strayed. It was so rough out there for his guys anyway. With the face of crime getting younger and younger, sometimes his men jumped the gun. Some assumed every black kid was a potential criminal, which infuriated Alex. Sometimes he felt as if he were always lecturing somebody about something. He was tired of it.

Alex shook his head and threw his plate and mug into the sink for later. He placed the folders in a locked filing cabinet in a walk-in closet. He removed the gun from the cabinet and placed it in the black leather holster, located close to his armpit.

His first appointment was at court, for a young woman who had beaten up another young lady so badly that she had to get her face reconstructed.

Alex put on the light-colored jacket. It fitted his frame perfectly. It smelled clean and was warm but not bulky at all.

He knew both girls pretty well. Tiffani was a boisterous fifteen-year-old and Jida was a twenty-six-year-old administrative assistant who became enraged when Tiffani had said her very expensive purse was not the real thing, that she actually had purchased it at a Korean store, along with the weave she had on her head. Without saying a word Jida had pounced on the young woman and beat her face till it was broken. The young men stood around watching the women fight. Some other women had stopped them.

Alex locked his front door. The air was rather chilly, the early morning sun being slightly covered by some clouds. He jogged to his Jeep and drove to the court building. His cellular phone rang incessantly. Minor crises, happening while he was away from the department. When he was off duty he turned off his cell phone and the department had to page him, unless something was really bad.

At a red light he began thinking about Affrica again. He was able to stop himself immediately. *Good,* he thought. *Women, I can't let them control me. Get all up in my head.*

Alex did not understand them. All his life, he had women basically throw themselves at him. He wasn't a self-absorbed man at all. It was a fact that he was attractive. It was also a fact that when he was a teenager, his friends' mothers would try to seduce him. Only one woman was obvious and came on to him outright. The rest would stay around when he came over to the sons' or daughters' houses. They would give him expensive birthday presents. They called him to mow their lawns, shovel snow, help paint the house. They always wanted him around. The women were very subtle in their flirting.

One of his friends' mothers, an attractive brunette, "accidentally" let Alex see her naked, for a full minute. Seventeen-year-old Alex simply stared at her in awe. He was entranced while one of her sons played video games in another room. He lost his virginity that same year to his friend Marlon's sister. She was a college student when Alex was a high school junior. She was head over heels for him.

As Alex walked through the courthouse, he focused on what he had to do. He walked through the beeping metal detectors, greeting the security guards in a friendly manner. His heels clicked lightly as he walked toward the courtroom. He entered the blue-carpeted room quietly. The proceedings had already begun.

"How do you plead?"

Neither girl had her own lawyer. The court-appointed lawyers both sat quietly by as each young woman spoke for herself, describing in her own words what had happened the day of the fight.

At the end the judge decided that Jida would have to clean up the park at 7 P.M. every night for a month. He told them if they didn't do it they would get arrested and thrown in jail.

That's such a weird ruling. It's so light yet humiliating for Jida. Judge Harelson was rough, but fair. He liked to give the offenders old-fashioned sentences. He tried his best to keep the young people out of prison.

Jida cried quietly as she walked down the courtroom aisle. She realized she had no choice. She
had no money to pay for Tiffani's surgery and she
did not want to go to jail. She would be embarrassed but not in jail.

Jida carried herself a little taller as she passed
Alex, her braids going down her back.

"Are you okay, Jida?"

"Yes, Mr. B."

Alex stepped outside the courtroom with her.
He folded his arms over his chest. He tilted his
head. "Jida, what the hell is going on with you
kids?"

"It was her, Mr. B. I didn't want to hurt her so
bad—"

"But you did!"

Jida saw the disappointment on Alex's face. She
wanted to please Alex. Even though he was a cop,
he was one of the good ones. He cared, she
thought.

"Mr. B., I'm sorry. She just kept pushing me.
Talkin' all this mess," she pleaded. "I had to defend
myself."

"I understand, Jida, but couldn't you talk back?
You could have easily dissed her rather than hitting
her." Alex hated even telling her that. He didn't
want her to think it was okay to go around cursing
out people. "Honestly, Jida, I wish I could tell you
to stop fighting altogether. Talk it out like people."

Jida pursed her pretty lips at Alex. She raised a
sculpted eyebrow at him.

Reading her mind, he replied, "I know it's hard,
but you could try."

"I ain't gonna be no punk, Mr. B."

A young man appeared in a brown suit and tie.

His short, light brown hair was neat. He did not look older than seventeen.

"Jida, at least apologize to her mother, if you can't talk to Tiffani," Alex told her.

Jida crossed her arms over her full chest.

"What's up, Jida?" The younger man appraised Jida openly.

"Nothin' much. Judge gonna make me clean up the park."

"Yeah, well, at least you kicked her—"

"Enough!" Alex stood between the two young people. The dialogue disgusted him. He pushed open the courtroom doors and shoved the younger man through.

It wasn't even 10 A.M. yet.

Five

Irving Housing was run-down. The United States Government in 1965 had built it specifically for North-migrating blacks. The four-building complex was never supposed to stay open as long as it was. The government thought the blacks would use this building almost as a hotel, a place to stay till they got back on their feet from the move. Most blacks never got back on their feet and lived at Irving Housing permanently. They had children, and those children stayed within the building complex or surrounding neighborhood.

The current residents were tired of the buildings falling down around them. They used masking tape, crazy glue, and whatever they could think of to keep their homes together. Most people were scared of the ceiling crashing in or a large water-main break and extensive water damage. They constantly complained to management, who listened with deaf ears. They knew it would take nothing short of a miracle to get the place fixed. The old mayor had made empty promises to them. When the citizens questioned him on his unkept promises, he appointed someone who cared even less about the people in Irving Housing.

But the place was run-down, literally falling apart. A large piece of the ceiling in apartment 4F was rotting. Water had been dripping slowly through the years and now, pregnant with years of water and filth, gave birth to a brown liquid mixed with cement and plasterboard. Little Kysha Miller had just left the bathroom and she heard something that sounded like a loud cough; then the entire ceiling came tumbling down around her. Luckily Kysha only got splashed with a little water and debris. Her mother, who was in the kitchen, came running in to see. Her heart skipped in her chest. Her eyes were scanning for the cordless phone, while her footsteps never wavered. She took a deep breath and when she rounded the corner she saw her little girl unharmed. She said a silent thank-you to God and picked up her heavy five-year-old.

"Mama, the ceiling is broke."

Chantay gingerly stepped on the mess on the floor. "Yes, baby, the ceiling is broken."

"Broken," Kysha repeated.

"Yes." Chantay was so upset she was shaking. She dropped her daughter off at her sister's apartment in 3M and proceeded straight to the management office. On Saturdays the management company, which was located in the basement, right next to the washers and dryers, closed promptly at 2 P.M. If they were even open. They were mostly closed. Vic was the manager of the building.

Chantay jogged a little so she wouldn't miss him. They would have to fix the ceiling today. Muttering and cursing under her breath, Chantay made her way to the basement. The smell of fabric softener assaulted her nose before she even opened the elevator door.

Chantay was an attractive woman. Her permed

hair was pushed back in a frizzy ponytail. She wore tight jeans and a T-shirt that said BROOKLYN in white letters. The shirt was two sizes too small. Her breasts were accentuated by the fit and by the bright lettering on the front. She still wore her house flip-flops. "Yo, Vic!" she muttered, *Where is he?*

"Vic! Where are you, man?"

"Over here." Vic had his head in one of the machines. "You know, someone left a crayon in here."

"Yeah, okay, Vic, listen, my ceiling almost fell on my child just now. What the hell is going on?"

Vic, never one to mince words, replied, "You live in the Projects, what do you want?"

"Vic, I can't believe you are saying this. How about some level of physical safety?" Chantay shot back sarcastically.

She couldn't believe the audacity of the older Greek man. He took his head out of the washing machine.

He pointed a thick, hairy finger at her. "Listen little girl, you needs to get the hell outta this place. You and your child. It's just gonna fall apart and no one is gonna do nothin' about it. I'm sick of you people complaining every minute about dripping faucets and broke ceilings. Trust me. I been working here a long time." He shook his head. "Just listen, save your money and go. You could complain all you want, but this place is gonna keep falling down."

What Vic was saying was almost incomprehensible to Chantay. She had lived in Irving Housing her entire life. Her mother had moved in when she was only sixteen and pregnant. It had been a cheap and halfway decent place to live.

When Chantay found out she was pregnant, she moved in with the father, who lived in the Projects, but he left her to go to Atlanta, and Chantay's mother took over the apartment for her. She got on welfare and was able to at least feed her child and have a roof over their heads. It was that or going back home to her mom and dad pregnant. She stayed at Irving and made friends with the people so close to her. They treated her as though they loved her. Watched her babies when she went to work, cooked food.

But now this place was falling apart. The cheap materials used could no longer be patched up. The entire complex had to be demolished and rebuilt with better materials. That was the new mayor's plan.

Affrica's plan was a simple one: she figured, instead of rebuilding the five-story buildings, two-story homes would be built and two families would live in each house. Some of the houses might be bigger than the others if there was an exceptionally large family. Everyone would get a small plot of land in the backs of the houses.

Even though the citizens would be paying rent, these homes would belong to them. They would have to maintain them, make sure everything was in working order. They would have to mow their own lawns. There would be no management and no more funding for upkeep of the Projects. In the long run, the government would gain money because of no twenty-four-hour supers and no builders. Free plumbers and electricians would be provided.

Affrica also wanted to build a community center where people would learn home repair techniques. The senior citizens would have their own room to paint, talk, and have a bingo night every week. The kids would have a room and art. An arcade would be provided, but it would be paying.

Chantay did not stay quiet and just move out as Vic had suggested. She was afraid that next time the ceiling would fall on Kysha or herself.

She had left the office motivated to do something about the situation—her child was almost killed. She harassed Vic for a whole week, made as many tenants as she could make noise about something they needed fixed at their apartments. She started collecting lists of dangerous problems within the housing complex. She was ready to take her complaints to the highest person she could. Tenants had complaints that ranged from the roaches to broken refrigerator doors. Some tenants had light switches that sparked whenever they were turned on, some had huge holes in their ceilings. The buildings also had rats—most apartments were armed with industrial-sized rat traps.

When Kysha wasn't in school she was with her mother ringing bells and interviewing the people of the complexes. At the end of her mission she had over 300 names on her new petition to fix up Irving Housing, and she had a list of violations a mile long.

"I bet it's small."

"You're probably right."

"Men who are that fine usually are either bad in bed or have tiny little ones." Affrica made an obscene hand gesture. "If my constituents could see me now." She was dressed casually in faded blue jeans and a fading tie-dyed T-shirt. It was Thursday night and the two friends had decided to meet informally at the mansion.

"Anyway, girl, I am tired. To get a moment like this is so necessary. I'll be working straight through next weekend."

The telephone rang. The concierge told her it was Delroy. She rolled her eyes at Ramona and mouthed *Delroy*.

Delroy sounded excited. "I didn't tell you the lady who's been making noise at Irving Housing has riled up so much noise that Watson has called an emergency meeting."

"Wait a minute, he did not confer with me. Why didn't he confer with me about this?" Affrica stood up. Ramona was looking at her inquisitively. Affrica was looking at her and shaking her head negatively.

"He had to get on it. The press was asking questions and you were not there."

"Excuse me, Delroy, I have been here from the get-go. How can you say that?" Affrica was upset.

"I didn't say anything. It was Watson's idea."

Affrica quickly hung up on Delroy and cursed.

"He did it. Watson called an emergency meeting for Irving Projects. That idiot!" Affrica looked up at the ceiling, her teeth clenched.

"What? He has no jurisdiction. He's not mayor anymore." Ramona scrambled for her phone, turned to her ignored laptop, and began typing and making calls. What had been a get-together of two friends now turned into a planning meeting.

"See, this is what worried me, Ramona. I knew that Watson was slick, but I didn't think he would do it in public."

Ramona was not listening. She was writing notes on a pad.

Affrica was pacing. She had an idea of what to do, but she would have to confer with Ramona before she made any calls.

"So this is the deal," Ramona said.

Affrica sat down.

"Watson had an interview with one reporter from the *Daily,*" Ramona continued. "He just mentioned the fact that we were having meetings concerning the Projects. Somehow they got to talking about this woman who's been complaining and leading a crusade of angry tenants of Irving Projects."

"So?"

"Since it seemed like you dropped the ball on the problem."

"How could that be? I've been busting my butt trying to make meetings and get going with Irving Projects. How—"

"Listen." Ramona touched Affrica's sleeve. "We have to figure out how to clean this up so you come out unscathed. This is very delicate."

Affrica looked down, barely breathing.

"Affrica, I know this is your baby, your pet project." Ramona paused. "But I think you might have to act as if you agree totally with August and thank him for making the meeting."

Ramona pulled the laptop off the desk and started typing again. Affrica snapped out of the trance and started to dictate to Ramona the rest of what she would say. She would call a press meeting that Friday morning. But right now, Ramona and Affrica had a conference call with the old mayor. He said he was pressured by the reporter to say something, so he did, not thinking it would be on record. It seemed trivial to him.

Watson decided he would agree with whatever Affrica said was the reason. They would also downplay the whole thing. They would tell the press the only reason they were talking to them was that they wanted to know about the meeting.

"Good." Affrica was getting into the planning. She got on her laptop and started to highlight her plans on Irving Projects. She and Ramona did a question-and-answer session. Affrica perfected the speech she would make. By the end of the night, Ramona had called all the reporters at home, to arrange the conference. No questions would be asked. Mayor Bryant would just make the speech and explain why Watson had introduced the idea of the speech.

Early the next morning she met with the press and explained about the housing committee meeting.

She told them that she and Watson had discussed an emergency meeting privately. They decided that whoever spoke to the press first would announce the emergency meeting. She then read a ten-point plan she had. The press responded positively.

Once the press conference was finished, Affrica and Ramona gave each other high fives for staving off a potential disaster.

Six

Chantay's entire apartment was repaired. Everything from a leaky pipe to the ceiling. Her shower actually felt like a shower. Before, the water didn't even spray. She was pleasantly surprised. Some of her neighbors were experiencing the same amount of attention. Some were even given new carpeting.

But what Chantay didn't know was that her repairman installed bugs around her house and tapped her phone.

It was two o'clock one afternoon when Kysha wasn't feeling well. Someone buzzed Chantay's door. The man said he was from the management company and would be fixing her ceiling and doing a routine check of her electrical sockets and light fixtures. Chantay left him alone a lot that day, since Kysha wasn't well either and she kept having to go back to her room to tend to her. The nerdy repairman was quiet and quick. Chantay hated loud, noisy repairmen who flirted with her. This man didn't really look like a repairman, more like a computer guy or an accountant. He worked quickly and cleaned up after himself. Chantay was more than happy to let him use the phone when he was done.

Chantay's big surprise came when she received a

messenger-delivered letter stating she was invited to the meeting. If Chantay had read the letter carefully, she would have noted that it also stated she was not going to able to speak or ask any questions. She was there simply to observe.

No press was allowed at this meeting. Because of the sensitivity of the situation, the planners felt discretion was needed. They would call the press and give them an edited transcript of the meeting.

This was a very tension-filled and confusing issue.

Chantay wore her only business suit, a pretty peach-colored two-piece with gold buttons. Her hair was neatly brushed back and her legs were encased in flesh-toned panty hose. Her earrings matched her buttons.

Everyone was seated once again at the large conference table. Affrica sat and assessed the attendees, coolly. She was surprised Chantay was so young and sweet looking. She expected her to be older, bigger somehow. Affrica could tell she was nervous. She had dropped her pencil and gone under the desk to retrieve it. She kept shuffling her papers. If Affrica could have comforted the young woman, she would have. Affrica reread her paperwork and conferred with Delroy about the meeting. Ramona had briefed him once on what he would say.

The chief of police was dressed in an impeccable black suit and maroon tie.

Affrica eyed him suspiciously. He caught her stare, and she looked away. She started to go over her notes.

Herbert Stone would be mediating the meeting. He was a judge appointed by August six years ago. He could not make any judgments here though. He was only here to make sure it was a fair meeting, with all sides represented.

Also attending was the head of the Housing Department, Beverly Tims. She was a very large woman and she wore a green dress. She wanted to see Irving Housing remain the same. She had even thought about the houses getting landmark status.

Inside the conference room, some of the participants were talking. The treasurer, Maxwell Townsend, was there, and Delroy, Ramona, and representatives from the dueling contracting companies. Chantay nervously arranged papers in her folder. She actually thought she would address the room, make a speech.

Herbert Stone cleared his throat and said, "Let the meeting begin. Let all parties be heard so a fair agreement might be put in place." He did not mean it. Herbert had his own agenda.

Delroy addressed the group first. He presented the case and described some of what was holding back the larger repairs of Irving Housing.

After Delroy addressed the group, Chantay raised her hand. Everyone looked at her and then at Herbert Stone, who refused to acknowledge the woman's raised hand.

Why is he ignoring her? Affrica thought. She frowned visibly, disgusted.

Finally directing his attention to the woman, she said, "Mr. Stone, I think Ms. Miller would like to address the table."

Without looking at the young woman, Herbert said, "As it was clearly stated in the letter, Ms. Miller, you are not allowed to speak. This is a forum closed to the public. You are here strictly as a witness." He cleared his throat roughly. He didn't see the shocked look on Affrica's face.

She was upset. *How can he speak to her in that manner?*

Chantay was visibly crushed. In the shock of the moment her hand was still raised and she placed it in her lap. She did not know how to hide this emotion. She took a shuddering breath and fought back tears. Affrica stood up while Herbert Stone was speaking.

"I elect that we—yes, Mayor Bryant?"

Affrica placed her palms on the table. She took a deep breath, having really felt bad for Chantay. Her voice cracked. "As mayor, I elect that everyone in the room get a chance to speak."

"I . . . I . . . she was told." Herbert Stone looked around the room for support. He found none. Even Delroy looked down at his palm pilot.

"Well, I . . ." the large man stammered.

Affrica held up her hands. She sat down and motioned to Chantay.

Delroy clenched his teeth. *Affrica was ruining everything. Who the hell did she think she was, silencing Herbert Stone? Of all people.* He felt like an upset toddler whose pail got taken at the sandbox. He needed Affrica to be quiet. There was another plan under way. Since Delroy had been so successful at talking her into becoming mayor and dating him . . . They now needed her silenced about Irving Housing, needed her to stop snooping around the old accounting file. Affrica had told Delroy she would be going over the entire budget from the time Irving Projects was built till now. She had some accounting friend who could figure out all the numbers. When Delroy had relayed this to Watson, Watson had yelled at him, calling him incompetent.

Delroy had accepted more money to find a creative way of shutting up this woman or at least slowing her down. And he swore she was making eyes with that pretty-boy police chief.

*Some police chief. He's chief of the most corrupt depart-
ment in the city and he knows nothing about what's going
on.*

But Alex had been suspicious for a long time.
That's why he had two stacks of folders in his
kitchen. Alex knew enough about corruption not
to say anything to anybody. He had no concrete
proof of anything wrong. People being hired into
the department that should not have been hired.
Palaski, for instance, had been caught selling drugs.
Alex had fired the man immediately. But when he
returned to work three weeks later, claiming he had
gone to rehab, Alex didn't care—he told the man
to leave.

"The commish told me I could come back," the
short man had told Alex smugly. The man took a
step back when he saw the venom in Alex's eyes.

"In my office now." As Alex had walked through
the station, everyone moved out of his way. He was
imposing.

The police officer was slow in walking. Alex had
not turned around, had just gone into his office,
leaving the door open. He paced.

The man had gingerly stepped into Alex's office.
He did not want Alex's wrath. He never yelled, he
was just so precise and razor-sharp that he could
cut down anyone in mere seconds.

"You *were* an officer of the law. You sold drugs
to a sixteen-year-old girl on the street, out of your
police vehicle. . . . And you think for one second
that you are going to . . . what . . . get into uniform with your gun?"

The man tried to interject.

Alex got real close, standing over the man. "You
are the type of trash that we try to get off the street.
Get the hell out of my face."

They stood for a moment. Alex put his hand on his gun. "Now!" He slammed the door after the man left, too upset to do anything but fume, the heat rising off of him.

The conference room was quiet and tense. Africa motioned again to Chantay, who stood and smoothed down her pretty skirt. She rustled the papers to camouflage her shaking hands. She couldn't believe how utterly nervous she was. *Pull it together, girl,* she thought. She took a deep breath and began speaking just as Herbert Stone cleared his throat. Everyone looked up at him.

He was embarrassed. "Go ahead, Miss Miller. I apologize." He realized the room had turned on him and thought he was a bully.

Chantay began. "Where I live, Irving Housing is so run-down, we can't play in the park with our babies. The swings are broken, there's no slide. My ceiling almost fell down on my five-year-old daughter." Chantay looked up from the papers and around the room. Everyone was looking at her intently.

"Someone fell off the fire escape in building three. The fire escape was rusted and could not take his weight."

They seemed far away. She was desperate. She knew if these people didn't hear her or didn't listen to what she had to say about her home, nobody else would listen.

Chantay took another deep breath and sat down. She looked down for a moment. When she looked up her eyes were ablaze and she had renewed energy.

"Okay, this is it. My ceiling almost crushed my

child. I know a woman with two kids . . . two kids, whose husband bashed in her front door a month ago and the door is still broken. Is that not enough to make you people do something to help us?"

She was much calmer and resolved. She looked at everyone's face. They were listening; she had them.

The chief of staff looked as if he had a question.

"Mr. Roberts, you have a question?"

Delroy shook his head. Then he abruptly changed his mind and spoke. "You know what? I do have a question. Don't you think, *Ms.* Miller, that you and your neighbors are responsible for the mess that is Irving Projects."

A few other people at the table nodded their heads in agreement. Some mumbled.

Chantay could not be shaken. "Yes, you are right. But only certain things. We can't repair the elevator—"

"Yes, but if you stopped throwing diapers out the windows, maybe it wouldn't be such a dump."

"Mr. Roberts, I don't throw diapers out my window. And maybe you haven't driven by Irving Housing lately—there is no garbage in the front yard."

Delroy only snorted and checked his classic museum watch.

"We have a community clean-up program and every Sunday afternoon some of us get outside and clean up. We rake up old leaves. Shovel the snow. We do all that. Sanitation doesn't even come by us after snowstorms. We get fifteen-foot snow hills that stay until the first thaw."

Affrica wanted to help this young woman, let her know that she was going to support the initiative to rebuild the Projects. After a lull in the speaking,

Affrica decided finally to share her vision with the group.

"Chantay, I have to commend you on, first, your courage to come here—it could be a little intimidating. Second, for speaking up for your home in an honest voice, not just numbers and papers." Affrica looked around the room, scrutinizing everybody. She wondered how honest she could get everybody to be.

"I actually lived in the Projects a very short time. It was my home and it was all I knew. But I remember certain things I hated. Where we lived was falling apart also and the bathroom faucet leaked hot water. No one ever came to fix it. Our refrigerator stayed pretty warm and the freezer was merely tepid. We used to put our eggs and milk in the freezer." Affrica laughed. The room relaxed and laughed with her.

"I have a plan that will change Irving Housing forever." She took another breath. *It's a damn good idea, just say it.*

"The people of Irving Housing need something. They need homes, not just a place to live. People need to feel as though where they rest their heads is theirs. There is a certain security in knowing that when you come home, your ceiling will still be there."

The people at the table smiled at her. Chantay was intrigued.

Affrica continued. "Restless children need a place to be besides school. A place where they can be kids and teenagers. A decent park. They need to have the privacy to grow—not have to grow up in the street. There is nothing wrong with living in the Projects. But why do people have to live in dilapidated buildings? Why is there no security, no grass to walk on?"

Affrica stopped and took a breath. She tried to check her emotions. Ramona gave her a thumbs-up sign inconspicuously. Affrica was sharing her dream with them.

"Instead of doing major repairs and fixing the swings in the park as was originally planned, I say we rebuild the entire thing." She paused, waiting for the murmuring to subside. She tried to gauge the reaction in the room.

Everyone nodded their heads, except Delroy. This was the first time he had heard about *this*. Affrica always went on about fixing the Projects, caring so much about the people there. She spoke to him about doing an overhaul on the budget. His plan had been to thwart those ideas and change her concerns, have her focus on crime or schools. Now she seemed so determined, he was afraid. He quietly formulated another plan. He couldn't listen any more to her daisy-age rhetoric. She was such a hippie, he thought. Thought she could change the world just because she wanted to. He was utterly disgusted and surprised by the revelation.

Chantay, who had listened to Affrica, had a beautiful image in her head about her and her child living in a decent place. But all those years of nothing ever getting done, all those years of broken washing machines and uncertainty. She wanted to dream but she knew the reality of Irving, of the people she dealt with every day.

"What are you planning to do?" Chantay asked timidly.

"Good question." Affrica gave her a smile. She was on, ready to answer any question, convince any detractor. "We would demolish the entire complex." The room was abuzz; it took a good five minutes before everyone quieted. The two contractors were calculating what they would make from that scale of a project. They were both ready to sign on the dotted line, no matter how low the city would offer them.

"We would demolish the entire complex." Affrica looked at everyone a moment. "And rebuild about one hundred and twenty-six two-family homes instead."

Delroy's mouth fell open.

Ramona took frantic notes. She already knew Affrica's plan. She was the one who told Affrica not to mention her idea to anyone until after she was elected. She didn't even tell that fool Delroy or August. She wouldn't mention it until *after* the inauguration party. Affrica had shared her dream with no one. Meanwhile she and Ramona had been having secret meetings on what the new Irving houses would look like.

Beverly Tims was upset that she hadn't come up with Affrica's idea. It was so simple and brilliant. She resisted though.

Everybody had his hand up, including the police chief, who had been silent all this time. But Affrica continued. "There would be backyards, with grass and fences." She looked at the notes Ramona passed to her. "Each home will house two families. People who were related, but lived in different apartments, could, if they wanted, be in the same house as their cousin or sister. They could reject the pairing anonymously. We could even pair single parents with other single parents."

"Are you trying to play matchmaker, Mayor Bryant?" Beverly sneered openly at her.

"No, Ms. Tims. I'm trying to give people a sense of community."

"I'm sure they feel a sense of community just fine," she offered back.

Chantay said, "No, Ms. Tims, there is no feeling of community. The housing meetings happen in the lobby, people always fightin', these guys always hangin' in front of the entrance. At least if I had my own house, they wouldn't be hanging out in front of anybody's house but mine. You have to step over them to get into the building. They don't help you if you have a cart . . ." She stopped midsentence. "I'm sorry."

"No, that's why we are here, to voice concerns and give ideas," Affrica said.

Alex raised his hand. "I agree with some of your ideas, Ms. Bryant. What about having twenty-four-hour security? It would make the residents feel safer as well."

"I agree, Mr. Bartholomew." She gave him a genuine smile.

She looked around the mahogany table. "What if the eighteen-year-olds who are causing so much harm in the city were so busy with activities that they had no time to deal drugs or threaten people?"

A heated question-and-answer session ensued after Affrica made her last points. Ms. Tims and Herbert Stone had to be convinced. Though she hated to admit it, Beverly Tims left impressed but unwilling to consider the idea. Delroy did not challenge Affrica. And Alex was interested in this woman.

Seven

After the Irving Housing meeting a few people stayed around, Delroy, Ramona, Alex, and Maxwell, even Chantay. Chantay had grown to like the mayor in the brief time she had known her. The mayor had defended the Projects and the people in the Projects.

The judge had suggested that the people living in Irving Projects deserved to live in dilapidated homes because they somehow didn't deserve more. And since they were there, they wanted to be there. Everyone thought that was ridiculous.

Chantay was not the only person impressed by Affrica's drive and conviction during the meeting. She felt inspired seeing this black woman with power and influence.

Alex had looked at her determined face, as she spoke of the real people of Irving Projects, the babies and the teenagers, whose lives were in danger.

After hearing Affrica, he thought about her a little differently. *Maybe she's not the stuck-up witch that I thought she was.* He had taken many notes on her ideas and realized that they did not disagree on the project. *I guess we've always been so at each other's throats that it didn't make sense to agree.* Any doubt that he had about Affrica's commitment to changing Irving Housing was gone. There could be no way she was involved with Watson.

He thought her somewhat naive thinking a community center was the cure-all for the rampant crime in the city. He wanted to talk to her about this. He didn't want to argue a point; he wanted to pick her brain. He found himself wondering what kind of past she had. Where was her father? Why had she lived in the Projects. How did she get out?

They all agreed another group meeting would need to be had, along with a joint meeting with the police chief and housing director. After individual meetings with the treasurer, the contractors, and the police chief, Affrica would have to make some decisions on when to start the rebuilding. She would also meet with an architect who could build a small-sized replica of what the new Irving houses would like. How the land would be distributed and plotted.

I swear I spend every waking hour in meetings or press conferences.

The idea Affrica had presented to the group seemed like a good one. *But it's so drastic. Tear down Irving,* Chantay thought. She was feeling good otherwise—she had presented her point flawlessly and she had the blessing of the mayor, that gorgeous chief of police, the chief of staff, and that handsome Maxwell Townsend. When she had made her speech he was staring at her so intently that when she looked at him, she tripped over her words. She felt happy to be able to have something to give to the tenants.

Maxwell later invited her to stay and have dinner with them. He was smooth. Chantay couldn't believe she was going to have dinner with the mayor and all these other politician people. *And* the treasurer made goo-goo eyes at her.

Maxwell helped her with her leather jacket.

Ramona was not happy about the current state of affairs with Maxwell. Since the last meeting, they had gotten together a few times. But now he was outright flirting with this Chantay woman.

He ignored her the whole evening. He acted as if the entire incident hadn't happened. That they never had dinner the other night, gone back to his house, and had sex. She didn't tell Affrica because she didn't want her friend to think she was easy.

How could he stand there in front of her drooling at this other woman?

The group made reservations at a restaurant and proceeded there. This group was the elite. They were the who's who of Passion politics. They were treated like royalty wherever they dined. The patrons were sneaking glances at the group, who were laughing and telling jokes. The mayor had entered the posh restaurant and immediately said good evening to all the people sitting at their tables. She didn't miss a beat.

Ramona went with them just to see what Maxwell would do. He ignored her. He joined in when everyone talked, but he never addressed her directly.

Alex and Affrica were once again trying to ignore each other. Delroy tried to usurp her ear. But Affrica wanted to talk to everyone.

The restaurant was one of the most popular places in the city. It was a soul-food West-Indian restaurant where you could get rice and peas with ham hocks.

The famous architect, Fred Harcourt, who designed the Gersheinem Museum of Modern Art, had designed this place. It was done in a post-modern style, filled with sweeping couches and intimate tables, vibrant and soothing all at the same time. Large elephant ferns decorated each table in a crystal vase. There was a waiting period of almost three week to get in, unless of course you were the new young mayor—then a table of six would pop up almost immediately. The food was so popular that some celebrities flew in personally just to eat and flew back to LA.

The group was ready to eat after such a long and draining meeting. Somehow Alex and Affrica wound up sitting across from each other. Affrica had removed her suit jacket and was wearing a pretty white blouse.

Delroy, who had been especially quiet, was waiting for a call. Earlier when Affrica had asked him what was wrong, he said only that he was not feeling well. Affrica had not probed. She had been so relieved that he did not want to talk. She had enough on her mind.

He was thinking about the next drastic move he would have to make. He would have to do it sooner than later. The meeting had shocked him.

The group engaged in lively discussions. The topics were kept very light, like which schools people had gone to and what outrageous things they did when they were younger, funny names their friends had growing up. They ordered shrimp cocktails and hors d'oeuvres.

When their dinners came, they ate heartily and laughed all through. Maxwell told a lot of jokes, as did Chantay. They sat very close and told anecdotes to the table. Both had a great sense of humor.

They were laughing when Delroy's cell phone

rang. The group was winding down and enjoying a little dessert and wine.

"Get your butt over here." It was August Watson. He was already briefed on how the meeting went and the vote to rebuild the housing project.

Delroy shot up. "I have to go. Important." He barely looked at Affrica, who was shocked at his abrupt exit. She knitted her eyebrows together.

Ramona stood up and turned to look directly at Maxwell, who had his arm around Chantay's chair, trying to make her laugh. Ramona turned her back on them.

She turned to the rest of the table and said a polite good night. Affrica got up as if to leave with her.

"No, I'm fine. Enjoy your wine," Ramona said. She then turned on her pretty heels and sauntered out of the restaurant, some male patrons admiring her round behind.

At the same time Ramona was leaving, one of Affrica's constituents greeted the mayor. Affrica stood up at the table and spoke to the person. A redheaded man with a bandage on his nose. He proceeded to tell her his idea on making the sewage treatment sound. Chantay and Maxwell waved, and she responded absentmindedly, wondering how she could make this man go away without being rude. Just then his wife, also a redhead, came and dragged him away.

"Come on, Henry, leave the mayor alone. I'm sure she does not want to hear about poop treatment." She turned to Affrica and smiled. "Good night, Mayor Bryant."

Affrica sat down and began speaking, not having realized everyone at her table had left, except one person. She looked at Alex questionably, then looked around at the empty chairs with a comical expression.

"How . . ." She pointed at the other seats.

Alex smiled at her. "Maybe it was all that talk of sewage treatment." Alex smiled at her again.

Why does he keep smiling at me? Affrica thought.

"You must think I'm so stupid. Just grinning at you. But you know what? At work I don't grin or smile. It feels good to have someone to smile at."

Affrica was curious about this annoying, attractive man. *Has he always been this beautiful?* She bit her lip and squinted a little at him.

He frowned slightly. "So, can we call a truce, Mayor Bryant?"

"I think we can, *Mr.* Bartholomew."

"Alex," he said.

"Affrica," she said.

"I think for the good of all involved, we need to find a common ground. In listening to your speech, it seems we don't disagree on this issue."

"Yeah, you know, you're right. When I heard you speak, I was glad to hear we don't disagree."

"So you lived at Irving Housing."

"Yes, it was fine, like I said before." She sat up. "It was great and horrible at the same time." She scratched her cheek lightly.

Alex followed her long fingers and for the first time noticed her mouth. Her lips were full. They looked shiny, as if she had just applied lip gloss. His eye trailed up from her lips to her nose, then her eyes. *Wow, what beautiful eyes she has. How come I never noticed before? Wait, what the hell am I thinking?*

Alex was confused.

"I really want to see people living comfortably," she said. "If we have the ability to give them more of a choice in their life, I really feel there wouldn't be so much crime." She looked at Alex with determined eyes. "Once I can make heads or tails about this budget, I'm going after education next."

Affrica looked at her watch. She started to get up to leave. "I think I better be going, Mr. . . . Alex." She gave him a warm smile, her eyes twinkling.

Alex couldn't stop himself. "Uh, Affrica, are you really tired or do you just want to get away from me?"

"Yes, this place is great, but I need to take off these high heels and my mayoral mask." She gathered her things and went to coat check for her coat.

"All right then. I'll walk you to the parking lot." Alex wanted to talk to her some more. It did not seem that it would happen tonight. They had planned another meeting.

Affrica looked deeply at Alex. She could have sworn he wanted her to stay. *Why? Even though we called a truce . . . there's so much bad energy from the past. Why would he want to be around me?*

"Do you really want to get some coffee or do you want my company?" Affrica smiled brilliantly.

Alex felt such a draw to her he was overwhelmed. He held his head down for a moment and said quietly, "I want your company."

She looked at him confused. "Look, Alex, I don't know what you're thinking. Are you planning some argument, some point to challenge me on? We were just at odds a few months ago, and now you want to take me out for coffee?"

"Yeah, you really irritated me."

"I irritated you? You're the one who kept every single file away from me. You're the one who instructed his staff not to speak to anybody. You were not a good sport, Mr. Bartholomew. You know what?

This should be interesting, Alex. You have succeeded in piquing my interest, you know. One of my favorite spots is down by Filligan Street."

"That cheesy diner."

"Yes!" Affrica said excitedly. Would you like to go and have some coffee over there in an hour? I need to go home and change my clothes. Then I can go past my house and see how it looks."

When they got to the parking lot, Alex's Jeep's tires had all been slashed.

This was the third time in a month his tires had been slashed. The culprits were always elusive—nobody ever saw anything. When Affrica drove toward him, her headlights hit him, crouching looking at the tires. He was shaking his head as he stood up. He seemed oblivious to the cold.

Affrica looked at him out the window. "You planned this, didn't you? So I would have to take you around with me. This is so typical." She got out of the car, looking at his tires, shaking her head. At least she would have a good excuse as to why she had the chief of police in her vehicle.

The sun had almost set and a chilly wind had set in. Affrica had a cashmere pink pashmina around her head. She looked like a movie star from the fifties. The sky was a plethora of colors and cloud patterns. Alex called his mechanic friend, who also had a tow truck. The department used his services and paid him well. Josh would come at a moment's notice to help an officer. Alex called him, telling him just to take it and he'd collect it later that night. Affrica let him into the car.

"I didn't plan to have my tires slashed. Why are you so mean?"

Affrica was silenced. She withdrew, then came back quickly. "I'm not mean. Listen, Alex, just because I'm not one of your many admirers doesn't mean I'm mean. Also I was kidding."

"What are you talking about, 'many admirers'?"

"Because I'm not—how do you say?—sweating you, you think I'm being mean." Affrica started the car harshly, pressing down the gas unnecessarily.

"I don't need you to sweat me."

"So why are you calling me mean?" She made a right, speeding out of the parking lot.

Alex sat back in the seat. *She drives like a maniac.* He shook his head and looked at her profile. He had to choose his words carefully. "Just with the whole police department investigation," he started slowly, "how you came in there and demanded all these duty-related folders and you wanted to interview my guys. You barked out orders like an army sergeant."

"Yes, well, I was only doing my job. Watson told me I had to do it," she said.

"Oh, Watson told you to do it."

They pulled up to her house. Through the trees she could only make out the outline of it, as it was so dark. Affrica's headlights lit up the trees.

She had left most of her casual clothes at her house, thinking she would be back to retrieve them, but she hadn't come back since leaving initially.

"You have to wait in the car." She slammed her car door. "You can turn on the radio. I have a cassette already in there. I shouldn't be more than ten minutes."

Alex got out of the car. "I'm not going to sit in the car."

Affrica was exasperated. "Why don't you walk ahead of me to the diner? I'll meet you there."

"Let's do that. Because I'm not going to just sit in your car. Let me escort you to the door."

"No, I'll be fine."

He looked at Affrica in the dark as he stood there, his senses keen. Together they walked down the path to her house. He waited until he saw she had safely closed the door behind her after entering. She turned her outside lamp on and it partly illuminated his walk back down the path. His stride was purposeful and confident. He walked the five minutes quickly, bracing himself against the chilly winds. The whole time he walked, he was observing like a stealthy panther.

Eight

Half an hour later, Affrica's car drove into the restaurant parking lot. She walked quickly up the short stairs and through the glass doors. She was wearing very loose-fitting black pants, a brown turtleneck, and flatter shoes. She was stunning. Her keys were the only thing she carried. Her obvious natural beauty floored Alex. *Why didn't I notice before?* He felt his manhood stir.

The waitress was leaning against the table chatting with him. She couldn't stop smiling at Alex. She had already told him the name of all her six cats. He knew what school she graduated from and her favorite ice cream flavor. Alex didn't really care to know all this personal information, but he was used to it. Women for some reason always wanted to tell him things, personal things. He was very cordial, asking questions, keeping eye contact.

Affrica smirked at Alex and scooted into the booth and looked at the waitress, who did not even realize Affrica was now sitting down. "Olivia, is that you?"

Olivia Jacobson turned around and let out a shriek. Luckily they were the only customers. "Affrica, baby. *Mayor.* How are you? We miss you so much over these parts. I made your usual for two weeks."

"I miss you guys too. Girl, no one can touch your quiche. I dream about the spinach pie."

Olivia, in her mid-forties, with two sons, was a rail-thin woman with a long gray braid down her back. She was a very friendly woman who cared about Affrica very much.

Alex looked at the two women talking and reminiscing.

Affrica was holding Olivia's hand. "How are Jason and Timothy?"

"Girl, they are teenagers getting on my last nerve. The twelve-year-old is trying to act like he's eighteen, the seventeen-year-old is acting like he's ten." She threw her hands up. I just leave them with their father and come over here, girl. I'd rather be at work than be in that house filled with men." She looked at Alex. "No offense."

"None taken," Alex replied.

"So, tell me, honey, how is it being the mayor?"

"Girl, I feel the same way I did when I was deputy mayor. I feel the same way I did when I was an intern."

"I hear that. That means you won't change on us, get an ego the size of Canada and refuse to eat at cheesy diners."

"Never." Affrica looked down at Alex. He had an amused look on his face. Olivia looked down too.

"Okay, okay, I'll let you two get back to your *meeting*. Want more coffee, sweet cheeks?"

"Yes, please." Alex almost blushed.

She left with a wink at Alex and Affrica.

Alex had chosen a pretty discreet place to sit. Affrica liked that. He had the common sense not to sit by the window. Sadly Affrica learned that most people did not posses that simple skill.

Alex cleared his throat and sat back. His jacket was hung up and he was wearing a long-sleeve black T-shirt, rolled up past his forearms. He had a little bit of hair on them. Affrica noticed a lot of things in Alex that she had never noticed before.

He smiled at her, and she saw the deep dimples on his cheeks.

He has dimples!

"Like I was saying . . . you were so demanding."

"Wait, Alex, I just got here and what do you mean 'like I was saying'? I'm the one who was making a point when we got to my house. I was the last one to speak in the car on this subject."

Alex held his hands up in surrender. "Okay, you got it. Do you know what you want to eat?" He changed the subject.

Affrica took note and let it slide. As he said it, Olivia made her way to the table with a side salad, a plate of fries, and buffalo wings.

When Alex looked confused, Affrica explained her frequent visits. "Order something else. Olivia always brings me this."

"No, this is fine." He munched on some french fries. Alex ordered the famous spinach pie and a soda. He drank some coffee.

"I didn't order this for you," Affrica said carefully.

"People usually share food when they eat out. Especially when the other diners don't have any food yet *and* the person has magical powers and food appears within two minutes of them sitting down."

"Yeah, well, too bad," Affrica said playfully.

Alex poured ketchup on the side of Affrica's plate

and dipped a fry in. "When my food comes, I promise to share."

"I'm the mayor, you know, I could get you in trouble." Affrica looked at him seriously and they both laughed, causing a lot of their tensions to melt away. They felt relaxed.

Affrica noticed a light scar on Alex's forehead. She took in his rugged good looks, his stubborn jaw, and his brown skin.

He looked at his pager. "Quiet night tonight."

"Huh?" Affrica was startled.

"I said it's a quiet night tonight. My pager has been quiet all day. The guys usually page me at least once."

"Maybe they're handling the station fine without you. Don't tell me you're a control freak too."

Alex ignored her comment. "Don't eat my food when it comes. I have to go make some calls." He was getting up to leave.

"Unless they're really personal, you could make them in here. It's cold out there."

"Nah, I can't stand when people do business in public."

"Oh, Alex, just make the calls wherever."

Alex went outside. He contacted the garage, who had his car ready with brand-new tires. There were benefits to being the police chief.

He called the station. Everything was under control. Alex was relieved and checked his personal messages. His mother had left him a message asking him to come over soon. Patrick had left a two-minute message about the advice Alex had given him, working.

He went back into the restaurant smiling and shaking his head at Patrick's foolishness. Affrica could not believe how beautiful his smile was. Those dimples. Affrica always thought men with dimples looked feminine or young. Alex looked neither. He had a face all to himself; everything fitted perfectly. *His parents must be gorgeous,* she thought.

"Is everything all right?"

"Yes, it's fine. The station is still standing. A friend of mine, Patrick, left me a crazy message." He rubbed his cold hands together.

"Tell me about the department." She was very curious.

"What do you want to know?" He folded his hands on the table, sitting up closer to her.

"Tell me whatever you want."

"Why do you want to know anyway?"

"Because I'm curious. I've dealt with cops, I was around your guys at the station for six weeks. I never went for coffee with any of them. I never sat down and talked personally with a cop. I've talked business, politics, but never personal."

"Okay, Affrica, I got you." He thought for a moment.

Olivia approached with his plate of food. She placed it gently down in front of him, smiling broadly. She left quickly to give the couple privacy.

He looked at Affrica, then down at his food.

"I'm telling you, the food here is good. Trust me," she said.

He put his fork into the hot food and brought it to his full mouth. It was delicious. He shoveled five more forkfuls while Affrica patiently waited for him to finish.

"You eat a lot. We just had dinner plus dessert and here you are scarfing down spinach pie," Affrica marveled.

He simply pointed to her plate of french fries, empty. After he was satiated, he ordered another soda. He wiped his mouth and cleared his throat. "My work is hard to describe. As the police chief I have to watch over these officers. Make sure they stay safe. Make sure everything runs smoothly. The sarge and I usually deal with big cases. Rape, murder, felonies."

"Wow, you said that so matter-of-factly."

"Yeah, well, I don't take any of those crimes lightly. But I've put it into its proper context. We're just talking about those things as ideas. No one is murdered in front of us."

"Okay." Affrica hoped he wasn't feeling as if she were belittling him. She really wanted to know what he was thinking. "How do you keep yourself from getting jaded about life?"

"I . . . it's hard, you know." He rubbed his beard, a habit Affrica was noticing.

"When I was an officer I handled a lot of domestic-abuse cases. Robberies and burglaries. I didn't think it could get harder, but it has." He ate some more. "What is troubling is the fact that it's children now. It's children doing the robberies, the drug dealing. They have no respect for elders or property."

Affrica nodded and let him continue. His words were so heartfelt and honest. She wanted to reach for him.

"You said something at one of the meetings, something like 'you get them before we do,' and I do agree with that." Alex thought about it and nodded.

"I think we've failed our children—the school systems are backward. They are underfunded, the teachers are underpaid, with overcrowded classrooms. School is no longer a place of learning. It must be so hard to be a child these days."

"I know I'm probably going to get my butt kicked for asking this but . . . how old are you?" He quickly cowered in mock fear.

Affrica laughed and poked one of his broad shoulders. "I am not afraid to say my age."

"So say it then." Alex faced her boldly, enjoying the teasing game they were playing.

"I'm thirty . . ." She covered her mouth when she said the last part.

"Huh? I didn't get the last part." Alex turned his head sideways toward her and placed his hand behind his ear. Speak up, granny, I can't hear you."

Affrica threw a dirty napkin at him. "Seriously, I'm thirty-three. Born on a lovely spring day in May. I am a Taurus. You?"

"I'm thirty-seven years old and my birthday is August fifteenth. I don't know what that makes me."

Affrica thought a moment. "You are a"—she counted on her fingers—"a . . . Leo. Oh, boy, hardheaded."

"You think?"

"So what do you do when you are not watching over your department and cleaning your gun?"

"I swim."

"Really?" This man was getting more and more interesting by the moment.

"Yeah, swimming helps get the stress out. I do about thirty or forty laps a day, depending on how my day went."

"So the harder the day, the more you swim."

"How about you, Affrica, what is your release?" He looked directly in her luminous brown eyes.

She felt her whole body tingle. "I work out . . . I like to dance . . . haven't done much of that in a while . . . stretching, yoga. I like yoga."

"Does it help?"

"You know what? It really does help. It's very subtle."

"That's all you do to keep up your body?"

"Wait, what do you mean by that?"

"I'm just saying . . ." Alex was embarrassed. He didn't mean to say that. "You have a very nice figure. I didn't think some stretches could do that, and you eat like a man."

"You would be surprised what yoga does for one's body and flexibility." Affrica looked at Alex. "Anyway."

"Being a cop is stressful. My father doesn't think so. He thinks I'm a loser because I didn't stay in the military."

Alex did not know what had gotten into himself. Why had he brought up his father? He never spoke about him.

"You don't get along with your father?" Affrica asked.

Alex clenched his jaw. Affrica noticed immediately. "I'm sorry, we don't have to talk about it."

He shook his head. "No, that is an automatic response." He drank some soda.

"My dad," Alex began, "thought that joining the Military Reserves was a cop-out. He didn't care that I was already a full-fledged military officer. He wanted me to be what he was. A marine. So I joined the Marine Reserves. He didn't like that. So I figured, no matter what I did, I would never make him happy. So I stopped trying." Alex was thoughtful.

"Parents can be rigid sometimes," Affrica said empathetically. She wanted to know more about this man. "So . . . what did you want to do?"

"I wanted to finish college. Climb mountains,

travel all over the world. Swim in the Olympics maybe."

"Did you get to do all of it?" Affrica asked.

"I've traveled and I've climbed a few mountains. I've never been to the Olympics . . ."

"And you're the chief of police," Affrica stated. Alex nodded.

Affrica was so impressed. She'd never met someone who had aspirations the way she did. A lot of goals. She smiled at him and shook her head. He wasn't bragging either. He was very matter-of-factly. Alex sat back.

Affrica got herself comfortable in the booth. "So what else do you have? I'm almost positive you have more."

He smiled at her. "I only have slight knowledge of Capoeria, I just started taking a class, but I've been so busy . . . you know, that Brazilian martial art?"

"I know of it, but I'm sorry, Mr. Bartholomew, you don't seem like the type of person who has *slight* anything." Affrica looked shocked at her own words. She began to stammer to clear up any confusion.

Alex just smiled at her.

"I mean, you seem like you would have broad knowledge instead of just general, okay?"

"I understood what you meant the first time." Alex was so intrigued by Affrica's honesty. It seemed she was trying to get a rise out of him, provoke him a little.

He imagined kissing her, parting her lips with his tongue. He couldn't believe how hot it was in the restaurant. Alex forced himself back.

"I was in the army for four years," he said seri-

ously. "And the marines on weekends. I really did
not want to go—"

"But your father made you go," Affrica finished
his sentence.

"Ah, you know about pushy parents."

"Very much. My mother was a hippie, Black Panther, communist. My dad is a CPA."

Alex laughed heartily.

"Yes, laugh at my pain." She joined Alex in the
laughter.

Alex sat forward and leaned into the table. He
could see the pretty mole under her eye.

"How was that, living with someone with so many
ideals?"

"It was hard. You know, she had me attending
rallies from the time I was born. I spoke two lan-
guages by the time I was five."

"Which?"

"English and Swahili. When we lived at Irving, I
was alone a lot. Mom was the type to go to people's
homes and counsel them. She talked to couples,
single moms, and teenagers. We finally moved out
when she decided it was time for her to go see the
continent of Africa."

"Wow. By the way, why is your name spelled with
two Fs?"

"My mom had a lot of friends in the movement
and some of them were naming their children Africa. My mom did not want to copy them, but she
loved the name and the idea of her child being
named after that great continent. So she added an
F."

Alex thought Affrica had a good head on her
shoulders. She was beautiful and smart.

Affrica had always been a confident woman. Usually she was the one making men stutter and ner-

vous. Not just by her looks, but her accomplishments too.

She had finished college by age twenty, got her master's and finished law school, and now at thirty-three she was the mayor. It was incredible, not just because of her age, but the fact that she was an African-American *and* a woman. A fact not lost on Alex. Even the strongest man would be intimidated. Alex was intrigued. She was conservative but not overly so. She had a sense of fun.

"I was raised in two different worlds. My mom, when she was around, was always going to rallies, trying to organize people. She was in all the marches and sit-ins. I mean, she did it all."

"Great."

"Yes, she did it all and my grandmother raised me to have solid goals and make changes in the world we live in. Good changes. You know, she's really for justice."

"That's why you went into law?"

"Yeah, but my mother was not too thrilled about me going into law and working for the 'establishment.' " Affrica fiddled with the rim of her mug, drawing circles around it.

"She wanted you to be on the outskirts of government, grassroots."

"Yeah, she did not think anything could be changed from the inside. She thought I would somehow become corrupted or unfeeling about the plight of poor people."

"Of course you didn't."

"Of course I didn't," Affrica repeated.

They stared at each other for a moment; then Alex looked away this time. Though he wished he could talked to her more, talk to her forever, he knew they had to stop. As much privacy as this section offered, what did it look like, he and the mayor in intimate conversation?

As if reading his mind, Affrica started to collect her things. She pulled on her pretty wrap. "I have to go, Alex." She loved saying his name. Her heart was pounding and she felt excited and hot. She knew she had to get out, now. "Will you be okay getting home?" Thinking about his car and flat tire.

Alex only nodded.

She put her hand on his as she stood over him. "Thank you, Alex. I enjoyed speaking with you."

The heat between them was almost unbearable. She wrapped her pashmina around her shoulders and walked away from Alex. He made a phone call to a unit in the area, and they would pick him up immediately to bring him to the garage.

Affrica stood at the counter talking to Olivia for a while and Alex laid a twenty on the table, walked back toward the women.

"Everything is on the table." He tried hard not to look at Affrica, but he did. The police car drove up and he walked away after bidding them a good night. There was no drama, no looking back.

Affrica sat at the counter with Olivia for almost an hour, catching up with her friend and gossiping.

Nine

He hungrily kissed her lips. Her soft mouth was beginning to hurt, his lips were pressed so hard on hers. He slowly licked his way up her face to her ears, leaving a moist trail. He lapped at her ear like a dog drinking water.

It was everything Affrica took not to gag. Delroy started kneading her breast over her shirt. She was looking at the ceiling.

After she left the restaurant, she had come home, to find Delroy waiting up for her, at her den in the mansion. It was an old-fashioned decorated room, which was so different from Affrica's more modern and ethnic way of putting together her home. He was watching a relationship movie. He never watched those. But she found him deep in the middle of one. He might have had tears in his eyes. The movie was about a black couple going through it and finally winding up together. She was suspicious of him. But he offered his hand after she took off and hung up her coat.

She stood by the couch with questions in her eyes. "What's going on?"

"I'm watching *Love Rules.*"

"You hate that movie."

"No, I never hated this movie. I just did not get it. Now I get it." He looked at her and patted the couch, indicating that she should sit down.

She sat next to him and crossed her arms over her chest. He placed his arm around her shoulder and brought her closer to him.

Now she was in bed being groped. She was upset she had let him get this far. She tried to come up with an excuse.

"I have my period, stop." She rolled from under him.

"Didn't you just have your period?"

"Yes, a, a few weeks ago. It's postmenstrual."

Delroy didn't believe her, but knew better than to question a woman about her cycle.

Delroy stormed out of the room. Went to the den. He really did not want to have sex with Affrica. He actually missed Evelyn, who was living in Chicago. Evelyn was a CPA working for a large accounting firm. She was a warm brown woman with small breasts and green eyes. Delroy thought her green eyes and naturally curly hair were her best features, though Evelyn was a college graduate and a certified public accountant. She was actually sleeping with the vice president of the company she worked for. Delroy didn't know about that, but she knew about Affrica.

Delroy just wanted to reclaim Affrica as his. He had seen the way Alex had looked at her. He knew she had stayed in the restaurant with him, had even gone to that horrible diner that she loved so much.

He had gotten three calls on his cell phone. Mayor
Watson told him he was messing up.

He thought if they made love, she would stop
thinking about that cop. But there she went with
that period crap. He had to do something drastic
to shut her up. He needed her pregnant.

Affrica was relieved. After Delroy had left she had
exhaled and lain on her back.

She tried to make herself like Delroy. She
thought about his smooth dark skin. His chest was
nice and a little hairy. Nothing. She thought about
his tall muscular body. She had to be crazy not to
want him anymore. She rolled onto her side and
looked out on the side lawn. Silhouettes of beautiful
bare trees waved slightly in the winter wind. She
thought about Alex. Alex was beautiful. A whole
man, he had a sense of humor, he was intelligent,
and he was so handsome her breath caught every
time she looked at him. She even noticed the dimples he tried to hide behind his light beard. She
wanted to stick her tongue in them. Kiss his face,
unbutton his shirt. She tried to stop and think
about Delroy once more. Delroy with all that co-
logne that got on her clothes, and on her sheets.

He was a decent person, she thought. He loved
dogs, never said anything bad about his mom or
dad. He never cursed. He had lived in New York.
But those fake contacts, it was so bizarre for her to
see him take out his eyes almost every night.

Her telephone rang abruptly, interrupting her
thoughts. When she answered she heard the voice
of the mansion concierge. Though a little wary, Affrica accepted the late call. *Maybe Ramona has business to discuss.*

"Yes," she said into the telephone. Affrica looked at her clock. Ten o'clock. A male voice responded. At the same time she heard Delroy coming up the stairs. She grabbed her notepad from the night table. When Delroy opened the door, she mouthed, *Ramona. Business.*

It was Alex on the other end. She was excited.

"Affrica?"

Her spine was jelly. She melted against the bed.

"Yes . . . um, Ramona," Affrica said once again into the phone. "I, I have those notes you wanted."

Delroy was still standing at the door, his hands on the doorknob. He closed it and stood behind it a few seconds. He proceeded to the den and opened the couch. There was no way he could hear the conversation. She had two phones in the house. The business phone was in the living room, the personal phone in the bedroom. There were no connections to eavesdrop on. He slammed the cushions of the couch on the floor. He knew it wasn't Ramona. Ramona never made Affrica nervous. He changed his mind about staying over at the mansion. He left the couch open and dressed. He was humiliated.

"Hi, Affrica," Alex said huskily.

"Good night, Alex."

"I had a question burning in my mind."

"Ask away." Affrica could not believe how happy she felt. She was dizzy. She tried to catch her breath.

"What kind of music do you like?"

"I know you did not call me at ten o'clock to ask me that."

"Yes, I did. It's very important that I know."

"Hold on a minute, one minute." She thought about it. "Give me four minutes." Affrica placed the phone on the bed, checked the window, and saw that indeed Delroy had left. She ran down the stairs to her office phone. She dialed Ramona's number with shaky fingers.

"Hello," said a breathless voice.

"Ramona, Ramona."

"Hey . . . Affrica, what's going on?"

"I need to ask you something."

"Max came home with me tonight," Ramona blurted out.

"No, you did not. . . . Why would you go home with him after the way he treated you?"

Ramona changed the subject quickly. "So you were asking . . ."

"Listen, I need your advice quick. Alex is on the phone. What should I tell him? He wants to know what kind of music I like."

"Wow!"

"What do you mean 'wow'?"

"Well, just the fact that he's calling you outside of the business setting. Second, the fact that he wants to know this personal information that really doesn't matter. Woman, you better go talk to your man. Good night." She hung up the phone in Affrica's ear. Affrica looked at the phone in disbelief. She walked quickly up to the bedroom.

Alex held the phone to his ear and waited exactly three minutes and twenty-three seconds. He had been staring at the clock. He heard her clear her throat; then her voice was in his ear.

"Sorry about that. Had some business to take care of."

"Oh, were you putting Delroy to bed?"

"So you called to harass me."

Alex felt horrible. "No, I'm sorry. That was petty." But he *was* curious about Delroy's where-abouts. She had pretended the call was from her girlfriend; then she spent three minutes doing something.

Alex had called on a whim. After dinner he had gone home, taken a very cold shower, and put on some Marvin Gaye. He was wondering if she liked Marvin too. He had her home number, like all the home numbers of all elected officials of the city. He had spontaneously dialed her number and heard her melodic voice before he could hang up.

"Marvin Gaye, John Coltrane, Aretha Franklin, Missy Elliot—"

"Wait, Missy Elliot and John Coltrane?"

"Hey, you asked."

"Go on, this list is very interesting." Alex sat on his couch, music playing lightly.

"Are you sure? I'm honestly not interested in getting a critique on what kind of music I like."

Alex was immediately sorry he had made the initial comment. "Affrica, I'm very sorry I was sarcastic. I really want to know what music you like."

"Missy Elliot," Affrica continued. "Elton John, Prince, Michael Jackson. I like the old Michael Jackson. Even after surgery, but before the Bad album. Yolanda Adams can blow. Jill Scott, Lauryn Hill . . . the list is endless."

"Do you like Davis?"

"I love Miles." Listening to Miles Davis always bought up strong emotions in Affrica.

Alex said, "Whenever I listen to Miles, I always start remembering things like when I was stationed in Bosnia. We had a boom box and one of the CDs that was always playing was Miles Davis's 'Kind of Blue.' "

Affrica began to hum the first bars of the album. Alex was impressed. "Ah, you know it."

"So what, Alex, do you think you know something about me now?"

"A little something."

"What do you know, Alex?" Affrica almost purred into the phone. She was lying on her side again. Looking at the trees. She felt very comfortable now and very flirtatious.

"Hmm," Alex said, his deep voice reverberating through the phone into Affrica's panties.

"I know you are a passionate woman, who disguises it under expensive, conservative suits. I know I would like to—"

"Hold on." Affrica's call waiting beeped. She clicked over, annoyed. "Yes?"

"Good night, Affrica," said a voice smoother than silk.

"Delroy?"

"Yes, baby. I'm just calling to tell you I love you and I hope you sleep well tonight."

"Uh . . . thank you. You too."

Delroy hung up quietly. He did as he had intended. Planted more questions in Affrica's mind and broke whatever mood they had created for themselves.

Affrica hit the flash button on her phone. "Hi, Alex. I'm back," she said dryly, unsuccessfully trying to pick up where they had left off.

"Once again, Ms. Bryant, good night." He knew just by her voice when she clicked back to him that things were not the same.

Delroy had soured it once more.

Ten

It was a very cold day in Passion. A cold, stinging wind was swooping off Lake Michigan and barreling straight into the city. The weatherman said below zero temperatures. "Anybody with compromised immune systems should stay indoors today and maybe for the next few days. Young infants should also stay indoors for this cold spell."

The residents of Passion took heed and by six o'clock most of its citizens were in their warm homes. Even the young men who usually milled around Irving Housing's courtyard had dispersed.

The six young men who called themselves Bloodhounds were always in the courtyard. They ranged in age from sixteen to twenty-four. Every one of them had been arrested at least twice, even the fifteen-year-old.

Jay Blow was the leader, an overly confident twenty-two-year-old who wanted to be a kamikaze. He wanted to die fighting for his cause. Until recently, Jay Blow's only "cause" was drug dealing and putting fear into the citizens of Passion. Those same citizens went to him for crack cocaine and marijuana. For his special customers he had cocaine, LSD, and psychedelic mushrooms. He delivered too. He would drive all over Passion, never leaving his car. One of his "boys" would always do the drop and collect. They would get twenty dollars for each delivery they helped him with. He didn't disclose how much he made for each delivery. The poorer customers had to go to him.

"Listen, ya'll." Jay Blow gathered his men around him. They were still in their large leather coats and knitted hats. They had escaped the brutal cold and joined again in the laundry room. Little Man, the fifteen-year-old, was barricading the laundry room door. He was a large boy, weighing at least 250 pounds. Every time someone would try to enter the laundry room he would lean against the door.

Jamie "Jay" Blow was a short man, the same height as the average woman. His girlfriend was an almost six-foot-tall blonde. One of his regular customers, she could afford the large ounces of coke she bought. Juliet liked to show him off, as he was a good-looking black man, with heaps of drugs at his fingertips. They drove to Chicago often and she would take him around to art openings and hip parties. Jay sometimes supplied these extravagant parties. He was nice looking, clean cut, and wore expensive clothing, his only piece of jewelry a diamond-encrusted watch with his name engraved on the back.

Most of the time he stayed with his mother, Reena, at Irving Housing, even though his girlfriend had a large home in Passion.

Jay paid his mother's rent and utilities, and for her food and clothing. She talked with him quietly about maybe leaving the drug-dealing scene, but she never pressed.

She was a poor woman who had broken her hip after falling off a ladder at work. Worker's compensation found a way to deny her coverage. She was on welfare for a while before she asked Jay to help her make ends meet. He constantly offered to move her out of the crumbling building, but she wanted to be around her friends. So she stayed and he stayed with her.

One of two fluorescent lights in the laundry room flickered, creating a strobe effect around six figures. Jay Blow cleared his throat and spat over his shoulder, "Yo, so D-day will be tomorrow night. They got some big party going on at Wyant. We have to strike then."

The young men nodded their heads. Jay Blow had decided that the Bloodhounds needed an initiation. He needed them to prove their worthiness in being Bloodhounds.

"Ya'll got to do something. I don't care what it is, as long as it's big and illegal."

"So what we need?" said the always efficient Mastermind.

"Yo, I can't tell you what you need. You *need* to know what you need. If you fail, you ain't down with me no more." He looked at the men seriously; they looked back somberly. "Whatever you do, I want heads talkin' about it for two weeks. And yo! If you fail, we will have the right to beat you down any time we feel like it."

Everyone was silent, their young hearts beating. Some were excited, but most were scared out of their minds. Resistance was futile. Most of them grew up in the Projects. They saw that either you were a player or you got played.

These lost young men were the terror of Irving Housing. When they wanted to have private meetings they locked down the laundry room and stood on the dryers, threw gum into the washers. They liked to sit on the front stoop of building 3 because it had three steps and a short fence in the front that they could sit on. Jay Blow didn't always hang out with them. The Bloodhounds always waited for him in front of building 3. They would wait moments or sometimes hours for him to show. They played basketball, harassed the young women, and sold Jay's drugs for him.

People accepted them as part of their daily landscape. The six men included Jay, Mastermind, Little Man, Tommy Weed, Hakeem, and Milton. Milton and Hakeem were brothers who lived on Baum Street, a middle-class neighborhood close to Irving Housing. Their parents were hardworking people with two other children to take care of. As far as they were concerned, the boys went to school and played basketball. Since they were teenage boys, their parents did not feel the need to restrict them with curfews that they would be breaking anyway.

The Bloodhounds were so unpredictable that some people were afraid of them. None of them had legal jobs. Only Mastermind was in junior college. They drank publicly, smoked marijuana constantly. Some nights they kept the tenants up, playing music very loudly and trying to rap. A few times the police were called, but after the young men were released they terrorized everyone and slashed their tires.

Melly, the young man that Alex was counseling,

used to run with the Bloodhounds, till he left the state.

Later that same evening, Jay Blow made his way to the apartment he shared with his mom.

Jay went home encouraged. He felt that the task he had put before his men would weed out the punks and the real. He knew he would lose some of them, because they didn't have the courage to go through with the challenges, but he was committed to building his future empire. Tomorrow night all was going to change. Those that were successful would be his first generals. After this test, he was going to go about the business of recruiting more young men for his street army. He had a huge deal on the horizon that could change his status forever.

"Ma! I got Chinese food."

The hallway light was on, but the rest of the apartment was dark. Jamie's mother, a short, middle-aged woman, appeared from the bathroom drying her hands with a napkin.

"Good, baby, I'm hungry." Reena smoothed his cornrows.

"Ma, I got you some wings and moo goo gai pan, and one bottle of bottled water from France. How do you drink that stuff? It taste like you're drinking from a metal cup."

"Jamie, you know I like it. Don't give me grief."

She opened up the Chinese food cartons. Jamie got the dishes out, preparing two trays for them.

"How was the session today?" he said, referring to her physical treatments. He placed two forks on the trays.

"It was hard with all that cold out there. I could

barely walk. My hands were freezing even with the gloves. Once I got inside, it went well."

"What'd they do, anything different from last time?"

"No, the same things."

They chatted amicably, then sat on the couch together catching the last minute of a basketball game. While watching the highlights from the game they just missed, Jamie started rummaging around in the box of tapes under the TV. Reena stiffened and looked at Jamie suspiciously.

"Jamie, I need to ask you something," she said softly.

"Yeah, Mom," he said without looking up.

"Jamie, look at me."

He stopped fiddling in the box and looked over his shoulder at his mother. She was so surprised at how young he still looked. The same square jaw and calm eyes. She'd mentioned a few times to Jamie her wish that he would quit selling drugs. She was resigned to letting him find his own way out. She loved him dearly but she couldn't think of anything else she or anyone she knew could tell Jamie to make him stop. She was put into a horribly awkward situation. Without Jamie, she would be unable to have her physical therapy, which was $200 per session. He gave her enough money to schedule one a week for six weeks. After that time they would see how she was feeling and if the therapy was working. If it helped, they would continue. If not, they would seek other options.

"I think you and your friends need to find a new place to have your meetings." She looked down at her hands. "Some people complained to me today. All they wanted to do was wash their drawers and they couldn't."

Jamie turned away from her, closed his eyes, and gritted his teeth. "Who said that? Who's complaining to you?"

"Never mind that. That's not the point." She leaned to one side and rubbed her hip. "You guys need to move, find someplace else to be. Go back outside, dress warm, and find someplace where you not bothering anyone."

"Mom, do you realize how cold it is out there? Just tell me who got complaints."

"Jamie, I'm not going to do that. Can you just do it for me, please? Good people just want to wash they clothes."

"I'll think about it." He looked at her untouched tray of food. "Let's eat, Mom."

"Don't blow me off, Jay Blow!" she shouted. "Yeah, I know what they call you. Everyone knows who you are. They know what you do. They know I'm your mother." She sighed. "You know I wanted to stay here to be close to my old sister friends, but one by one they stoppin' talking to me."

Jamie sat on the floor by the TV and spun around to face her. He rested his elbows on his knees and pondered her over his clasped hands.

"Mom, those people are just jealous because I'm getting mine," he said.

"Son, listen to me. It ain't just them. The police are watching you. I've seen them. They were out there yesterday, just sitting in their car at the corner. They probably got files on you and the rest of your—"

"Who! Jackson and that other cop?"

Reena's eyes squinted and her jaw dropped slightly. *Oh God! He got cops on the payroll!*

"Ha! We call him 'Jack the Pig' 'cause he'll jack you. They just want a piece of my action. So I give them some. And they stay off my back." Jamie stood to his feet. "I'm taking care of business, Ma! I'm taking care of us."

"Baby, I just want you to stay alive. This is getting too dangerous. The police? You dealing with crooked cops? They could change their minds at any moment and lock you up . . . or worse." The images that flew across her mind forced her face to hide her trembling lip and watery eyes.

Jamie just stared at her. *Damn! I told her too much.*

"You know they got this new mayor who wants to clean up the complex. The cops are gonna have to start doing their job. They not gonna let you do what you been doing. It's gonna be different around here."

"Nah, that ain't gonna happen. Those mother-fu . . . those people that hold those offices are just like us. They do what they have to do to survive and get paid! They just have the so-called law on their side. It's the same stuff, they just hustle on another level. But soon I'll be untouchable. I got plans, Ma. Soon I won't even need to be on the street. Just don't panic. And don't pay any mind to the small-minded people around here!"

Reena stood up and without another word walked unsteadily into her bedroom and shut the door. Jamie heard her settle into her bed.

It had been a long time since Jamie had lost his composure in front of his mother. It made him angry at himself. He took a deep breath and put away her food, vowing once again never to tell her about details of his business. He pulled *The Godfather* out from the box of videos and popped it into the VCR.

While watching the movie, he visualized his empire, and the steps he would have to take to make it reality. *Yes, I have work to do,* he thought.

He fell asleep on her couch holding the remote. On the TV screen, someone was screaming as he woke up to find a horse's head on his bed.

Eleven

The next night a party was being thrown in honor of Mayor Bryant by LAAW, the League of African-American Women. It was going to be held at 7 P.M. at the Grand Wyant Hotel, a large upscale hotel, with buffet-style food and an open bar, and a live band would play jazz the entire night.

Affrica and Ramona decided they would go to Chicago that morning to purchase their dresses. Affrica drove them there, excited about the party and a chance to finally unwind. Also glad for the chance to catch up with Ramona, happy that there was so much to talk about. The first few miles they rode in relative silence, enjoying Gregory Isaacs, the reggae crooner.

They got business out of the way first, though neither of them really wanted to talk about work. But great things had happened since Affrica had revealed her plan to rebuild Irving Housing.

"So, your interview with *Essence* will be this coming Thursday at three-thirty. They'll be taking lots of pictures, nothing fun though, you at a desk or behind something official looking."

"I love *Essence*. That magazine has great articles. Susan Taylor is amazing."

Ramona pressed her pen into the palm pilot screen. "Did you read the *Daily?*"

"Yes, I saw the article, pretty fabulous. They wrote that article as if they never doubted my skills when they put me through the damn ringer!" Affrica slammed her hand on the steering wheel for emphasis.

"Well, my mayoral friend, they are kissing your feet now. Enjoy it while it lasts, because I'm telling you it won't last long."

"I saw the little snippet on the news about the 'New Twenty-first Century Irving.' That was uplifting." Affrica smiled.

"Let's see . . ." Ramona mused, "the tenant association of Irving Housing is not in total agreement about the demolition and rebuilding. It seems a few . . . more than a few . . . are outright opposed to the idea."

"But this is such a good thing. I understand though, it's such a tremendous change. I'm sure they don't know where they'll be staying while the place is demolished. I understand, there are so many factors to consider." She took her hand off the steering wheel a moment. "But that place is about to collapse. Those buildings need to be condemned." She looked at Ramona, the car never wavering. "I looked at the old architectural drawings for the buildings and the builders' comments, and, girl, that place should have been torn down thirty years ago, and those buildings were built thirty years ago." She shook her head, her eyes growing misty. "We always get the short end of the stick."

"All right, Affrica, I didn't want this trip to be all business and depressing. Let's talk about something else."

Affrica was staring straight ahead, hypnotized by

the road. She wondered what Alex was doing. *He* had liked her idea about the buildings. She felt her body heat up when she imagined him. She opened her window slightly, the cold wind stinging her face.

"Girl, it is not that hot in here." Ramona was dressed casually. She had removed her coat once she entered the car. Ramona wore brown suede pants with a form-fitting black sweater. The outfit suited her large-boned body perfectly. The dark sweater contrasting nicely with her light skin and emphasized all that was great about her voluptuous body. Her hair was loose around her shoulders.

Affrica looked at Ramona and rolled up her window. "I think I like him," she admitted.

"Who . . . Chief? Wow, I should have guessed, the way ya'll were at each other's throats." Ramona turned to look at Affrica. "Repressed sexual frustration!"

"No . . . you think?"

"Yes, people who usually argue like you two did want to have sex."

"That's bull, Ramona."

"I know it is." Ramona grinned sheepishly. "So, did ya'll?"

Affrica whipped her head around. "No!"

"There would be nothing wrong if you did."

"Not with Delroy in the picture. Besides, I still have to get to know him. I might not even like him once I know him better."

"I doubt that. He is soooo fine."

"He is, isn't he?"

"What have I been saying all this time? I slept with Maxwell and I still don't have a date for the party," Ramona said abruptly.

"I know. Remember you confessed when I called you about Alex."

"Oh yeah, so I screwed him."

"Why are you getting involved in that mess? Maxwell is such a player."

Ramona shrugged and turned away, looking at the trees rushing by them in a green blur. Affrica was a fast driver. They kept passing cars that looked as if they were still. But she was always safe and calculating.

"I just like him a little," Ramona said.

"But he was flirting with Chantay at the meeting. How could he just do that in front of you like that, Ramona?" Affrica looked at Ramona while trying to keep her eyes on the road.

"He's a jerk," she said sadly. "He was right though, we're not boyfriend and girlfriend." Ramona shrugged her shoulders.

Affrica could not understand Ramona's rationalization of the situation. "I don't understand."

"He's not my man. He can do whatever he wants. Even flirt with other women openly."

Affrica looked at the green highway sign. They still were a few miles from their ultimate destination.

"Listen, Ramona, you are my friend and if I see you getting disrespected I'm going to say something about it."

"He's not disrespecting me."

Affrica looked at her seriously.

"Look, didn't I curse him when he pulled that stuff at dinner? I'll keep him in check," Ramona said.

Affrica looked at her once more.

"I will. Really. I'll drop him like a hot potato if he pulls anything like he did," Ramona stated emphatically. She decided to change the subject. It was a bad habit she had when she didn't want to deal with something.

"Tell me about Chief."

"No, I want to talk about you and Maxwell."

"Stop being such a Taurus. Stubborn. Let it go please."

Affrica frowned at her. "I may be stubborn, but you're my friend."

"Yeah, yeah, yeah." Ramona waved her hands. "I'm not in love with him and I can cut him off any time I want." She looked at Affrica. "The sex *ain't* all that great anyway."

Affrica laughed so hard the car swerved. She shook her head in disbelief. "Oh, I'm so sorry."

"It's not horrible sex, it's just not . . . fireworks." Ramona chose her words carefully. "There's no . . . bang. Pun intended."

"You are so wrong." They smiled at each other and laughed hysterically.

They were quiet for a moment after that. They listened to music, Ramona enjoying the passing scenery.

She really did not like Maxwell that much. She thought she had handled the thing with Chantay very well. *Just because he flirted with that woman didn't mean we had to stop seeing each other, but I need to check my own reaction to it. I can have sex with who I want, so can he. Affrica forgets I've been married before, and that player cannot rattle me. Please.*

Ramona was forty-two years old. She knew *something* about men, she thought.

"Alex really is an interesting guy." Affrica wanted to talk more about Alex. "He's cool."

"Cool? Affrica, I don't think in the years that I've known you that you've ever used the word 'cool' to describe something or somebody. What's up?"

They pulled into the large parking lot of the Michigan Express, a mall with over a hundred stores. Ramona felt her heart quicken. *Shopping.* Ramona loved to shop. Affrica found the perfect parking spot, close to the mall. As they walked toward the doors, they formulated a plan.

"Okay, so where are we hitting first?" Ramona had her own list. They rushed in to get away from the whipping winds.

After the plan was formulated, they figured they would do all the stores on the north side; their three favorite ones were located on that side. They knew they would find what they wanted within those stores. Then they would roam around, maybe get a bite to eat. They liked just to walk and look at people. This would be their catch-up time. As luck would have it Affrica found her dress at the first store, a designer boutique that was up with the latest styles but not trendy.

"Ms. Bryant, so nice to see you again. And congratulations on winning the election." Mrs. Harpermyer ran the shop. She was a very short woman who wore fabulous dresses, most of them mini. She liked Affrica, who not only was a good customer, but did the shop's dresses justice. Affrica's body made every dress look nice.

Mrs. Harpermyer clasped Affrica's hand in her liver-spotted one. Ramona was looking at the bridesmaids dress section.

"Thank you, Mrs. Harpermyer. How are you? How's Mr. Harpermyer?"

"He's fine," Mrs. Harpermyer said dismissively. I don't talk to him when I'm in the shop."

Ramona ignored the two. She didn't like that shop much. She followed the two women down the aisle looking at the extravagant dresses. She wanted something slinky and scandalous. Most of the dresses were nice but she wanted something with the back out and low. She entered a large dressing room with mirrors on all sides. Affrica was disrobing and Mrs. Harpermyer was holding a lovely-looking purple frock.

After Affrica was standing only in her bra and panties, Mrs. Harpermyer helped to lift the dress to Affrica's head. It was beautiful.

"Wow, you look great!" Ramona was impressed by the way her friend looked.

Affrica twirled around. It was a perfect twirling dress, a strapless, silk dress that puffed out at the hip. It wasn't exaggerated, either too long or too puffy. She looked like a true princess, as if she should be on stage with a flower in her hair.

Affrica smiled. "I like it."

"It's elegantly simple." Mrs. Harpermyer held her hands to her chest. "I knew it would fit, I knew it would look just superb on you." She fluffed the dress up some more.

"We'll take it," Ramona said with a big smile.

"Girl, isn't it divine?" It was so far from the suits Affrica wore all the time.

They walked out of that store, convinced that Ramona would also be lucky and find her dress as quickly. Fifteen stores later, both were exhausted. Ramona had purchased clothes for work but no clothes for the party. As they once again made their way to the north side, Mrs. Harpermyer beckoned the two women.

She pointed to Ramona. "I've found something for you, deary. Come in, both of you." She held Ramona's arm and pulled her through the same aisles she had been down earlier.

"You know what? Thank you, Mrs. Har—" Ramona started saying no, but when she saw the dress hanging in the large open dressing room, her jaw dropped. Hanging in the dressing room was *her* gown. Her dress for the party. Mrs. Harpermyer shook her head. Ramona disrobed immediately. Affrica walked into the dressing room. The dress fitted Ramona perfectly. It wasn't tight, but was clingy, molding Ramona's body exquisitely. It was black with silver sequins, with a split that went up the leg and stopped at the knee. It plunged perfectly; a nice necklace would have to be added.

Affrica nodded her head approvingly. Ramona turned her head—her butt looked perfect in it. She did a little salsa move. They all laughed.

"I feel like I should be in some kind of salsa dance troupe. Someone should be spinning me around and picking me up over his head."

Affrica shook her head. "It's time for some grub."

They thanked Mrs. Harpermyer again. Ramona thanked her by paying $700 for the dress.

Affrica wanted Italian, and so did Ramona. The food court was grand. Greek pillars overhead and a full skylight gave the place a very bright atmosphere.

Affrica's stomach was growling as she waited in line. They stood back patiently though. Affrica was glad she had come out. Not only did she get a beautiful dress for the party, but she didn't think about Alex once. *Oh, Alex. Damn, I'll stop thinking about him.* But she couldn't get him off her mind. She placed her order for fettucine alfredo and an espresso. Ramona ordered the manicotti and a glass of red wine. This was the only place in the entire food court to serve wine. One of the young men was kind enough to bring the ladies their food.

They quietly tipped him. Needless to say he was very happy.

"Whatever you need, I am here." He backed away from them smiling ear to ear. After he turned around, the two women laughed.

They began eating, relishing their food. When they felt a little satiated they stopped and started talking, eating slower. The food court was filled with people, but there wasn't the usual din. It was relatively quiet.

"So, Alex?"

Affrica looked up at the skylight. "What about Delroy?"

"Who? Who's Delroy? Affrica, you've been trying to figure out a way to break up with him, so here it is. You are not sure about the relationship; you have feelings for somebody else. That's it. He's going to have to accept that."

"But, Ramona . . . we put two years into this thing. I can't just let it go."

"Yes, you can. Let go."

"I wish I could let go because Alex makes me feel like . . . energetic."

"Energetic? Okay, first it's 'cool'; now it's energetic. Please explain." She twisted the pasta around her fork.

"I feel like I have boundless energy. I feel like telling him off-the-wall stuff just to see what he would say." Affrica's fork was in the air, her hands dancing as she spoke.

"When I spoke with him, I didn't feel like I was the mayor. I felt like I wanted to climb a mountain."

"You're getting a little fairytale-ish."

"Sorry. I just feel like a princess."

"Girl, those dresses are so beautiful." Ramona looked at her garment bag dreamily.

"I know, I know . . . and the way old lady Harpermyer came with your dress, my goodness."

"Affrica, I've looked around that store and I've never seen a dress like that."

"Maybe she's your fairy godmother. Oh, by the way, how are the specs coming for Irving?"

"They are coming along. I should have e-mailed you. They're three-D drawings."

"Send them to me tonight, any time."

"Ramona, this is great, I get to work on *the* project. I mean, it's been a dream of mine to change that place." She balled up her napkin and threw it onto the empty plate. She pushed the tray to the empty table next to them. When Ramona finished she did the same. She slowly sipped her wine, relishing the flavor.

Affrica looked at her friend intently. "Are you thinking about Maxwell?"

"No, I'm not, Affrica. I was just enjoying my wine." Ramona rolled her eyes at Affrica.

"I have to see Alex again," she said quickly.

"About?" Ramona examined her manicured fingernail.

"He has to see the specs and to make sure the security station is placed correctly."

"Why don't you just e-mail it to him?"

Affrica smiled. Just then a group of rowdy teenagers walked by the women's table.

"Wow, remember that?"

"Don't want to," Affrica said. "It was too much of a confusing time. I like being an adult."

"It was such a time of learning and growing."

"You're right, but I like being an adult. We can do what we want, get paid for working jobs we love, live where we want."

"It's true, you're right. We can be our own person. No one can force their agendas on us."

They were both thoughtful for a moment. Affrica took out her organizer-purse and started to look at her receipts.

"Oh, I spoke to Holly," Affrica said, remembering.

"Holly! How is she? I miss her dearly."

"She'll be back from London . . ." Affrica looked at the calendar on her organizer. ". . . in March."

"I can't wait for her to get back."

"Me too."

A good-looking man was approaching their table. Over six feet tall, he moved like a cat and resembled a sports figure. His bald head was polished to perfection. He wore a dark-colored suit with brown leather shoes. As he swaggered toward them, they straightened up.

"Good afternoon, ladies." His voice was deeper than Barry's.

"Hello," Ramona said flirtatiously.

"Good afternoon," Affrica said politely.

The man beamed at the women. He looked them over respectfully and said, "I'm really not trying to make a fool out of myself, but you ladies are very attractive."

Ramona said thank you for both of them. He looked at her with soft eyes. She kicked Affrica under the table without looking away from him. She got the hint.

She stood up. "I think I need to use the . . . ladies' room." Affrica left the two to their own devices.

She pushed the door open to the ladies' room. It was garishly painted with three stalls. It wasn't four-star, but it was clean, had toilet paper, and had soap for her hands. She waited patiently in line, looking at herself in the mirror.

I don't look like a mayor.

Her hair was braided and her outfit was far from conservative. She moved up a little in the line.

Mentally she felt ready—she was young in numbers only. It seemed as if her life had prepared her for this great responsibility. As far as she could remember, her mother had never spoken to her as if she was a child. She always spoke to Affrica in full sentences.

She looked at her watch. She would give them fifteen minutes. *I bet she sleeps with him.*

Not only was Ramona going to sleep with him, but he was going to the party tonight with her. Affrica did not know that yet.

While Affrica was growing up, her mother, Zembemba, had tried to hold jobs but could never keep them. She had refused to move in with Affrica's grandmother even after the landlord threatened them with eviction. Instead her mother found a rare vacancy in building 2 of Irving Housing. Affrica was six going on twenty-five. She was attending the Freedom School for African-American Children. Even though the people of Irving Housing thought they were strange, they were well liked. The citizens had come out in record numbers to vote for Affrica as mayor. They felt as if she was one of their own.

Her mother was never pretentious or preachy. She talked with everyone. She talked to everyone from the drunks to the other moms. She arranged community meetings (which still happened to this day). She pushed the management to repair and exterminate. She would organize block parties and food drives. The food would always be discreetly distributed to any families within the Projects that were in need.

With her eight-inch Afro always picked out and oiled, Affrica ran around, played like the other children. Some made fun of her hair, but most paid it no mind, especially when she told them something about the juicy jheri curls they had in their own hair.

They left the Projects when her mother decided she was needed elsewhere, out of the country. She went to the continent of Africa. With a kiss and a fist in the air, she left her astute nine-year-old daughter in her grandmother's charge. Jerimia was a widow, her husband having died five years before Affrica moved in with her. She was ready for company. The first thing she did once Zembemba had left was braid Affrica's thick hair into neat plaits that were redone every two days.

Affrica had those same plaits even through high school, when she decided to cut all her hair off. Male attention never wavered. Her short hair only drew attention to the physically beautiful things about her, high-sculpted cheekbones, impossibly long, curled eyelashes, wide, sumptuous mouth. She was an attractive woman.

After the bathroom she walked around the floor she and Ramona were on and looked at housewares.

What am I thinking? I need to try to work things out with Delroy. He's not a bad guy. What will it look like, me breaking up with Delroy and starting to date the police chief? What if we get caught sneaking around? I'm too old for this. I need to at least try. Affrica felt resolved. She would forget about Alex and concentrate on

Delroy. Tonight's party would prove just the place for making up and having some fun with him.

Her fifteen minutes were up. Affrica went back to the food court. As she walked toward them, it seemed the man was saying good-bye to Ramona. He glided past Affrica and with a tilt of his shiny bald head he said, "I'll see you tonight, *Mayor* Bryant." He sauntered out of the food court.

Affrica rushed to Ramona, who just looked at her coyly. "I found my date for tonight," she said.

Affrica looked at her with intense confusion. She thought about it for a moment. She understood.

"No, you didn't. You just met him and"—she whispered—"he looks like he's half your age."

"Not exactly, but close, baby." Ramona flipped her hair, looked at her nails. The two women considered each other for a moment, then exploded in laughter, tears streaming down their pretty faces. Between gulps of air Ramona said, "*And* his name is Richard Princeton the Third."

Affrica burst into new laughter, just as she was collecting herself.

Twelve

That same afternoon, Alex drove to his parents' home in Kalamazoo, a two-hour drive from Passion. He was still debating what he should do about the dance. Judy Bloomberg and Penelope Matthews both had left long messages on his machine inviting him to the dance. Alex could not help but compare the two woman to Affrica. He wanted to go to that party to get away from work and to see Affrica, though he would probably beg to differ with himself on that.

He went to Judy Bloomberg's bungalow first. *If Patrick could see me now, knocking on this woman's door to tell her I'm turning her down for a party.*

Alex shook his head at the ridiculous situation he found himself in. On the one hand, he did not want to go to the dance alone; on the other hand, if he went with one woman and not the other, there would be hurt feelings. So he was going to invite both women to come to the dance. He would encourage them to bring a friend and he would try to dance with them, but he did not want to lead the women on.

Affrica. What about her and that Delroy? She'll probably be so busy, she won't even see me.

Judy opened the door. She was a semiattractive woman. Her brown hair was held up by many barrettes and her brown eyes were as luxurious as cashmere. She had a horrible crush on Alex that caused her to lose her senses, to throw herself at him outright.

"Hello, Jude."

"Hi, Alex," she gushed. "Come in, come in." She opened the door wider but did not move out of his way. He had to get really close to her in order to pass.

She had on gray slacks and the twenty silver bracelets she was known for always wearing.

She knew Alex did not like her in that special way, but she did not know how to look at him as a friend. *He's so bloody handsome.* Her heart pounded at the idea of him being in her house. Anything could happen. Alex's eyes danced when he looked at her, but they always danced. *He made a point to come to see me. He did not have to do that. Maybe he does like me.*

She was fooling herself. She and Alex had never gone on a date. They had met when he helped her after her house had been burglarized a few months ago. He called her a few times, to see how she was doing, and went to visit her only to check on the house. She was smitten.

"So, Jude," Alex began, "thanks for asking me to the party tonight."

"You don't want to go?" she said incredulously.

Alex saw the disappointment in her face. He had to be careful. Though he liked this woman, it wasn't anything romantic. If he said this the wrong way, she would be crushed and would lose a friend.

"Jude, I'm still going to the party . . . but I have to ask you something."

"What is it?" Her dark eyes were wide.

"Did you ask me to go to the party as a friend or as a date?"

She nodded and smiled at him as if she understood. "Date." She looked down shyly. "I have a confession to make. . . . I know you don't like me like *that*, but I thought maybe once you saw me in my gown"—she swept her hands over her body—"you would be sooo entranced by me." She laughed at herself.

"Jude, you're a beautiful woman—"

"I know, I know." She waved him off and smiled.

Alex looked at her intently to make sure it was okay.

"So who are you going to the dance with, Alex?"

"I'm going alone, I'm going to be on duty."

He did not mention the fact that he was deeply excited about the mayor.

Judy looked insightfully at Alex. She did not want to let the opportunity of spending time with him slip through her fingers, but at the same time she wanted to respect his honesty.

"Good, that means I can get a couple of dances without some jealous woman throwing visual daggers at me."

"Judy, you know I don't dance in public."

"Yeah, we'll see."

"You're a great person. It's just such a weird time, with so much going on with my life and work. I'll tell you honestly, I'm still trying to figure your kind out." He stopped. "I hate sounding like this. I'm going to shut up now."

Judy laughed heartily. "Sorry, hon, you never will figure us out."

"So I'll see you tonight?"

"Yes, you will, Alex. Where are you heading now?"

"To see my parents." He offered nothing else.

Judy waved at him as he backed his Jeep out of her driveway. She had a bittersweet feeling. She wanted to continue the charade and be in the dark about whether he liked her or not.

Alex attempted to call Penelope two more times after he left Judy's house but she wasn't home. He left messages telling her to call him on his cell phone, because he would be leaving Passion for the day. He hoped she wasn't counting on him to be her date. He was wishing he could get a single moment with Affrica even for a few seconds.

Ancient pines, winding streams, ravens, deer. Alex wished that the best part of visiting his parents were his parents. He always enjoyed this trip out of the city. The roads to his parents' house were lined with a paradise of nature. But sometimes, it was like a candy-lined path to an ogre's cave.

Without any effort, Alex was generally an intimidating man. His height, his eyes, his physique, his very presence made one feel hesitant to try anything dishonest. Many times he had inspired a confession from a perpetrator simply by standing quietly in the corner of the room.

In all of his life, there was only one person that had intimidated him. Frank Bartholomew. His father.

Frank Bartholomew was a highly decorated veteran of the Marine Corps. He had spent his entire life in the marines and had only retired because he was forced to. Four generations of Bartholomews had dedicated their lives to service in the military. From an early age, Alex and his brother had been groomed for a life of military service. It wasn't until

Alex's junior year in high school that he started to consider that he may have had a choice, but he couldn't imagine discussing his feelings with his father. At home, Frank was constantly expressing his views on the ungratefulness of the masses of mindless civilians. To be unpatriotic in the Bartholomew household was to be evil.

Alex's parents had children relatively late in their lives. Frank held a stationary post for the latter part of his career, and after the children were born, the Bartholomews did not travel around much. Prior to their first pregnancy, Frank was content to be childless. Camelia Bartholomew, Alex's mother, had actually threatened to leave the marriage before Frank agreed to do his part in the conception of their child.

Camelia had been from a large family in South Carolina. She was a performer in a dance troupe that was on tour when she met Frank. They were young and got married quickly. She moved around with him from base to base teaching dance in the civilian recreation centers after hours. Usually her classes consisted of a few young girls and one or two bored wives. Camelia wanted a family for many years and Frank had always talked her out of it. After nineteen years of marriage, the routine life of a civilian wife on a military base became too monotonous. She decided that she would have a baby with or without Frank, and she told him. He agreed, and they conceived.

Two years after their first son was born she convinced Frank to try again, for a girl. When she birthed a very beautiful second son, her girlfriends on base joked that Frank's testosterone level would not permit the conception of a girl. But Camelia was content with her two boys and she did what she could to balance the influence of her husband on them. They loved her, and respected him.

Alex went from high school to the marines, traveling intensely with them. Then he went to the reserves and back into the civilian population in about five years, much to the dismay of his father. A year later he was training to be a police officer. He was a young man of strong convictions and he wanted to work in his own community. For the first time in his life, he felt as if he was doing what he wanted, and making a difference in the world. He rose in the ranks quickly. By the time he was thirty-four, he was chief of police. Now, at thirty-seven, he was happy with where his life had taken him.

The Passion Police Department needed an overhaul, but he was working on it. He regretted nothing about the paths he chose, because every decision led him to where he was now. He only wished that his father were more accepting of his career decisions. Frank thought that police officers were wasting time and resources, and that the real day-to-day battle was with foreign countries and foreign influence. During a heated debate, Frank once said, "What America needs is another good war to get our economy back on line. Why are you flat-footing it around the neighborhood? You should have been brass, planning for the survival and prosperity of your country." They butted heads every time they met.

The only reason that Frank intimidated Alex was that Alex allowed himself to stay vulnerable. He wanted healing in their relationship. He wanted understanding. And as remote as the possibility seemed, he wanted some semblance of father/son intimacy. He never gave up. And every time they met he would dare to be hopeful that his father would suddenly be more accepting of his son. The son that did not follow in his family's grand tradition of military service. The son that came home one day criticizing America's foreign policy. The son that chose instead to be a soldier for justice in his own community. Alex had seen that there were few African-Americans on the police force and he made a decision to join. Unconsciously, he still felt the pressure to serve his country in a manly capacity. He thought that joining the police force was a fair compromise.

Alex did not understand why his father did not look at the police department with the same respect as he did the armed forces. At the end of every argument he would realize once again that it was not that Frank did not respect the police, but that he was hurt that his son did not follow in his footsteps, and worse, his son cited moral reasons for not doing so.

Alex's Jeep was now on the dirt road that winded its way to his parents' house. The houses here had hundreds of feet between them. He slowed as he passed frozen farmlands, pillars of smoke rising from chimneys to fade into a pastel purple sky. Up ahead a column of at least three hundred ravens flew high above the road, noisily making their way to their nightly communal nesting grounds. Alex almost pulled over to get out and watch, but he knew he would probably not want to get back into his Jeep. He opened his windows as he passed under them, listening to the raucous cawing. The smell of the pines and the invigorating winter chill hit him harder now. It was a familiar sensation, stirring memories.

Shady Duck Pond was coming up on his left now. The pond was a marker. Once he passed it, he would be in sight of the house. Every time he arrived at the pond he knew that it was the point of no return. If he did not proceed, he could turn around and go back home, fabricate an excuse, and spare himself the inevitable conflict with his father. He resented the cowardly thought. He never turned back, but yet every time he reached this point, the thought came. His foot mashed down on the accelerator.

Camelia Bartholomew was sitting in the front room of the two-story Italianate house working on her latest painting. When Frank retired from the service and they moved to this house in the country, she was thrilled with the prospect of getting into something artsy. She turned one of the front rooms into her craft studio and started painting immediately. She began with still-lifes and landscapes that became increasingly surreal. After a few years she started to show her work in galleries and was surprised by immediate success. She decided to take a break from painting last year following a three-month "creative block" during which she did a lot of reading and studying African art. But now, she was back in the saddle.

On the large canvas before her, an image in oil paint was slowly emerging. A lone figure stood on a beach facing the water. Behind the person was a forest, the trees of which were her current focus. The figure was bowing in a gesture of respect to an approaching tsunami. As if with an intuitive urge, Camelia stood and looked out of the window. She saw Alex's Jeep round the bend by the pond. She smiled and gave her work in progress a look-over, vowing to continue in the wee hours. By the time she covered the tubes of paint and put all of her brushes in the bucket to soak, Alex was at the front door.

Alex knew he had been seen, so he just waited on the porch until the door creaked open.

Camelia greeted her son with a kiss and a bear hug. "Hi, my big baby."

They hugged each in silence for a while, and then Camelia took Alex's hands in hers, examining them the way she always did.

"How are you doing, Mom?"

She had to bend her head way back to meet Alex's eyes. "Oh, I'm fine," she said with a grin and twinkle in her eye. "How are you, son?"

"Good, Ma. Painting trees?"

"How did you know?"

Alex held up her paint-stained hands. "Burnt sienna, and at least three shades of green."

"Well . . ." said Camelia with a chuckle, "I guess you've been painting too. Come in, it's cold." She pressed the doorbell and walked inside. Alex stared at the wet paint spots on his hands, then caught the door just in time to slip in after his mother.

Camelia was standing at the bottom of the steps leading to the second floor. She pitched her head to listen for the sound of Frank stirring.

"It's good to see you painting again," said Alex. He gave a lingering glance into her studio. "Wow! Mom, this is great work." Alex heard his father start down the steps, accompanied by a whispered exchange between his parents. *Mom is trying to talk him into having a pleasant evening No arguments, she's probably saying.* He walked down the hall to the foyer to meet his father.

Frank was standing on the landing.

"Well, you guys sit down and catch up," Camelia said. "I'm going to start supper." And she practically jogged off toward the kitchen, the hint of a grin on her face.

Start! was the thought on both men's minds, as they both looked after her. She usually had dinner ready by the time Alex arrived.

"Since she picked back up the brush, nothing gets done on schedule anymore," Frank muttered. He was wearing a pressed shirt and slacks, polished shoes. Less than formal, not quite casual. His typical home attire.

"Hi, Dad," said Alex

"Hey, buddy," Frank returned.

"How is the car coming?" Alex asked, in a swift attack against the awkward silence that often came on the heel of their greeting.

"Oh, great. Almost there," said Frank. "Just need a few more parts and she'll be completely restored."

"Did you check that Web site I told you about?"

"No, I don't think the computer is connected properly. I can't . . . uh."

"Let's have a look at it," said Alex, and they both walked off to the den, happy to have something practical to talk about. Ten minutes later they were on-line. Alex was giving Frank a refresher course in navigating the Web. Ten minutes later they had purchased the auto parts necessary to complete Frank's restoration of the classic car.

The smell of southern-style home cooking was wafting through the house like a seductive spirit. The aroma of sweet potatoes, collard greens, macaroni and cheese, and baked chicken beckoned Alex and Frank from the computer. They shut down the computer and followed their noses. They tried to enter the kitchen.

"Oh no, no entry. You can set the table," said Camelia, meeting them at the swinging doors to the kitchen. She held a pile of plates topped with utensils, extending them to the two snooping men.

The two had the dining table set in under two minutes. "We're ready!" said Alex. "Do you want us to come get the—"

"No, thank you. Dinner will be ready in twenty minutes," Camelia shouted from the kitchen. "You two go do something. Play cards or something."

Frank and Alex looked at each other. "How about a game of chess?" Alex asked.

"I'll get the board. Let's sit in the den." Frank walked off.

The den smelled like cigar smoke. It was a large room with all antique-looking wood furniture and wood wall paneling. Plaques and awards lined one wall, and framed photographs lined the opposite wall. The photos were of military buddies, some in formation at a base, others in the bush during some campaign. A few photos featured the Bartholomew sons at the height of their father's pride, in full military dress.

A small tile-covered table sat in the middle of the room accompanied by one comfortable-looking leather chair. A cylindrical green lamp hung over the table, suspended from the ceiling. A display case of medals and certificates sat at the back of the room framed by large, full bookcases.

While waiting, Alex found himself staring at a picture of Taylor, his brother. Taylor was stationed in Florida where he lived with his wife and two children. He had another child in Thailand. Alex had not seen Taylor since last February. Taylor was the son that fit snugly into the mold. He went from high school ROTC straight into the Marines Corps and there he stayed. He got to see the world. China. Thailand. Hawaii. One morning at four o'clock a woman in Thailand called looking for Taylor. She said she had been hunting him down for two months and eventually got his parents' number. The woman claimed to have had a baby with Taylor, and then Taylor disappeared. The boy's name was Hinsu. When confronted, Taylor initially denied that he could be the father of Hinsu but he eventually changed his story. When it became evident that Taylor was not interested in his responsibilities, Alex took a trip to Thailand and visited with Hinsu's family. He was amazed at the beauty of the land and the humble sophistication of the Thai people. Hinsu's mother and family were surprisingly welcoming. They treated Alex like family. He visited them again three years later, and planned to go again, but he hadn't been able to take the time off from work to make it happen.

"Okay, here we go," said Frank entering with his special collector's-edition crystal chess set. He placed the board on the table that Alex had quickly cleared. Alex pulled up a chair and they began to set up the board.

Frank put on his reading glasses, and cleared his throat. "So, what do you think of Passion's new mayor?" Frank said, while arranging his row of pawns.

"Well, let's see . . ." said Alex, gathering up his pieces. "She is pretty young and inexperienced, but determined, and I believe she is competent. Reminds me of Paige Allen."

Frank paused. "You mean that vicious little Girl Scout that wouldn't leave us alone until we bought a dozen boxes of cookies?"

"Yes, that's Affrica, maybe not so neurotic though." Alex grinned while placing his king and queen on the board.

"Oh, you know her like that, do you?" Frank said, looking over his glasses, one eyebrow raised. "Affrica," he repeated, "not Mayor Bryant, or Ms. Bryant, just Affrica."

"Come on now, Dad, I just met the woman."

"Yeah, but you went crazy over Paige the first time she came to the door, and you only saw her through the curtains." Frank neatly placed his rooks on the board, barely taking his eyes off of Alex's face.

"I was twelve!" Alex protested, putting his bishops and knights in place.

"You're the same," Frank said dryly.

"Am I?" *What the hell does that mean? I'm not the same!* Alex resisted the impulse to look up at his father. He felt that this was turning into a challenge. The inevitable challenge from Frank.

"Well, have you had an unofficial, informal meeting with her yet?" Frank sneered.

"What? Ha, ha." Alex was flabbergasted, and did his best to hide it, keeping his eyes focused on the chess pieces. He placed his rooks in position and started to line up his pawns. *I am not that transparent.*

Frank smiled broadly now. If anyone on the planet could pull secrets from Alex's face, it was Frank. "You rascal! She's the mayor, for God's sake, boy! You want some kind of scandal to knock you off of your little police chief pedestal?"

Alex had to remind himself that his own keen eye, attention to detail, and jet-speed deductive reasoning came from this man. There was no lying.

No hiding. He looked up at his father. "Dad, nothing happened, we just sat in a diner and ate. We have to know each other. We'll be working closely, you know."

"But . . ." Frank left his questioning one-word accusation to hang in the air like a noose.

Alex knew he had to place his head in the noose. No doubt his father must have already read the subtle facial expressions that indicated emotional involvement. Alex took a deep breath. "Yes, she is attractive. Yes, I am attracted. No, I'm not a fool. I have a job to do in Passion, and so does she."

"Hmph!" Frank snorted. He straightened the pieces on his side of the board, centered each one in its respective square. Perfect formation. Ready for battle. Frank sat back in his chair and pulled a cigar from a drawer.

Alex placed his final pawn on the board. "What do you mean, *I'm the same?*"

Frank stood up. He walked over to the panel of light switches on the wall. He nonchalantly reached up and flicked the room into darkness. Another click, and the shaded lamp that hung from the ceiling threw a beam of light straight down onto the chess board. The rest of the room was bathed in a dull green glow.

Frank came back to sit opposite Alex. "Your move," he said, lighting his cigar.

Alex was breathing deeply to stay calm. He looked up at Frank's silhouette, focusing on the place where his eyes would be. "You heard me, Dad. How am I the same?"

Frank answered, sending a cloud of smoke into the bright beam of light. "When you were twelve you didn't know what you wanted. Did not know the consequences of your actions. You thought you knew. Thought you had it all figured out. I tried to guide you, show you the way. But you never committed. Never saw the glory of our family's values."

Glory! Alex thought. He felt that that word was only used in political and religious propaganda. *How does glory have anything to do with making decisions about life, except egotistical gratification?* This was what he was hoping would not happen.

Frank took another pull of his cigar as Alex sat silent. "All throughout your school days you resisted. It was subtle, but I saw you. Ha! You probably didn't even realize it yourself. I thought surely before you left high school you would come to me and tell me that you wanted to be a veterinarian or some kind of hippie nature photographer or something. But you didn't have the nerve. So again I tried to guide you to the path of true glory. You enlisted and excelled. I was almost proud. But still you weren't committed."

Frank leaned into the light, smoke curling around his head. "I could see it in your eyes."

Alex was shocked. *He knew. All of this time, he knew!*

"And now . . ." Frank sat back in his chair. "Now, you are chief of police of a pathetic police department!" The cigar tip flared red, followed by another billowing smoke cloud. "And you're going to let that fall too because of this Affrica broad. Mark my words."

Alex tried to get up. He tried to speak but he couldn't. He was paralyzed. He had joined the marines because of his father's expectations, though he secretly hated doing so. To a certain degree, even joining the police force was an acquiescence. And all of this time, his father knew it. *He knew it, watched me fumble my way through life trying to satisfy him. But I never did. I never can. He has never forgiven me for not being him. And he never will.*

Alex was engulfed in smoke. His head was spinning. He stared at the chess board trying to get his bearings. He felt as if he were lost on a smoking battlefield. Visibility was low. The enemy was hidden in the haze. Where was the next attack coming from? When would he feel the blow? How could he defend against such an enemy?

Alex looked up at the thick smoke before him just in time to see the next attack coming. His father's face, surreal and contorted in a grotesque expression, poked through the smoke at him.

"Yes, you are the same," Frank growled. "That Girl Scout knocked on our door and scrambled your brains. The next thing we knew, instead of running track with your brother you were sneaking out to the woods to look at chipmunks, and streams and stuff. And now it's happening again. This new mayor is just another Girl Scout trying to get everyone to buy her stupid cookies. And you come in here cheesing as if she's the Wiz."

Alex had had enough. He felt an anger blossoming inside him, tensing his arm, clenching his fist. The next thing he knew, the room exploded in a bright light.

"Frank, stop it!" Camelia yelled from the doorway.

It took Alex a moment to adjust his eyes to the light, but he saw his mother take three long strides and slap Frank in the arm with a wooden spoon. "Damn it, Frank, you promised!"

Frank stood up and whirled around to face her. Alex also stood to his feet.

"Ya can't be soft on them, Cam. Ya have to be hard! Life is not soft. It's hard."

"I'm leaving, Mom," Alex said, walking toward the door.

Camelia ran after him. She caught up with him at the front door and grabbed his arm and tried to pull him back inside, saying, "Wait, Alex. Please, don't go like this."

"I've been a fool, Mom." Alex removed her hands from his arms and continued walking.

"Your father is ill, Alex."

Alex stopped at the edge of the porch steps and looked at his mother. His face was stone and emotionless. He waited.

"Just come inside and let me fix you a plate to take home." She walked up to him, taking him once more by the arms. This time Alex let her lead him inside.

Three minutes later Alex was sitting in the kitchen while his mother was preparing some food to go.

"Alex, a lot of people have this disease called fear. They feel out of control in their own lives and they cling to something, anything, that gives them a sense of purpose. It could be political ideology, religious dogma, whatever, as long as the ones diseased don't have to think for themselves, figure it out for themselves. They want to rely on tradition or laws to tell them what to do. I'm not saying that these things are bad. They are often necessary structures for an evolving society, but some people, many people, get fanatical. They start thinking only within the confines of that structure. They become gears in the machine." Camelia brought the bag of food to Alex and sat down at the kitchen table with him. "It's sad. Perhaps your father was never given a choice. Don't hate him. That's a disease too."

The words had a remarkable effect on Alex. He felt much calmer.

Alex took the bag and stood. "Thank you for your wisdom, Mom." They hugged in silence, and then Camelia walked her youngest son to his Jeep and waved at him until his vehicle rounded the bend by the frozen pond.

Thirteen

While Affrica was out shopping in Chicago with Ramona and Alex was at his folks' house, Delroy was in Passion, and he called his girlfriend and did some shady business with August.

"Hey, baby." Delroy had just dialed Evelyn's number, and her high-pitched voice crackled into his ear.

"Hi, honey bunny. I miss you so much, baby cakes," she cooed into the phone.

"Plans are not going well. I need to revamp my angle."

"English please," Evelyn said gruffly.

"Affrica's not buying us, this. I could feel her trying to pull away. She kept a lot from me."

"What? What's going on?" Evelyn was looking at herself in her mantel mirror. *I should take that modeling job. I'm so much prettier than that Tyra.* She ruffled her curly hair. She couldn't care less what was going on with Delroy. He kept promising her all this money. He sold her dreams about her living fat, quitting her CPA job, and becoming a celebrity. *I haven't seen anything. Just some dumb drawings and a plan that confused me.*

"Well, Affrica has a ten-page outline on the

changes she wants to make to the city department. She has an architect already for the rebuilding of Irving Housing. She's acting suspicious toward that pretty-boy cop friend of hers . . ."

Evelyn's head was going around in circles. She swore Delroy was like a horrible soap opera where excessively elaborate plots were created just to confuse the viewers. Evelyn was almost through with all of it. She would give him one more month to come up with at least ten thousand dollars. *If he can come up with at least that, then maybe he'll have a chance.*

"Mhm. Really?" Evelyn tried to sound interested, while examining a potential pimple on the bridge of her nose. *Damn, I thought I was too old for these things.*

Meanwhile Delroy was on the other end spilling his guts.

"So, I'll be coming to see you next week."

"Huh, what?" Evelyn stuttered. "You're what?"

"I said I was coming again next week sometime."

"Uh, okay," Evelyn said slowly. She rolled her eyes at the naked muscle-bound man on her bed. She jumped on the bed into the man's torso, and he rolled her onto her back. He mouthed for her to get off the phone and threatened to pull it away.

"Uh, Delroy, I gotta go."

"What? Oh, okay." Delroy thought they had been having such a great, intense conversation. "Bye."

He hung up the phone and thought about their conversation for a moment. He exploded in a loud "yes" and gave himself a thumbs-up. *I got Evelyn. She's mine. I can't wait to get back to her for good. With all that money I'm going to be getting, she'll be sweating me. I have to get this money quick.*

* * *

The muscle man held Evelyn's arms over her head and kissed her passionately.

She freed herself from his grip and tapped him on the back. "Baby, listen."

He continued to kiss her neck. She shoved him gently. "Listen, *he's* going to be coming next week. You gotta move out again."

The man rolled over onto his broad back. "I'm tired of having to come and go from my own home. You need to tell that knucklehead something."

"Sure, baby. Sure." Evelyn rolled on top of him and he forgot what he was tired of.

Delroy called August and was yelled at as if he were a preschooler.

"This is what happens when you send a boy to do a man's job."

"Sir, what are you talking about?"

"What's going on, Delroy? Why isn't Affrica busy with other things? What happened to your making her forget everything? She's not forgetting anything."

"Sir—"

"I swear if this fails . . ." He held himself. He'd almost threatened Delroy's life.

August Watson had a large crack cocaine shipment coming from Italy. The man on top was trusting Watson to make good on his promise to make crack popular again. With Affrica making all those changes she had proposed in all the departments, there would be no way she didn't spot all the defects in the budgets, especially in Irving Housing and in the police budget. With all the snooping she'd been doing he was surprised she didn't know. *Any day now Ramona will be talking. Who would have known they would grow to be close friends? They have nothing in common. She's going to fold and implicate all of us, I know she is.*

August Watson was livid. Delroy was failing miserably. It was as if he were invisible.

"When was the last time you saw Affrica?" Watson said calmly.

"Just this morning."

"Why aren't you with her now? You should be everywhere she is. You don't let her out of you damn sight! Where she turns, there you are! When she lays her head down, when she wakes up . . . you be there smiling at her! When was the last you had sex with her?"

"Excuse me?"

"I said, when was the last time you guys had sex?"

"Uhm, sir, I don't think that's relevant." Delroy was embarrassed and upset at the line of questioning.

"Did you put the holes in the condoms?"

"She's been taking birth control pills, sir, and she has an IUD."

"Damn, Delroy. I guess you're not 'rocking her world,' as you put it."

Delroy's grip on the telephone receiver was deadly. He clenched his teeth.

"Maybe not, sir." Delroy could barely breathe.

"Well, you better think of another way, since it seems you are sexually dysfunctional or impotent now. Just take care of it, of her, or I swear . . ." He hung up the phone violently.

Delroy threw the phone down and cursed profusely.

Fourteen

That evening Affrica dusted her soft shoulders with a little facial powder. *Don't want to be too shiny.* She admired the dress from the back. Her waist was sculpted, and the way the skirt came out emphasized her hourglass hips and a really nice butt. Affrica felt like a movie star. Her dark hair was being held together by two porcelain combs her mother had given her from Japan. She wore a thin diamond necklace. Her father had given her the extravagant gift when she finished law school. Her mother had chastised him for buying diamonds knowing full well there were starving children in the world. Affrica had taken the gift and worn it only a few times. She decided tonight would be the night.

After she and Ramona had shopped, they went to their own hair stylists. Affrica usually did her own hair, but tonight she wanted a more formal hairstyle. Teresa had already washed Affrica's earlier that morning and unbraided her mass of hair. One strand of Affrica's hair could be pulled down past her shoulders.

"Your hair is growing fast, baby," the hairdresser had remarked proudly, as if by her very hand, Affrica's hair were growing.

"I'm thinking about cutting it all off."

"No!" Teresa had shouted. "I know it's thick and unmanageable, but we could put in a light relaxer or I could use a hot comb."

"Are you crazy! My hair has never been permed, nor my ears burned by the evil hot comb. I like my thick *nappy, kinky* hair, thank you very much." Affrica rolled her neck at Teresa in the mirror. They both grinned at each other and burst into laughter.

Teresa had finally straightened up and said, "Okay, let's see what we can do with this 'thick, *nappy*' hair."

Affrica had laughed and shaken her full mane.

As Affrica lightly touched her hair she was impressed. Teresa had it all gathered tightly in the back and had let a little of the front and top cascade slightly. It looked a little eighties, but the style suited Affrica so nicely that even Delroy's breath had caught in his throat when he first saw her emerge from the room.

"Affrica!" He blinked.

"You like?"

"Wow!" This was one of the few times that Delroy had shown a true emotion. Most of the things he said to Affrica were very calculated, every smile a frown away to draw her in closer to his trap. But now he was very impressed.

The dress was unbelievable on her. It seemed the first time he was really seeing her.

Affrica's dress was a lavender silk strapless. It hugged her top and flared at her hips. The top was straight cut so as not to show immodest cleavage.

Delroy helped her with her elegant cloak. A large wide hood covered her head, but did not lie on it.

In the car Delroy and Affrica chatted amicably. They caught up with each other.

"It feels like I haven't seen you, Affrica." Delroy put his hand on Affrica's knee.

"It's been so busy, Delroy."

"I know, I know . . . you're not just the mayor. You're my lady too. I need some time. I need some lovin'."

"What are you talking about, lovin'? You know better than to ask me to put you before my career." She crossed her arms over her chest. "You know better than that, brother." Affrica knew that line very well. She had broken up with countless men, because they acted as if the time she spent working on herself were nothing and all that mattered were the time she spent with them.

"No, no, Affrica, you know I wouldn't ask you anything like that." *Uh-oh, that didn't work. Plan B.* "I was just hoping when things slowed down a bit, maybe real soon, we could have a romantic dinner and I could give you a massage with warm oil . . ."

As Delroy described the romantic night, all Affrica could do was guiltily think about Alex doing those things to her. His big hands rubbing her smooth body all over till they were both shiny with heat and oil. All leading up to a night of . . .

"Affrica!" Delroy called out her name loudly. He had been describing their night of passion when her eyes seemed to glaze over.

"Huh?" She turned around, startled. "Yes, yes, that sounds great, Alroy."

"Did you just call me Alroy?" Delroy knew what he had heard.

"I called you what? We should lower the radio," Affrica stated. She stared out the window.

Derloy did not want an argument so he did not

pursue her slip-up. If that pretty cop was there, he would make sure there was no way he got to her during the party. *I know they're going to try to dance some slow song together. I'm going to have to do a lot of blocking.*

Affrica stared at the foggy window and imagined what it would be like to slow dance with Alex. To have her head against his shoulder taking him in. Feeling his heartbeat against her ear. The heaviness of his hands on her hips. Maybe a hard rise on her thigh. She shuddered at the thought, then smiled. She refused to look at Delroy's expression.

Chantay Miller stood looking at her lovely reflection in the full-length mirror. She was downstairs at her sister's apartment as usual. What was unusual was the fact that tonight she would be going to a big political party, being thrown for the mayor of Passion. Maxwell asked her the same day they had met, and Chantay said yes so quickly they both had laughed.

"I feel like a black Cinderella."

"You look great, but hold still before your ear gets singed." Erica held the curling iron to Chantay's glossy hair. This was the last touch. Chantay wore a long, satin, champagne-colored dress. She had worn it as a bridesmaid last year and it still fitted and looked absolutely amazing on Chantay. The wedding had been a winter wedding, so the seamstress who made the dresses made beautiful matching wraps.

"Girl, I can't believe he asked me to go with him. He's so smart, so *mature.*"

"You mean old."

"He's fine, trust me, and he acts like them old-style men. He likes to bow, hold the door, and help me with my coat on. Girl, he even pull out the chair at dinner."

"He pays or you pay?" Erica asked flatly.

"He pays!"

"You sure he's straight? He sounds too good to be real."

"He's as straight as an arrow. He made sure I didn't miss it." She looked at her sister guiltily.

Kysha came out of a room dressed in Kermit pajamas. "Wow, Mommy nice." She nodded at her mother with large eyes.

"Thank you, baby." She touched her little girl's hair.

The telephone rang and Erica answered formally. "Good evening." She hung up the phone quickly.

"It's him?" Chantay said expectantly. "He's here?"

"Yes, Cinderella, the *limo* is downstairs." They screeched. "Wait, wait. Your purse. Check your purse."

Chantay looked at her small purse, confused. Then she understood.

"Okay." She opened up the purse, examining its contents. "Gum, car fare home, lipstick, two quarters, safety pins, and a small lotion. I got it all.

"No, I think you forgot something," Erica said mischievously. She pulled out a condom.

"No, you didn't just . . ."

Erica waved the condoms in Chantay's face.

Chantay laughed and swiped at them. She quickly grabbed her long winter coat.

"Kareem, I'm going out with Chantay, keep an eye on the kids."

Chantay's skinny heels clicked loudly on the hallway's black and white linoleum, as they waited at the elevator banks. People were coming out of their apartments to look at Chantay, after learning the person who was about to get into the limo was living on their floor. Her sister held the lobby door open for her, but ran back inside. She wasn't wearing a coat.

Chantay unsteadily made her way to the limo, its headlights brightening up the evening. Maxwell exited the toasty limo and stood in the blustery wind as she made her way to the car. He extended his hand when she came near, and he gave her a bow and kiss. He assisted Chantay into the car and waved to the small group of people who had gathered in the lobby with Erica to see Chantay off. They did not wave back.

The long slick car made its way slowly to the Grand Wyant Hotel. The fifteen-minute ride was pleasant for both Maxwell and Chantay. They spoke softly and drank cold wine.

Alex decided to go stag to the party. He wore one of his tailor-made suits. Alex had three, gifts to himself. He had grown tired of department-store suits, so he had three made up especially for him at a men's boutique in Spain. They were shipped to him priority three months later and they were worth the wait. He wore a midnight-blue tweed suit that sat perfectly on his broad shoulders. He was comfortable in whatever he wore. He purposefully went to the party late. He made sure dinner would have been served and eaten. Everyone would be in a good talking mood. He had a few questions to ask some city officials and he needed people to have at least one drink in them and a full stomach. He needed to get more dirt on the police commissioner.

When Alex entered the dimly lit ballroom, he realized he was right on time. People were milling about, and live jazz music was playing. There was an eclectic mix of people in the room. It was still very crowded. Lines at the bar. The ordinary citizens mixed with senators. He noticed everyone. By the time he had walked past the dance floor toward a few congressmen, he already knew where everyone he needed to talk to was.

The talk was political but light. Alex knew it would not be light toward the end of the night. After two drinks, most people's lips became loose.

He felt something soft press up behind him. It was Judy Bloomberg. Alex turned around surprised.

"Oh, don't act surprised. With that sharp hearing of yours, I'm sure you heard me miles away."

He looked at her dress. She wore a long green dress with sequins that reflected the chandeliers' frosty light. She looked positively radiant.

"Judy, you look striking."

Judy waved her hand at him and blushed terribly. His sincerity was overwhelming.

"Would you like me to get you a drink?"

"Yes, please. Scotch and soda."

Alex whistled. Judy smiled.

Alex walked purposefully to the bar. He said good night to city officials and the like. He spotted Oprah Winfrey leaving with an entourage.

As he waited in the line, he grew angry when he saw the police commissioner. *I'm going to get him out.* He would have to be crafty, but this was the time and place to get any information on the commissioner that he needed. A lot of his pals were at this party. He was finally able to order the drinks. He had a soda and got Judy her strong drink. He walked back to Judy and gave her the drink. A friend of hers asked her to dance and she went out onto the floor, dancing to a Cab Calloway type of dance ditty. Judy moved pretty well; too bad her partner kept stepping on her feet.

Alex heard laughter, and his head immediately shot to his left. Affrica and a group of Republican and Democratic senators were exchanging anecdotes. Affrica was a lucent sight. Alex was mesmerized by the vision of her. The dress found curves and incredible dips in her body, rose at the two hills and flowed down to the polished floor.

She looked like a queen and seemed very much at home talking to these Republicans. He was sure she had issues with most of their agendas. But here they were, Republicans and Democrats gathered around this woman. He was deeply impressed by that. A person with that kind of personal power and charisma. It turned him on. He straighten up and pulled his vision away from her. He fingered the cassette tape he had made for her. He cleared his throat and like a hawk started to zero in on the people he needed to talk to. He spotted one looking very tipsy pointing to another man that Alex didn't know. When Alex walked toward him, the other man quickly left and Alex was left alone to talk with Mr. Herbert Stone, the judge from hell. But the judge was so wasted that Alex could barely understand a word he was saying. He just kept pointing at Alex mumbling things. Alex kept asking and soon he was able to get some more information.

Chantay was in heaven. Her head was swimming with so much information to process. She marveled at the large floral designs decorating the entire room. The lights were dimmed warmly and the candles on each table gave the room a glow. The party was kept intimate and jovial at the same time. Chantay danced with Maxwell all night. He seemed very much the Don Juan type. He said poetry into her ear as they danced slowly to the jazz band, and he massaged her feet when she told him her foot hurt. The only bad thing the entire evening was the evil looks she kept getting from Ramona, who at times stared at her with so much venom, Chantay thought she would approach her and hit her. *Did I just step on some toes?* she wondered.

But when she looked she saw Ramona all over some fine baldheaded brother in a tuxedo. *Why would she trip over the old guy when she has that on her arm?* Chantay did her best to ignore Ramona and enjoy herself, and she succeeded. She saw so many famous people, just walking around or dancing. Oprah was so much more beautiful in real life; Hillary was so much smaller than she thought she was.

Affrica and Ramona finally had a moment and were whispering to each other.

They both looked remarkable in their own way and every time they had a moment, someone would ask one of them to dance or they would be engaged in conversation. Delroy tried to remain glued to Affrica but he found her whirlwind pace dizzying. First she was talking to a group about the Environmental Protection Agency. Then a group of six people wanted her opinion on an issue they were debating. Everywhere he went someone was vying for her attention. Even Hillary Clinton extolled her virtues, saying she was making women all over the world proud.

"Girl, he will not leave me alone. I came out of the bathroom and he was outside the door waiting for me. I swear he had this weird smile on his face too."

She was having such a great time, it seemed every single African-American in Michigan politics had come to the party. Detroit's mayor was even there. *LAAW really knows how to throw a party.* Every single thing had been magnificent. The dinner was not regular catered food. They had flown in an entire restaurant staff from New Orleans to cook and serve the Cajun food. The spicy food kept everyone alert and dancing.

After she had not seen Alex during dinner, she gave up hope that he was coming and went about her business. When she felt a tickle on the side of her face, she turned and saw Alex across the room looking at her. He nodded lightly when their eyes locked. She felt a great rush of heat hit her and her legs turned weak. She looked away quickly, but Delroy had noticed and he stepped in front of her and asked her a stupid question.

Affrica's face felt hot. She needed something cold and asked Delroy to get her something with ice. Before he could come back, Affrica was back on the dance floor doing the salsa with David Dinkins, the black ex-mayor of New York.

Ramona had succeeded tenfold in making Maxwell jealous. She whispered to Affrica on the balcony after they snuck away from the crowd to gossip.

"I swear Maxwell turned purple when I walked

in in all my glory." She raised up a hand. "It was all worth it just for that. Just for that look. Ha, ha."

"You look so nice, girl." Affrica sighed. "But I am tired. I swear if I smile any more, my face is going to freeze this way." Affrica pasted a fake smile on her face.

"You are working it, woman! Your mama is going to be proud. You didn't kiss up, you didn't brown-nose. You were mannerly and accommodating, but you weren't a pushover. You weren't overly sexual, but you flirted. There is no way you won't get monu-mental support on all your ideas for Passion."

Affrica did feel confident that she did well. She really did enjoy speaking to all the people she did. She learned so much about what went on in other cities and counties, about what was being done. She could seek counsel with anyone now. She felt as if she wanted to talk to Oprah some more one day if she could. They had spoken a few moments in pri-vate, but they didn't sit down and gab, as Affrica would have loved.

Affrica stared out into the ballroom. The whole night had been so magical. The chandeliers were sparkling cut glass and were elaborately designed. Two wall mirrors were on each side of the room, with magnificent palms on the four sides of the ball-room. The food had melted in her mouth and spiced her tongue. The chef took an ovation from the dinner guests. Affirca appreciated the work that had gone into the party. Before dinner, Hillary Clin-ton had presented Affrica with an award and vote of confidence. Affrica felt very blessed.

She searched around the tops of heads milling about for one particular perfectly shaped head. When she found him, she felt a hand on her shoul-der.

"Hey, Affrica, I was looking all over for you, love."

Affrica didn't even look at him and started to walk away.

"Let's go back to the party." Delroy looked down at what he thought Affrica was looking at, but he saw nothing. He was getting very upset and wanted to leave, but he did not want to leave Affrica. He had to do this.

The jazz band played the entire night. An all-black ensemble who took requests and played music out of the Harlem Renaissance era. They all wore white tuxedos and sounded great, and they also played some of their own compositions. It was an electrifying and exciting night.

The people at the party felt happy and confident about this new beautiful mayor. She was witty and engaged everyone in dialogue. Some had been reluctant to talk at the meeting, but with this new forum, they felt relaxed enough to talk to Affrica. Some were very concerned about the budget crisis that no one was talking about. They were worried that once again their department needs would not be met as they hadn't been with the last administration. Some of the concerns Affrica had not been aware of. When she spoke with sewage management, the word *misappropriation* was used, and this troubled Affrica. But she remained confident and talkative, never missing a beat. Some of the conversations were light, people sharing their childhood memories of Passion.

The reason most people were drawn to talking to Affrica was that she listened. She listened and let them speak, even with the heated issues.

Affrica was interested. Ideas were what made the world go round and the sharing of information and ideas were how good things happened. This was one of the main reasons she wanted to talk with Oprah some more. That was one person who knew how to implement good ideas, and Affrica wanted to be able to implement her ideas with fervor and support. She shared her ideas freely too.

Alex always knew where Affrica was during the party even when he couldn't look at her. He knew where there was laughter or a small group discussion, Affrica would be there somewhere. Even later on in the night she still seemed fresh.

At 10:15 Alex's cell phone vibrated. Alex walked out to the terrace to take the call. It was the sergeant.

"Chief, shortly after 2200 hours the P45 bus headed north on Charles Street was diverted from its path by two armed men. The bus driver was instructed to park in a darkened area of Washington Street and everyone was robbed at gunpoint. There are no injuries, just a lot of shaken-up people. I've dispatched officers into the surrounding area and we're getting everyone's story. Perpetrators are described as two hooded black males with large coats and one having a backpack. They stole wallets and purses from the passengers and left the scene on bikes that were hidden in an alley. It was well planned." The sergeant relayed this information to Alex but wanted to handle this one himself. Alex usually took over most large investigations. Sarge really wanted this one for himself.

This sergeant was one of a handful of police staff that Alex had total confidence in.

Alex gave it to him. "Okay, handle it. Keep me informed if anything further develops." As he

pressed the button that hung up the phone, he was
slightly disturbed. He was glad no one was hurt, but
angry that once again black men had committed a
crime. He was tired of the description of the "usual
suspect."

Outside, it was freezing cold. The moon was
bright. He breathed deeply of the frigid air and felt
invigorated. Being in the military had built up his
tolerance to cold. He took another cold breath and
headed back into the warm party and stood in a
corner, pondering the sarge's call. It came to him
with strange delight that he had a perfect view
through the crowd at Affrica.

Affrica did not realize Alex was staring at her.
The only reason she knew he was there was that
when Ramona saw him she came and told her
"Roots" code name for Alex. Alex Haley had written the book *Roots*. Affrica nodded and pretended
she did not care. Ramona cleared her throat and
nodded. She knew better.

By 12:30 A.M., most of the party-goers were thin-
ning out. A few remained, talking quietly or dancing very, very slowly. After Affrica was done saying
her good-byes to a young senator and her husband,
she finally had a moment to herself. She looked
down and made a beeline to the bathroom. She
kept her head down, even as she saw the figure
move toward her.

Alex bumped into Affrica "accidentally." He was
watching as she made her away from the couple,
and he began walking ever so slowly toward the aisle
she was coming out of.

"Excuse me," she said before looking up into
Alex's dark eyes.

"Hello, Mayor Bryant. My apologies," he said formally and flashed her a wicked smile.

She blushed. "You smell good," she said without thinking. Alex smelled fragrant, yet only if you were standing close to him, as she was. She took a step back and looked into his spectacular face.

"Oh, really?" Alex tilted his head questionably.

"I just meant you smell like . . . the beach and trees." Affrica regretted the words as soon as they came out of her mouth.

Alex was laughing gently now. "Well, thank you, Mayor Bryant. I actually got it when I was in another country."

"What country?"

"Thailand."

"Thailand. How long were you there?" After spending the entire evening getting to know so many people, Affrica realized she did not spend any time getting to know Alex. And she so wanted to get to know him. She was asking him about his perfume and travels, but she was searching his face, capturing every contour of his face to take to bed with her tonight. Standing this close to him in very high heels, she was still much shorter than he, and she liked that. But she knew she could easily rest her head right there. She looked at his shoulder.

"I've been to Thailand. A few times. I went with the military and a few times by myself."

"Did you ever go to Thailand during the rainy season?"

"You know what? Yes, I have."

"My mother told me about it. She had lived in the jungle for two months."

"Your mother lived in the jungle?" Alex said.

Affrica nodded. To see the two of them talking would not seem suspicious at all since this *was* a social event. Ramona came by them, smiling broadly, her broad hip gyrating seductively.

"Hello, Alex."

"Hello, Ramona."

"This is Richard." Ramona introduced her handsome man.

"Hey." The two men shook hands.

Judy Bloomberg came sauntering over to them. The group stood and had an interesting conversation about the party. They spoke about the people they had met. Drunk Judge Stone dancing like a ballerina on the dance floor. They cracked up at that one. Affrica turned and started chatting with Alex. Judy excused herself to the rest room. Ramona and the young man were gone.

Delroy was quickly making his way toward them with Affrica's jacket. He had seen them "bump" each other. He was humiliated. He had prematurely ended a conversation he was having with Nettie Wilson, the head of LAAW. He made his way toward them after having retrieved Affrica's coat from the coat check.

They had quickly changed the subject when they both saw him approaching. By the time Delroy was putting Affrica's coat over her shoulders, they were talking about the Irving Housing demolition.

"I have some specs to give you, Alex," she said.

He found it very difficult not to look at the slight cleavage—the dress left a lot to the imagination. "You could have a messenger deliver it to my house or station."

"What would you prefer?"

"Either. Send it to my home."

They stared intently at each other. The magnetism between them was unbearable. Affrica was actually a little relieved when Delroy rudely interrupted them.

"I'll have Ramona call you in the—"

"Good night, *Mr.* Bartholomew." Delroy gave Alex the look of death.

Alex looked down at him and nodded. Delroy put Affrica's coat on and started to walk away.

Affrica frowned after him, and continued talking to Alex. "I'll have Ramona call you, and you two can arrange a drop-off. She'll call you Monday." She shook Alex's hand and said good night. She gave him a beautiful smile filled with promise. She walked away toward Delroy.

Alex could not believe how this thirty-second conversation could shake him up so much. Judy came back from the ladies' room and took Alex's arm.

Affrica's warm feeling dissipated the moment she caught up with Delroy. *Who does Delroy think he is? I'm supposed to leave now because he wants me to. I'm not his child. He can't make me go home if it is not time for me to go home.*

Affrica did not leave as Delroy had proposed. Instead, as they almost made it to the door, she began speaking with Thomas Needleman. He was the mayor of Valleyview, Michigan, one of the neighboring cities. He had heard of Affrica's plan and loved the idea.

"What about space?"

Affrica removed the coat Delroy had placed on her shoulders and threw it on a chair. Councilwoman Hilary Fausto and her husband, Terrence, joined them. They too wanted to hear about the radical plan the beautiful mayor was proposing.

"Let's get some drinks," said Thomas Needleman. The group walked to the bar with a reluctant Delroy holding up the wall. All the while Thomas made stupid golf and stock jokes. They ordered a few more drinks and continued chatting.

Delroy began gesturing to Affrica that it was time to go. He waved frantically at her and pointed to his watch. He was fuming, so enraged he could barely restrain himself.

Affrica tried to remain calm. She knew she was still being watched. She remained stoic-faced.

"Excuse me for a moment." She left the group. She walked quickly back to him.

"Listen, Delroy. I can't leave these people here, no matter what time it is. I am the mayor, I have to be the last one here. Or someone from my office, and I'm the only one left. Even Ramona is gone."

His hazel contacts bore into her face. "No, you don't have to stay. I think they would understand if you had to leave now."

"But I don't have to leave now. You have to leave now."

"Fine." He almost threw her purse at her. "Bye." He kissed her lips harshly, a hollow gesture, attempting to keep up the happy couple image.

Affrica returned to talk to the group, who were anxiously awaiting her return.

"So tell us, Affrica," the councilwoman said, raising her drink to her red-stained lips.

Affrica gave them a radiant smile and stood up straighter. She held her glass of wine in one hand and gestured with the other. She explained that the renovation plans could be altered to turn three blocks of high-rise apartments into eight blocks of two- and three-family houses.

"But what about the space?"

"Well, I don't know if you know this, Mrs. Fausto, but there are two very large plots of land behind Irving Housing. As of late they've been unused. There is available space. I actually got to see the space. I went with some planners."

"How convenient."

"It really is."

The group Affrica was speaking with were very impressed. She was articulate and had the perfect blend of professionalism and humor. What they had heard and read in the press reports about her was nothing like what they saw before them.

Alex left with Judy and walked her safely to her car. She was reluctant to leave the party, hinting that maybe Alex should spend the night with her, but he politely bade her farewell.

He purposefully made his way back to the party and stood in the hallway for a while before he called Sarge to see how things were going with the bus. They spoke for a while when Alex heard voices coming toward him. He looked toward the voices and nodded politely to the crowd. Affrica was part of the crowd and looked calmly at Alex as she walked down the chilly hallway. The group stood together another moment and bundled up their coats, making their way to the blistering cold. Affrica rubbed her arms and looked boldly at Alex talking on his cell phone. He followed her form as she entered the almost empty ballroom, and he tried to pay attention to his work. He took a deep breath. After he hung up with the sergeant, he headed back in. He immediately spotted Affrica. The jazz band was packing up their instruments and had popped a CD in.

Alex didn't hear Affrica politely refuse the ride home. When she saw Alex still there, she had other ideas besides going home. She walked the group to the door, knowing full well she would have no car. *He'll take me home.*

On the dance floor the two drunk couples were barely holding each other up. Affrica sat at a table, took off her shoes, and looked at Alex, who was walking to her table.

"Were you waiting for me?" She smiled coolly.

"Yes, Affrica, I was."

His honesty turned her on. What was happening? She hadn't been this hot-blooded since college. She looked at her watch. Almost 2 A.M. No press would be around at this time.

At first he sat across from her, but when he realized he could not see her through the table centerpiece, he moved next to her. They sat side by side at one of the tables closest to the dance floor. Affrica did not want anyone to suspect anything. She was glad he did not speak. After spending the night talking, the last thing she wanted to do was have a conversation. She also knew that as much as she wanted to get to know Alex better, Delroy was still her boyfriend and she was the mayor. She felt so confused.

"You look great, Affrica."

Alex's comment snapped her back to reality. "Thank you, Alex." Every muscle in Affrica's body was tense. "You seem to always revisit the scene of the crime. You can never just leave, always have to come back."

"That's me, I never leave till the job is done."

"Is that a fact, Alex?"

She turned to finally face him and he handed her a cassette tape. It was in a clear case. She searched his face for answers. They stopped looking at each other as one of the couples walked past them. They paid Alex and Affrica no mind. The jazz band from Indiana did not even realize Affrica was the mayor. They were just happy for the $9,000 they had just made. The bass player had called a taxi for the drunk couples. Alex was keeping an eye on them anyway.

"What is this?" she said, fingering the smooth plastic.

"It's a cassette tape."

"I know what it is. But what *is* it?"

"It's music, some of the ones you told me you liked and some that I really like."

Affrica was moved. She couldn't believe he had gone through all that trouble for her.

"You mean you just made a . . ." She looked at the label. It said 120 minutes. "A 120-minute tape for me?" She thought about it for a moment. "Thank you, Alex."

"You're welcome." He opened his mouth to speak when he felt a strange vibration in his pants. Someone was calling his cell phone.

He pressed the speak button. "Yeah?" He knew it was the sarge.

Affrica only heard one side of the conversation and it sounded serious. Alex stood up while he was still on the phone. He gave some orders and hung up.

"We have to go." He was all business.

"What's going on?" She was feeling nervous. She wanted to know what was going on in her city.

"Listen, some bad stuff just went down. Put your coat on and I'll tell you in the car."

Thirty seconds later they were in Alex's Jeep. "Put on your seat belt," he said as he whipped the

Jeep backward and out of the parking space. He was very serious. "Earlier tonight a bus with six passengers was robbed. I just found out that two burglaries were just reported in Old Oak Hills," Alex said as he flicked on the police radio in his Jeep. It sounded like a lot of chattering and police code.

Affrica was stunned. She had not expected to have to deal with anything like this so soon. Alex clearly implied that he could not tell her any more at that time but would call her immediately if he thought the situation warranted it. He sped through Passion, breaking the speed limit by at least twenty-five miles an hour the entire way to the Mayoral Mansion.

Alex masterfully decelerated the Jeep to a stop without screeching. He distractedly walked her to her door and started to rush back to his car. After three steps, he stopped and turned to face Affrica. "Good night, Mayor Bryant," he said in a cool voice that did not match his temperament of a few seconds ago.

In her mind, Affrica froze the image of him standing there. She knew he had to go and yet the whole damn city could wait. She waved at him to go. He jogged back to his Jeep while pulling out his phone. By the time his Jeep had reached the corner of her block, it was doing sixty miles an hour and had acquired a spinning red light.

She stood on the foyer before her door, listening to his engine race into the distance; then she closed her eyes, summoning the snapshot image of Alex, standing there. "Good night, Chief Bartholomew," she said softly as smoky wisps of her breath flew out into the cold night air.

Fifteen

2:15 A.M.

In the shadows of the closed Chinese food store on Jackson Street, Tommy Weed crouched between a dump site and a pay phone. His body was steaming from his long run through the night, but he was not out of breath. Something in his hand glinted in the light of a distant lamp. He leaned forward slightly, fierce eyes scanning the terrain. The street was clear now.

An old score had been settled, and a new allegiance had been formed. He emerged from the shadows and ran off into the night.

3:09 A.M.

Alex was just leaving the site of the first burglary to check on their progress at the site of the second house when he got a call from the station. A car that was reported stolen had crashed into an empty parked police car and then hit a pedestrian while fleeing the scene. They had put out an APB on a silver Benz with a dented front end and a smashed rear window. Alex got the details and hung up. He called the sarge. "Hey, buddy, sorry to do this to you, but I need you to go over to the second burglary site and oversee the investigation. . . . All right. Good. Call me when you get there. . . .Yes, I know, I'm heading to the hit-and-run site now." Alex hung up his phone and made a screeching U-turn.

3:10 A.M.

Milton was startled into consciousness by the car horn he was leaning on. It was wet with his tears. He was still very high and it took him a few moments to get his bearings. *Where the hell am I?* He looked around frantically but saw only the fogged windows of the luxury car.

What just happened? Damn! Where the hell am I?

He wiped the windows and looked out at green grass that stretched back to large, expensive houses. He was in a residential area, on a dark, quiet, tree-lined street. Everything was still. There were families inside, safely asleep in their beds.

He looked at the car he was in. A silver Benz. Stolen.

Milton sat back in the leather seat and tried to reconstruct the recent past, but his drug-induced haze started to drag him down into unconsciousness. His closing eyes came to bear on the rearview mirror. Bits of a horrific realization came to him. He opened the door and scrambled out of the car. He staggered around to the back of the vehicle to see that the rear window was smashed and caved in.

Milton again surveyed the area and found that he was on a dead-end street. His memories came back to him slowly. He sat down on the frozen grass, holding his head with both hands. *Okay, Okay, I was trying to get away from the police. 'Cause . . . I had hit one of their cars. The police car was parked at a Dunkin' Donuts. I did some dumb stuff.*

A halogen porch light came on, brightly illuminating the area where Milton was sitting. He immediately stood, pondered the stolen car, and decided to walk away swiftly. He was two houses down when he heard voices coming from the house by the car. When Milton reached the corner, he saw that four blocks away there was a lot of police activity. At least three police cars and an ambulance were parked in front of a Dunkin' Donuts store. *I only drove four blocks? Ambulance! Oh, man! I hit somebody! Now I remember. I had stolen the car to bring it back to Jay Blow, but I decided to hit the parked police car for fun. I got stuck. The cops were just watching in shock. Somebody was running up behind me yelling to find out if I was okay. When I tried to back up to free myself, I hit them. Damn!*

Milton was shivering, but not from the cold, as he turned away and walked off into the night.

3:27 A.M.

Little Man stared at the blue and purple flames. He dropped another card on the pile of melting plastic.

"Yo, son! He is still not answering. He must have his phone off. Yo, son, what are you doing in there? What's that smell?" Louis a.k.a. Mastermind rushed into the kitchen. "Yo, son, I know you didn't light that stuff in the sink!"

"You said to burn it, son. What?"

"Not now, and definitely not here! Damn!" Louis turned on the faucet and pushed the aluminum tray of smoldering credit cards under the running water.

The loud sizzling and resulting foul smoke woke up everyone in the apartment. Louis's two brothers and his grandmother all came out to see what was going on. They nearly tripped over all of the new merchandise from the shopping spree that Mastermind and Little Man had been on for the two hours after they robbed the bus.

"Don't just stand there, open the windows. This smoke is toxic," Louis yelled at his brothers. If anyone had bothered to replace the batteries in the smoke detectors, they would have woken the entire building.

"I ain't ready ta die yet, boy," said Louis's grandmother as she went back into her bedroom and shut the door.

On the twelfth floor of building 3 of Irving Housing, windows slid open and smoke billowed out into the cold night.

3:31 A.M.

The Dunkin' Donuts parking lot was a mess. The site had not been made secure. Civilians were still in the store, and so were two cops, getting food. The ambulance was still and the pedestrian who had been hit was sitting there with only a small cut on his hand. And it seemed that the whole neighborhood was out at 3:30 in the morning walking all over possible evidence.

Alex pulled his Jeep into the parking lot prepared to pounce on whoever was in charge and then take the names of everyone else. The police conduct here was simply a shame. However, before he left his car, he heard on the police dispatch that a suspected drug dealer was just admitted to the emergency room at St. Francis

Hospital in Clinton Heights, two towns away. He knew that there was some beef among gangs there and gangs in the two adjacent towns. One of those towns was Passion. The thought that these various crimes could be related danced across Alex's mind. It occurred to him that the night's crime spree may not be over.

He called in to the station and told them to wake up some off-duty cops. This was turning out to be one of those nights. He searched the sky for the full moon. As he opened his car door, prepared to begin the barking of orders to his officers, he thought, *Poor Affrica, what a welcome Passion has given you. We have our work cut out for us.*

3:45 A.M.

The sound of gunfire dominated the room.

Jay Blow's eyes moved from the TV screen to his cell phone sitting on the table. *They should all be done by now.* He had turned it off just in case one of the Bloodhounds became fool enough to try to communicate with him during the night's festivities. It was agreed that he would meet with them at Mastermind's apartment at noon.

Wearing nothing but pink panties, Juliet emerged from a dark hallway rubbing her eyes. "Can't you turn that down some? Can't a woman get some sleep?"

"Sure, honey," Jamie said in a chipper voice. He picked up the remote and turned up the volume four notches, then slumped back into his chair. Juliet produce her middle finger simultaneously with her extended tongue, then spun around and stomped back into the darkness. *Back at you!* Jamie thought, without ever looking up.

"Say hello to my little friend!" announced Al Pachino in *Scarface*. Then more endless gunfire.

Sixteen

That morning, Affrica talked on the phone to Ramona at length about the party the night before. They went through every single detail. Ramona guaranteed the press was going to write some really great things about Affrica and the job she was doing.

Ramona was in Chicago at Richard the Third's house. Richard had gone out to get breakfast for Ramona and himself. Affrica was getting ready to go to the cemetery to see her grandmother. That entire morning and afternoon, whenever Affrica got the chance she listened to the cassette tape Alex had made her. It was an amazing mix of music, all toe-tapping, swaying music. He had recorded Cassandra Wilson and Minnie Ripeton, even Lenny Kravitz. She was so moved by the cassette.

An officer from the precinct had called her to give her the low-down on the crime spree that happened the night before. To her chagrin it kept her on the phone most of the morning, until she finally turned it off when she got to her grandmother's grave.

She had called Alex, twice, both times leaving messages. James, the architect who was handling the

3-D models, was getting on her case and she knew if she could get them to him by Monday, then he could get right on it. First she had to get Alex. She knew he lived in the Linden Hills neighborhood. A nice neighborhood, not rich but not poor either. The people were mostly black and Latino.

Affrica tried to call Alex one last time, before she headed home.

He picked up the phone gruffly. "Hello."

"Hi . . . Alex?"

"Yeah, who is this?"

She couldn't believe how rude he sounded. "It's Affrica." When he didn't respond, she continued. "I just had the specs and I need to get it to my guy so he can start building the three-D models."

"Specs? Hold on. Affrica, bear with me, I just got home a few hours ago. I've been at crime scenes all night and morning."

Affrica understood the gruffness. She was disappointed she couldn't bring the pictures by. "Fine, Alex, I'll have them sent by messenger early tomorrow. I shouldn't be bothering you on a Sunday. What's the latest on the investigation?"

Alex was fully awake now. He wondered if he had time to take a shower before she got to his house.

"It's a very long story, Affrica. Come by my house and drop them off. I'll fill you in on the investigation." He yawned quietly. As tired as he was, he would love her company.

"No, Alex, I don't want to bother you."

"Bother me. If you knock and I don't answer immediately, I'm in the shower."

"Alex, it's freezing cold out here. I'm not waiting outside."

"Listen, I'm going to do something really stupid,

but I'll leave the door open for you since you're so close and hopefully you're the only one who gets in."

She pulled up to his house four minutes after they had talked on the phone. Alex had been listening out for a car or a slamming door and he heard it when Affrica drove up to his house. She parked in his driveway and stepped out of the car. She was dressed casually and warmly, her hood covering her ears. She reached into the backseat and picked up the drawings. *Nice house.* His front yard extended right to his backyard and she could see trees. There were no decorations on the front of the house. His blinds were made of wood, as she could see. *Hmm, looks like bamboo. That's different.* Affrica scrutinized Alex's house. She was curious about the backyard. But she made her way inside, pushing the brown door open. She immediately smelled the delicious fragrance of the oil that Alex had on the night before. His house impressed her. She felt like a snoop looking around. She heard the shower still running.

"Make yourself comfortable!" he yelled when she was inside.

He heard me come in? She did as she was instructed. His house was warm. He had a fireplace; she wondered if he ever used it. There were records everywhere. There was an archway that led to another room that she presumed was the dining room. Instead of a table he had what looked like a turntable and endless books. *Books?* The pillows were all dark and ethnic looking. He had some African-American art on the walls, mixed with art from other places. It looked Asian or Aztec, she couldn't tell. He had one large burgundy rug on his shiny wood floor.

She wanted to take her boots off and walk barefoot. It was such a welcoming house. There was a staircase and on the walls were a few pictures. She could make out an older woman and an unsmiling man. *I bet that's the military father,* she thought.

She put the rolled-up drawings down and leaned them on a very comfortable-looking couch. She sat down and fell into its pillows. The shower had stopped a few minutes ago and she had heard him padding upstairs. Her breath caught when she heard him moving about. She was so nervous her hands were shaking. She took five cleansing breaths. *I'm too old to feel like this and I'm dating Delroy. Nothing is going to happen between me and Alex.*

She heard him at the top of the stairs. She stood up in anticipation. Alex walked down quickly. He was dressed in flannel baggy pajama pants and a long-sleeve T-shirt. He looked comfortable and warm. Affrica could see how toned and muscular his body really was. She was dressed pretty comfortably herself. She had just come from the Linden Hills Cemetery, where her grandmother was buried. She was wearing jeans and a bulky wool sweater. She usually spent hours visiting the grave site.

As Alex approached her, giving her a disarming smile, all her nervousness disappeared. He gave her a quick hug. *I get a hug.*

Alex couldn't imagine Affrica could look more beautiful than the night before, yet here she was in his house looking a hundred times more beautiful. Her crinkled hair was held loosely in a ponytail. Her skin was radiant from the cold. She had such a mixture of emotions on her face that Alex felt drawn to kissing her. He wanted to ease her knitted eyebrows, kiss a smile upon her thick lips.

"I apologize . . ." They laughed because they just

said the same thing at the same time. They stopped and then laughed again. Alex held his hand up for her to continue.

"A few things. One, I apologize for disturbing your Sunday. Two, I should have thought you might be caught up in the investigation last night and were not thinking about specs or drawings. And finally, three. That tape had to be one of the most beautiful things I've ever heard. Just the way the songs blended into each other, even songs that were from different eras . . . I'm babbling."

Alex was smiling down at her sweetly. "I'm glad you liked it, and you weren't babbling. Before we go on, I want to apologize for being gruff this morning. I was just mentally fatigued."

"Do you feel like talking about what's going on?"

Alex shook his head yes.

"Why is there what seems to be this crime wave?"

"Affrica, I have a feeling this isn't the worst of it. We have to find out who's behind this and nip it in the bud. Otherwise I'm afraid some lives might be lost next time."

"When the police department called me this morning to fill me in on all the episodes, I was so shocked."

"Affrica, I bust my butt in the department. I make sure my men are posted in high-crime areas. I have two units who are constantly watching Irving Housing to make sure nothing is going down. I've counseled some of the kids in there. I've personally arrested some of the kids in there. . . . Most of my men are decent cops, but a few of them I don't know about anymore. They dropped the ball on this."

They were sitting on the couch. She looked at Alex's large bare feet. They weren't spectacular feet, but the nails were cut and his heels didn't look grungy or ashy. Delroy's heels scratched her when they were in bed. She suggested he find a pedicurist along with his manicurist. She stared at Alex's feet and listened to him talking.

"Are you looking at my feet, Affrica?"

Affrica bit her lip and nodded, and they both laughed.

They looked at each other a few seconds. And turned away.

"Would you like something to drink?"

"Yes, please. Some water will be fine." She hoped he would invite her to the kitchen. She wanted to see the rest of the house.

"If you're hungry I was about to whip up something neat and easy to munch on."

Affrica's stomach growled as he said it.

"Come on." He gave her a hand off of the couch. She stood up and for a split second Alex held her hand and stood close to her, her face close to his neck. It took every ounce of strength she had not to place a gentle kiss on it, to put her hands on his chest. He broke the spell and let her hand go.

She trailed behind him as he walked through the dining room. It was a relatively empty room. On the left there was a wall of records. A polished wood shelving unit held the hundreds of records, CDs, and cassettes that Alex had. He even had a turntable. He had a small end table stacked with books and three more shelving units filled with books. She had seen that from the living room. She had stopped and Alex watched as she appraised everything. He could watch her all day. She put her hand in her pocket. She looked as if she was trying to make a decision either to look at the books or at the music. She went for the music.

"Wow, Alex, you sure have a lot of music . . . stuff," she yelled from the dining room.

"Yeah, my mom got me into music really young and it never stopped."

Affrica was flipping through the large albums. He had Public Enemy next to Earth, Wind and Fire, which was next to the flamboyant Elton John.

She found an old *The Wiz* soundtrack. She really liked the movie and thought Michael Jackson was perfectly handsome before all that other stuff he did to himself.

"Oh, Alex, I have to put this on." She walked to the kitchen doorway with the album cover.

He smiled wide when he saw what she was holding up. He was cutting up some vegetables and putting them in the pot. The kitchen was large and clean. A counter ran along an entire wall and a table sat in the middle of the floor. Two large stacks of folders sat on and around a tiny table with a desk lamp. Alex sat on a tall stool cutting up spinach and onions.

"Press the red button, the top flips off, click, and it will play."

Affrica went back into the music room and figured out his system immediately. He was almost ecstatic when he heard Diana Ross singing about home. Affrica was the only woman to figure out his system. It really wasn't that hard. There was just a lot of stuff, but it was all pretty self-explanatory. He heard her humming. She was not talking much. His house had a lot to take in. She walked by the kitchen door toward the books. He couldn't see her from his vantage point.

The telephone rang. It was Sarge for Alex.

"Hey, Alex, I found a file here that I want you to look at tomorrow. Everything else is fine. We checked Jay Blow's whereabouts and he wasn't near any of the crime scenes. He had an alibi that checked out. We know it came from Irving. But so far no one in there is ratting out the perpetrators."

"Okay, Sarge. Good job. Get some rest, man."

"All right."

Alex had been positive Jay Blow was involved somehow.

Affrica walked toward Alex. She had a book in her hand and her shoes were off. Alex felt a remarkable elation by the simple gesture.

"Smells good."

"It's just some canned soup with my flavorings and I cut bigger chunks of veggies into it."

"Still smells good." She eyed the crackers on the table. "May I?"

"Of course. You must really be hungry, you're about to eat a dry cracker with water." Alex got off the stool and poured the vegetables into the pot. He washed his hands and dried them on his pants. He opened up his fridge, contemplating for a moment. He pulled out a Granny Smith apple and washed it. Pulling out a knife, he sat down on the stool and shared the peeled apple with her.

"What were you doing in the neighborhood, if you don't mind me asking?" he said.

"I don't mind. My grandmother is buried at Linden."

"Oh, you went to put flowers down."

"No, I don't put flowers. I just sit there and talk to her. Even though I know she's with me all the time, I go to see her resting place and clean it. I talk with her." Affrica stopped abruptly. "I know it sounds crazy but . . ."

"It sounds like you're keeping your grandmother's spirit and memory alive."

Affrica stopped and scrutinized Alex. "You understand that? Why do you understand that, when everybody else patronizes me when I mention talking to a dead woman?"

Alex looked up at her from the peeling. "I think it's the same reason you understood how to work my stereo with minimal instruction when every other woman who's been here couldn't figure it out with detailed instructions or after seeing me do it thirty times."

Affrica was thoughtful. Alex put the apple and knife down to check on the boiling soup. He turned the flame off and grabbed two ceramic bowls. His handsome face was awash with emotions. He wasn't sure what to do with all the information he had and all the feelings he was experiencing.

He placed the items on a tray. "Let's sit in the living room."

The Wiz soundtrack was still on in the background. Affrica followed him into the living room. It was brightly lit with the end of the afternoon's sunshine. They heard the wind begin to whip. They sat next to each other with a considerable amount of space between them. They quietly observed the sun and looked at their steaming bowls of soup.

Affrica grabbed hers with a napkin and blew into it. She held the warm bottom with two paper towels that Alex handed her. The soup was delicious. Even if it was from a can. They stared at the sunlight as if it were a movie. It danced on his mirrors and created rainbows in crystal. The soup and company were enjoyed in silence. They were deep in thought and comfortable. Alex couldn't remember the last time he had felt so comfortable with someone else in his house. He stared at Affrica's face and hair, her beauty outstanding. He felt as if he wanted to tell this woman every secret he had. He wanted to feel her breath on his face, taste her.

The last woman Alex had dated was on a mission to change him. She acted as if she liked him, but she was always cleaning his house. Moving things, putting things away without telling him. She had removed an Aztec mask from his wall. When he had returned home he immediately noticed it was gone. He had confronted her on it and she had huffily told him she put it in a closet because it scared her.

"It's a mask the Aztecs used to scare off evil," he told her and went back to the closet to retrieve the colorful mask. It was a little scary, with long brightly painted horns and a tongue sticking out. But Alex didn't care. It was his house. And it continued on, with her complaining about his beard, his clothes, and his movies. She had even complained about his attractiveness drawing attention from her.

Affrica sipped the last of the warm soup. "Good soup." She placed the bowl on the tray and sat back satiated. She took a deep breath and pulled her feet under her. She was getting very warm with the hot soup in her belly. Without giving it another thought she pulled off the bulky sweater. Underneath she wore a soft cotton shirt that clung to her curves. Alex could not help but look at Affrica's body. Her high breasts were beacons. The curve of her waist called his hands. Affrica caught him looking at her. She blushed.

"I'm sorry . . . I wasn't trying to be lewd. . . . It was just one minute, you're fully covered, the next minute I'm seeing curves and . . ." He smiled at her and stopped. "You have a very nice body, Affrica."

"So do you, Alex." They laughed at each other's silliness.

The record stopped abruptly. Affrica had found another album to put on. She gracefully got off the couch and offered to take the tray with the now empty bowls. Alex watched her every move, not hiding his interest. Affrica felt a surge of heat hit her and she wondered if it would be forward for her to take off the shirt and remain in her pretty yellow tank top. But she didn't trust herself that naked with him.

She took the tray and sauntered out of the room. She deposited the tray on the kitchen table and put on a Prince album. Alex liked Prince's music a lot.

Alex's phone rang again. *Popular, isn't he?* she thought. She tried not to eavesdrop on his conversation, but he lowered the music slightly and paced the room.

"Listen, Penelope, I left two messages for you to call me and you never did."

"Alex, I was dressed and waiting for you! How could you do that?"

"There must have been some misunderstanding. We never talked after you left the message inviting me to the party."

Oh, he stood somebody up. Wait, who was he going to take to my party?

"I assumed you would be *flattered* that I would ask you, Alex."

"I was very flattered you asked me—"

"So why didn't you just come and pick me up?"

"What's up with your answering machine anyway? Did you get my messages?"

"I got them, but I didn't really listen to them. I

assumed you were calling to ask about my dress. I was thinking no matter what I wore we would both look outstanding. But you did not pick me up! You're such a pain!" She started crying into the phone.

Alex did not want to be mean, but how could she assume he was going with her, without even asking?

"Penelope, you know what they say about those that assume."

She stopped crying immediately. "So you didn't go to the dance."

"Yes, I went to the dance, alone." He was getting a headache talking to her and he wanted to get back to Affrica. He peeked at her through the kitchen. She had her back to him doing the dishes, trying to act as if she weren't listening. He balled up a napkin and threw it at her butt. She didn't turn around; she just shook her butt slightly. He laughed out and into the phone.

"Alex, I know you are not laughing at me."

"I have to go, Penelope."

"Where are you going?"

Alex walked to his music equipment and turned the Prince album back up.

"I have company that I need to tend to. Goodbye." He hung up quietly.

She called back immediately. "Don't you hang up on me. I hang up on you!"

Click. She hung up the phone loudly in his ear. Alex could only stand there looking at the cordless phone. He was so disgusted with the whole thing.

"I'll be right back." Alex ran back up the stairs and changed into a lightweight T-shirt. After Affrica finished the dishes she looked at his incredible book collection. Some of his books weren't even in

English. She was getting even warmer. She gracefully pulled the shirt over her head, leaving the yellow tank top that showed lots of cleavage. She folded the shirt and put it into her leather bag. Alex came down the stairs in the same pants, and now he was wearing a dark T-shirt.

Later on that same evening, after the sun had gone down in the winter's sky, a large moon rose and brightened the night. It had been over five hours since Affrica "came by to drop of the specs." Most of the five hours the two spent getting to know each other outside of their professional masks. Alex shared his fear and guilt about his relationship with his brother Taylor and his father. Affrica shared her fears about being in the public eye and failing. They felt a deep connection.

Alex's house was dimly lit. John Coltrane's music quietly intermingled with the moans and grunts of the couple on the floor. They were sitting on Alex's floor leaning against his couch, arms and legs intermingled. Alex licked Affrica's neck and took slow, deliberate bites of her flesh, causing her to moan and arch her body deeper into his. He could not get enough of her. He licked toward her ear and trailed the line of her neck down to her soft breast and rested there a bit, one hand in her hair, the other gently kneading her breast. It fitted perfectly in his hand. She pulled his head up to meet hers. She slipped her tongue into his mouth, finding his, and they played, pulling and pushing. Teasing. She gripped his head, her hands in his shirt, trying to memorize his form by touch. She gripped his arms as he lay over her. He kneeled between her legs and slowly peeled off her flimsy tank top, freeing her breasts. Affrica was dizzy. She felt as if she were floating on an orange cloud, and every time Alex touched or kissed some part of her, the cloud changed color. Her body was pure passion. She thought of nothing but his body on hers and wanting him deep inside her. Alex had both her breasts in his hands and licked her dark nipples as if they were made of rich chocolate. He teased them with his thumbs, causing her heat to rise even higher. She begged him to suck them. He obliged happily, greedily.

She flipped him onto his back, pulling off his shirt roughly. She straddled him, moving her hips gently. His hands reached up and touched her loveliness. Her hair was loose now, wild. His hand roamed up her body and she kissed and teased him to shuddering. He unbuttoned her jeans. She stroked his manhood through his pants.

"Take them off," he said huskily. She stood up and started to undo her jeans button. He stood up, his long body on fire. She was unzipping her pants when he backed her against the wall. Affrica's stomach flipped, her panties getting a little wetter.

She roamed his body some more, touching the hard stomach, brushing him lightly. His head was buried in her breasts, squeezing them together, licking the cleavage he created. He trailed up her neck. But he stopped her as she tried to pull his pants off. She was holding both his butt cheeks in her palms, crushing him deeper into her.

"Wait, Affrica. Wait." He held both her hands for a moment and she continued exploring him with her mouth. "Wait," he said again.

"What, Alex?" Affrica was frustrated at him for breaking her flow. She looked at him.

He remained close. "What about Delroy? I'm not trying to get in the middle of your relationship."

"It's too late," she said into his mouth. She ran her thumb across his lips, biting her own. She didn't remember the last time she felt such desire overtake her, making her take leave of all her senses.

"Are you sure, Affrica?" He started kissing her neck again. "Are you sure you want to do this?"

She showed him just how much she wanted him. Taking her to the top and back down, then quickly back up, till she had screamed and arched her back in a final orgasm. She couldn't take anymore. And afterward as they lay there on a blanket Alex had brought out for their lovemaking, Affrica shuddered still in her bliss. He held her from the back, touching and kissing her lightly. Every time he did so she would shudder some more. They took a deep breath together. She turned on her side to face him and he did the same. They beamed at each other, neither of them sure what to say, but filled with questions.

"Have you ever . . ." Affrica asked.

Alex shook his head seriously. "I've never had that. I've never felt it like that."

"Don't you have orgasms?"

"I have orgasms, but that's it."

"How?" Affrica said in a choked voice.

"It's all in the control and mental focus."

She frowned slightly. Then her face brightened. "You have superb mental focus, Mr. Bartholomew." Affrica stroked him.

Seventeen

Hakeem's fingers blurred across the buttons of the video game controls. The two-inch gash on his forearm still throbbed but he'd be damned before he let Mastermind beat him at any game. His body contorted slightly as he focused on the digital battle on the screen. "You can't buy anything with radios and video games. I'm talkin' 'bout paper, son! Dead presidents! Mula! Loot! Greenbacks! Cash money! What the hell is Jay gonna do with toys?"

"We didn't get this stuff for Jay Blow. This is ours," Little Man retorted. He was putting another new CD into the new CD player. "He don't need us to get nothing for him. It was just a test, yo. Don't hate because we got mad stuff and you got a bandage."

"Ah, ha, ha, you got played!" cackled Mastermind.

"Yeah, but I'm kicking butt," replied Hakeem as he decapitated Mastermind's computer counterpart.

"I wish ya'll would just shut the hell up!" came a deep voice from the dark figure of Tommy Weed sitting in the chair by the window. Tommy was still wearing the clothes from the night before. He sat there slouched in the chair, his coat zipped up, the hood pulled down over his face.

"I told you not to sit there, yo. My grandmother don't want nobody sitting there," said Mastermind.

Tommy looked at the clock on the wall, 11:57 A.M. Then he nonchalantly turned his head and looked out of the window. "Is she here?"

"No, but that's not the—"

"Anybody heard from Milton?" Tommy asked, cutting off Mastermind.

There was a sharp series of raps at the door. Jay Blow had arrived. All eyes turned as Mastermind stepped over two CD players and a camcorder to undo the locks and open the door.

Jay Blow stepped in wearing a large black leather coat. He had his right hand in his coat pocket as he often did when entering a room, and he was also wearing shades. He stood in front of the TV. Hakeem quickly turned off the video game. Mastermind had already locked the door and returned to his seat.

No preliminaries. Jay Blow pulled off his glasses with his left hand and looked them all in the eye, each in their turn. "One could say that I made a mistake. One could say that I was lazy. I could have jacked up everything by letting you choose your own initiation. But it was the only way to know what you are made of. Not just your resolve to do what you were told but what you would do by your own design."

Little Man jumped in, "Milton didn't come, and nobody—"

"Milton is not ready to sit in your ranks. He did some dumb stuff last night," Jay Blow said. "However, the rest of you . . ." He yanked his hand out of his pocket, a nine-millimeter pistol gripped in his palm. He pulled out the clip with his left hand and pushed out four bullets with his thumb. He caught them in the same hand, and slid the clip back into the gun. He quickly slipped the gun back into his coat pocket.

"The rest of you . . ." Jay Blow paused again. ". . . are my first street generals." Jay flicked the wrist of his left hand four times. Each of the other young men in the room caught a bullet in his palm.

The tension in the room gave way to audible sighs of relief. "I know what you all did. There is no need to make any report. I listened to the police radio and got the word on the street. Keep that bullet, it's your membership card."

The guys made a lot of noise, gave pounds to each other. Only Tommy Weed stood aloof and sober. Jay Blow's and Tommy's eyes met through the animated gestures of the other three. Jay appreciated the forethought that went into Tommy's actions of the previous night. Besides their just stabbing and robbing a rival drug dealer, Jay came to find out that someone in the middle of the night wrote graffiti on a gang message wall indicating that another rival gang threatened to attack the man that Tommy stabbed. Now there was a gang war between Jay Blow's two top competitors. Yes, Tommy Weed displayed qualities that Jay Blow wanted in the officers of his street army. They nodded solemnly at each other. *The next order of business is recruitment procedures,* Jay thought.

Eighteen

Early the next morning Affrica held a press conference about the crime spree. She and Alex had talked about it in the shower the night before. They had decided Alex and Ramona would speak the most to the press. Affrica would speak only a little in the beginning. They thought it would be better if the public didn't associate the mayor with the crime spree.

The press conference was being held at City Hall. A podium had been set up and myriads of media were present. One hour before the press conference the three of them had sat down and formulated a plan. Affrica and Alex were very polite and businesslike. They never touched and reduced eye contact to a minimum.

Affrica spoke first about crime in the city and her renewed effort to stop crime before it started. She called for increased counseling quality in schools. More career development and college tours. She spoke about crime management in terms of offensive instead of defensive. She said, "If we could stop them before they commit the serious crimes, we could find adequate rehabilitation for those that cannot be helped." Affrica looked at a blank piece of paper on the podium. She wanted them to think she had written something. Affrica introduced the chief of police and presented him to the press.

Alex never enjoyed these press conferences. Too many times his words were taken and twisted before being printed. Too many times he had to hold another press conference to get the story straight, and put down false rumors.

The questions came fast and furious.

"Why is the crime rate of Passion rising?"

"What does the rising crime rate have to do with Irving Housing?"

"What are you going to do about it?"

Alex took a deep breath. "I think I can answer most of your questions with the following statements. If there are any outstanding questions after my statements, I will be happy to answer them." The press put their hands down, and prepared to record Alex's words.

"As we know, crime of these proportions tends to exist in conditions of desperation. The Irving Housing Projects is a small community complex in Passion in need of revitalization. They have been promised revitalization funds, which were allocated to them from the city's budget, but they still have not seen one penny. We have a community here that is literally on the brink of collapse. One of the buildings had been deemed unsafe by the housing commission three years ago, during Mayor August's term. The commission reversed their decision, because it is cheaper to keep the people there than it is to relocate them. These people are mad. Gangs are rampant.

"Police presence has been stepped up. However, this is not a long-term solution. I urge everyone concerned with this to be diligent in your resolve to make better the quality of life of all residents of Passion. As you know, Mayor Bryant has been working tirelessly to bring about a solution to this crisis, and make good on the promises of the last administration to revitalize Irving Housing. I challenge you of the media not to target the residents of Irving Housing for bad press, but to look sensitively into the issues concerning this situation and open your publications to community dialogue. I urge you to consider that your primary role is to serve this community. Be mindful of your words; you can start mass hysteria or contribute to healing and understanding. We need to begin to act like a community if we are to have a future for our children in Passion."

Before Alex left the press conference he handed Affrica a large envelope. Affrica nodded a pleasant good-bye and casually added the envelope to the things she already had in her hands. She didn't open it till she was in her office. She wondered why she even had an office when she was never in it for more than five minutes a day. She would be leaving soon with Ramona to the *Essence* magazine photo shoot. Affrica had talked Ramona into bringing a few changes of clothing. They were going to go to the mansion first and see if they could shoot there. If not, they would take the pictures back at City Hall.

Affrica had a quiet buzz. She felt so light and happy she could barely restrain herself. Alex made her feel so good. After they had made love the night before, she called the mansion to see if Delroy was there, but he didn't pick up the mansion phone or his cell phone. She left a simple mysterious message on his machine.

"I'm okay. I might not come home tonight. All is well."

Alex had reminded her about Delroy and she had called to let the concierge know she was fine. A discreet professional security group did the security at the mansion. They were known for keeping politicians' secrets safe, no matter what wildness they did.

I have to call Delroy. I have to break up with him. Even though there's nothing to break up. I don't want him to catch us sneaking around.

Affrica sat back in the large leather swiveling chair writing notes from the meeting on her palm pilot and starting to reorganize her paperwork. She came across the note Alex wrote her. It was such a small piece of paper. It said *Tonight. If I can, I want to come over. I'll call your cell phone with two rings and hang up. You let me in through the back door.* Affrica wondered how he would get by the security officer, but since he was the chief of police, she would let him worry about that.

Alex sat at his desk draining his third cup of coffee. Piled before him were the reports, testimonies, and accumulated data relating to the recent crime wave. The testimonies and police sketches from the bus robbery were spread out before him. Alex had just finished reviewing surveillance tapes from two electronic stores in Passion. The evidence was conclusive.

On the night of the robbery three of the victims were able to point out one of the perpetrators in a mug-shot book. The young man was identified as Melvin Thomas a.k.a. Little Man. Melvin was a fifteen-year-old resident of Irving Housing. He was prosecuted in juvenile court for two accounts of vandalism.

According to the testimonies, Melvin was taking cues from the other person. Alex had the sarge collect transaction reports from stores that had purchase activities with the stolen credit cards. He was also able to get copies of surveillance tapes from one of the stores. The tapes confirmed that Melvin Thomas was seen entering Music Emporium, a late-closing record store, minutes before purchases were made with the stolen credit cards. Melvin entered with another man. The other man fit the description of the second perpetrator in the bus robbery who was positively identified because of his police record. Alvin Washington a.k.a. Mastermind, a twenty-year-old resident of Irving houses. Alvin had a prior conviction for grand theft auto. Both he and Melvin were suspects in connection to the drug traffic in Irving Housing.

Alex sighed. *They don't know it but they are already caught.* Such young men. Their lives forever tainted by criminal actions.

Alex was waiting for Officers Jackson and Mills to arrive. They had been assigned to patrol Irving Housing for the four weeks leading up to the night of the crime. Alex wanted their input before moving in to arrest the two suspects.

While waiting, Alex reviewed the reports on the two burglaries. The houses of the victims were only eight blocks apart in one of the upper-middle-class neighborhoods of Passion.

Alex considered the facts.

The owner of the first house worked the night shift.
The residents of the second home were on vacation.
Chances are, the perpetrators knew this.

The time of both break-ins occurred between 12:30 A.M. and 1:45 A.M.

It's possible that the same perpetrators struck at both houses.

The burglars knew where hidden valuables were located. Jewelry, money, etc.

Alex concluded that there was a strong likelihood that the perpetrators had knowledge of the homes and their residents.

They were probably someone that the home owners knew, Alex thought.

His phone beeped. It was his secretary's line. He picked up the phone.

"Officers Mills and Jackson here to see you, sir," the secretary said.

"Send them in," replied Alex.

Alex realized that he hadn't spoken personally with these officers for a few days. They tended not to hang out at the usual off-duty spots. Alex had made it his business to know his officers. He would pass by the two bars, the bowling alley, and even the fishing dock to fraternize with the off-duty officers that frequented these places. However, the last few weeks had left him precious little off-duty time.

His office door swung open and the two officers walked in.

"Hey, Chief, what's up?" Jackson had a patronizing smile on his face as he closed the distance to stand in front of Alex's desk. Mills, who came to stand at his side, followed him.

Alex's sharp eyes caught the fading remnants of a subtle scowl on the face of Officer Mills.

Mills nodded at Alex. "Sir."

Alex stood to his feet and shook their hands, before inviting them to pull up a chair and sit. Alex saw them exchange quick glances as they retrieved the chairs from the corner of the room.

They are acting suspicious, Alex thought. He knew that some of the officers did not fully appreciate a relatively young black police chief giving them orders.

Alex had made it clear from the beginning that he would expect nothing but their full cooperation from his staff. He was tested early and had responded quickly. *"I earned this. Damn it. If you have something to say to me, say it to my face. If you wish to challenge my authority, be prepared to find other employment."*

He knew that he never gained the respect of some of the older officers. These two definitely had question marks above their heads. Alex knew he would have to watch them closely in the next few hours.

"Okay, men, as you probably know by now, the investigation into the bus robbery has turned up two suspects. Both have records. Both reside at Irving Housing." Alex turned the folders on his desk around so that they were right side up for the two officers to inspect them. Alex noted another strange expression flicker across the face of Officer Mills.

"Do you recognize these suspects?" Alex asked casually.

"I've seen the big one around the complex," said Jackson, donning a thoughtful expression. "Can't say much about his activities though."

"I have plainclothes officers tracking both of them now," stated Alex. "We will move in for an arrest within the hour. You two have been patrolling the neighborhood for the past few weeks. I want the benefit of your experience in making this a low-conflict arrest."

"Yes, sir," said Jackson.

Alex noted that Mills was letting Jackson do all of the talking. *Did they arrange this before entering? What's up with the scowl?* Alex wondered.

Alex decided to confront Mills. He looked him in the eyes. "Have you noticed any gang activity that could compromise or complicate this arrest?"

Mills shot a look at Jackson. Jackson knew that Alex was probing. Jackson kept his gaze focused on the chief. *You're on your own, Mills. Don't mess it up,* Jackson thought.

Alex's cell phone rang, but did not break the tension. The three men sat still.

Something is off here, Alex thought.

Mills began to mutter, "Um, well, we really haven't . . . uh . . ."

Another ring.

"You gonna get that, sir?" Jackson pointed to Alex's hip.

Alex's hand was already on his phone. Without removing the phone from its belt case, he turned it to see the number of the incoming call. Alex then snatched the phone and brought it to his ear. "Bartholomew here."

"Chief!" the voice on the phone snapped. "The two suspects just met up with each other. They joined with three others in the courtyard, and the four of them are heading into building three."

"Melvin's apartment is in building three," said Alex, keeping his eyes on the two officers. Again there was a subtle reaction of recognition in their faces.

"We might have to move on this fast, Chief." The voice on the phone was shaky. The plainclothes officer was probably running or speed-walking to keep the suspects in sight.

Alex stood to his feet, swinging his coat on with one arm. "We're on the way. Don't move in until I get there. But don't lose them."

Jackson and Mills were out of their chairs.

"You two ride with me," Alex said calmly as he rushed past them.

"Didn't Jay tell y'all to get rid of this stuff?" Tommy kicked the boxes that contained the new CD player and boom boxes.

"Yeah, I got some clients coming by later," said Mastermind. "It will all be gone by tonight."

Little Man started singing "Mo Money, Mo Money, Mo Money," pantomiming counting a wad of cash.

Hakeem started laughing. "What, you wanna see some real loot?" He reached into his pocket.

Tommy Weed found his seat by the window. "Shut the hell up!"

The four Bloodhounds were waiting for their leader to arrive. They were expecting Jay to present to them procedures for selecting and testing new recruits. "We have to increase our numbers. But you are my generals," Jay had said.

Tommy Weed looked at the way Jay Blow was handling things. He thought it was sloppy, too rushed. *Is something big going down soon?* Tommy thought. *Jay is scrambling to have people in place for something big.*

Suddenly the door to Mastermind's apartment bent and buckled with a loud crash. The four young men jumped out of their seats.

Tommy had the window to the fire escape open before the next crash sent the door sliding across the floor.

Uniformed police spilled into the room shouting,

with guns drawn. Hakeem and Little Man were already on the floor, frozen in fear. Mastermind ran into the kitchen and pulled a gun from his waist. He crouched in a corner, fumbling to switch off the safety from his weapon.

Tommy Weed had already rolled out onto the fire escape. Despite threats from the police that they would shoot him, he started climbing to the roof.

Hakeem and Little Man were already handcuffed and being dragged out of the room by four police officers, while four others were taking positions in the room, to try to flush out Mastermind. The police could not get to the window because they would have to cross the kitchen threshold. They had been briefed, and considered Mastermind to be armed and dangerous.

Tommy Weed climbed the fire escape stairs to find two plainclothes cops waiting for him on the roof. Their guns were drawn and trained on him. There was nowhere else to run.

Alex had entered the apartment. He told the rest of the police to be quiet.

"Alvin, there is no escape," he said. "If you want to try and shoot your way out like some kind of punk gangster, you will not even make it out of the kitchen. I know you just got caught up. Sorry, son, but you've got to be a man now, and deal with the consequences of your actions. Throw your gun out. It's not too late to salvage your life." Alex heard Alvin sobbing. He waved back the other officers. They retreated to the doorway. Alex crouched against the wall five feet from the kitchen entrance. His gun was drawn and aimed at the kitchen doorway.

"No one here will hurt you. Throw out your gun, son. It's not too late."

Silence. Sobbing.

The small handgun slid across the floor, out of the kitchen, and tumbled across the living room carpet.

"Good choice, son. Now lie down on the floor, Alvin. Lay both hands flat in the kitchen doorway."

Alvin did as he was told.

Alex did not expect the mob scene in the lobby when he emerged from the elevator with Alvin in custody. He had left Jackson and Mills in the lobby with orders to keep it clear. People were all over, yelling, cheering, and jeering. Children ran unattended all over the place. Some came close to tease Alvin.

Alex scanned the area for Jackson and Mills. He thought he saw one of them on the other side of the lobby. He gave custody of Alvin over to Detective Plant, then barked commands at the other officers to clear the area of civilians and create a police line. The suspect from the rooftop was still being brought down.

Alex was furious about the chaos. He moved through the crowd to the area where he saw Jackson. He got there but Jackson was gone. He was surrounded by a lot of loud and animated residents, many yelling at him. Suddenly from the din of overlapping voices he heard, "You can't hold them. You've got nothing on my men."

My men? Alex isolated the voice. His mental radar indicated that it came from behind him to the right and approximately ten feet away. He turned and gently split the crowd with his hands. He saw the figure of a man with a black leather jacket, walking through the crowd, away from him. Alex pushed through, following the man.

"Hey!" Alex yelled.

The man stopped in front of some elevator banks and turned around slowly.

Alex recognized his face. Jay Blow.

"I heard what you said."

Jay just stared at Alex, an unsure grin pasted on his face. "What have you got on them? Nothing. They'll be home for dinner."

"I doubt it," said Alex. "Are you the ringleader?"

"Are you the pig leader?" Jay sneered. "You ain't doing anything different than me. We pay your little piggies and they pay you big pigs. What! Now you come busting in here like you all high and mighty."

"Are you saying that you bribe police officers?" Alex thought of Jackson and Mills.

"Hey, if the shoe fits . . . Don't front like you don't get down. Everybody has a price."

"You're wrong, police officers that take bribes are criminals. And people who sell drugs and destroy lives are criminals."

"Oh, please. You gonna tell me that you don't sell drugs? The illusion that you provide safety and justice. That stuff is a drug. You go around sellin'—"

"You know what? The day I stand around and listen to some knucklehead boy tell me about the philosophy of cops and drug dealers will be the day they take my gun and put me in jail." He turned around, walking away from Jay Blow, shaking his head.

Nineteen

Very late that night Affrica's cell phone rang twice. Her heart was beating a mile a minute. She felt as if she were in a *Mission: Impossible* movie. She walked down the long corridor to the stairs. The rooms were all brightly lit. She nonchalantly entered the large dark kitchen to the back door and let Alex in. His hands were cold as he grabbed hers, the moon playing shadow tricks on both of them. They didn't speak, just walked casually up the stairs to her very large bedroom.

Alex could see where Affrica had tried to insert her own personal style into what she had inherited. The bedroom was the size of Alex's living room and dining room. Affrica had tapestries displayed to make the room look warmer. His coat was hung behind her closet door. She was dressed comfortably in a black tank top and gray jogging pants.

They kissed passionately, then both started talking at once.

"How are you?"

"I'm busy as hell and loving it. What's going on, Alex? I heard something today, but I couldn't get you on the phone."

"We caught the guys who did the crime spree."

He held her hands. "Damn, Affrica, they are so young! They're children with these crazy ideas of allegiance to some gang."

"Yeah, they have no place to belong, no initiation into manhood. Of course they're going to create their own initiations." Affrica put her head down. "I almost don't blame them. . . . I mean I blame them for doing illegal things, but I don't blame thing for wanting to belong. I don't blame them for feeling they need to do these extraordinary things, in order to be 'down.' "

"But what happens nine times out of ten is the kids who do this wind up hurting themselves or others pretty bad. They haze, they have to do a drive-by to be part of the gangs." He shook his head. "I've seen the results of drive-bys, I've seen the remains of a sixteen-year-old who was dared to jump off the roof of one building to another building. He slipped and fell the six stories."

Affrica's breath caught and she shook her head sadly, feeling slightly ill.

"I'm not saying it to disgust you or scare you, but this is so serious." Alex sat with Affrica on a mud-cloth-covered sofa. It had the designs of a Queen Anne sofa, but again she had added her own flavor.

Alex stared off in the distance. "I know for a fact they have a leader, Jay Blow. Real smug, thinks he's Al Capone or the don. Dangerous because these boys pulled that mess because of him. We interrogated them for three hours. They've changed their stories five times already, refusing to tell us the truth." Alex laughed without humor. "Even pointing the finger at some rival gang leader." Alex's face looked slightly pained, his eyes far off and distracted.

She wanted to soothe him, to kiss away his frown.

But she knew this was not a situation that could be fixed with hugs and kisses. This was life. This was why her mother worked so hard trying to help people. This was why she worked. For the first time she realized they had something so much in common. Service, they were both in public service and in positions of power to make large differences in people's lives. She felt a surge of positive energy.

"Do you think the rebuilding of the Projects will make any difference?"

Alex looked at her face, wanting to say yes. "I think it will make a difference in the lives of the people living there. It's going to be up to them really."

"What do you mean?"

"Well, people have to police their own neighborhoods, if everyone has a house and some land. They *are* going to feel a sense of ownership, a sense that the place is theirs. They might be more likely to tell a group of idiots to get off their stoop and stop throwing garbage around. People won't want the crack heads coming around even more now."

"Oh, I get it." She shook her head and imagined the citizens of Irving Housing driving out the vermin. She imagined old ladies yelling at the boisterous young men to get up from her stoop, maybe waving a cane at them.

"Cops can only do so much. When I've gone to Irving Housing and asked questions about crimes, people all of a sudden didn't speak English or they were legally blind. They don't know nothing, didn't see anything. We all have to be active in the retrieval of criminals."

"But people are afraid, Alex."

"No, I know. Even if they wrote a letter or gave us an anonymous tip."

Affrica was glad Alex was talking about the police department. She wanted to ask him about the cops.

"The people in the neighborhood have to trust the police. A lot of people don't trust the police," she said slowly and carefully.

"I know, Affrica, I'm not blind," he said quickly.

Affrica tried to diffuse the situation. "I'm not saying that, Alex. What I'm saying is there should be checks and balances. The community should be able to evaluate the cops. There should be public forums on how crime is handled, *and* cops should have to answer to them."

Alex thought that was a really good idea. He realized how much his hands had been tied at the department. He thought about the quiet investigation he had been doing, the large stack of folders that he had been stealing and copying out of the budget, old crime scene reports, drug deals, and he knew he would have something soon. Alex knew it was huge, something that would bring everything to light.

They talked about the police department some more. They discussed strategies and changes they could make to help the situation. They realized they could do a lot. Even more if they worked together. Finally Alex stood up and stretched. Having gone straight from outside to the couch, he had not seen the entire place. He looked at Affrica sitting down, and stared at her pretty brown face, drinking in her intelligent eyes. He really liked this woman. No one had ever made him feel the way he did when he was with her. He gave her a hand up, and she reached her arms over her head. Her little top pulled up and exposed her flat tummy. Alex noticed and tickled her belly button.

Alex put his arm around Affrica's shoulders as

he looked at the rest of the room. She had a private bathroom, and a minifridge next to an established office area.

He said her name and turned around to kiss her. She smelled clean.

"I took a nap. I had a feeling this was going to be a late night."

"You were right," Alex murmured into her hair. He let her go slowly and started looking at some of her artwork. Next to a Victorian flower painting, she had a large lithograph, an authentic Dirk Joseph lithograph painting. He was one of the most sought-after black artists in America. Alex thought he was a great painter. His mom had two of his pieces. He analyzed the painting intensely. It was of a black woman standing on water. Her hair was wild and she held a flower in one hand and a sword in the other. He stood for a long time looking at the art piece. It was so well painted, the colors incredibly vibrant.

Affrica came up behind him and kissed the back of his neck. "I look at that piece every day. When I see it, I feel like I can do anything."

Alex nodded his head in approval.

"I'm lucky I got this one a few years ago and I paid some money for it, but the price of it has tripled." Affrica went to a bookshelf and threw him a catalogue of Dirk's paintings. He knew he would be buying a couple of lithographs.

Alex had spotted a picture of an older woman when he had first come inside Affrica's room. He walked to the small-framed photograph and observed the smiling woman. Her hair was in two stark-white braids. Her brown skin was weathered and looked soft.

Affrica sat on the large bed giving Alex and the

picture a sad smile. She sat back against two large, colorful pillows. She had at least six pillows on the bed. Alex joined her on the bed after removing his shoes. He cuddled her from the back. She started talking about her grandmother.

"Jerimia was so different from my mother in so many ways, yet they were very similar. She was affectionate, where my mother was standoffish. I was able to sit in her lap at twelve years old. She was gentle when she braided my hair. She would sit me between her legs and try to distract me with stories and songs, great games that I was able to teach my friends."

Alex looked at her, then at her braided hair. "Thickheaded people are always tender-headed." He gave her a broad grin. She hit him with a large pillow. He playfully tumbled onto her quilt.

"Do you have your gun on you?"

"Are you going to shoot me!" He threw himself down on the bed and laughed.

She laughed too and lay next to him. He turned on his side and put his hand on her waist. "Tell me more about Jerimia," he said seriously.

Affrica gave Alex a weak smile. She loved talking about her grandmother, but it was a bittersweet thing that made her heart long for her grandmother's arms, her voice.

"She was really a great woman. She didn't have to take me in, she could have told my mother she raised enough children. But she didn't. My mother left me on her doorstep, and she loved me just as if she were my mom." Affrica paused momentarily.

"She was cleaning the yard at eighty-six years old. She complained about arthritis. She felt working was the best cure for any ache or pain. I was back in Passion by the time she passed." Affrica's nose was running.

Alex felt he wanted to share something precious with her. Something to show her she could trust him. He was so happy she felt comfortable sharing her grandmother's story. He found her tissue box and handed her a few.

She looked at him sadly. "You always make the ladies cry, Alex?"

Alex smiled brightly at her, glad she felt good enough to joke around.

"What's up with you? Do you have any stories that would make you cry? If you do, please tell them to me now." Affrica smiled at Alex.

Alex looked thoughtful, as if he was actually thinking of a story.

"I'm kidding, Alex."

"I know, I know." Alex lay on his back. "I never knew any of my grandparents. Which is sort of sad. But they all passed before I was born. I think about that sometimes, how hard it must have been for my mother and father to lose both their parents before they were thirty." Alex put his hands under his head and stared at her ceiling.

"Oh boy. This is going to be a depressing evening. Such serious thought, from two serious people." Affrica made a comical serious-looking face. She hugged Alex on the bed, and put her ear to his heart, listening to the thumping.

"Alex, I tried calling Delroy all day and he is nowhere to be found. I want to break up with him."

Alex's heart started beating a little faster.

Affrica continued. "I was confused, but I am no longer confused. I want the relationship done with."

"Do you care about him?"

"Yes and no. He's not a bad person, he's never done anything bad to me. We actually met in New York, long before I worked for the mayor." She looked at Alex, who was no longer staring at the ceiling but was focused on her. "He was the first one-night stand I ever had." She covered her face, laughing.

"You mean of all the millions of people on this planet and in New York, you picked Delroy for your one-night stand." He looked at her in disbelief.

"Yes."

"If you don't mind me asking, was it hot and sordid?"

"No, actually it was like . . ." Affrica looked embarrassed. "I don't remember the sex that much."

Poor Delroy, Alex thought. "So what did you do, when you came here and saw him?"

"I blushed horribly. But only for a moment. It was the initial shock of seeing him. We weren't really interested in each other. I don't really like Delroy's type. I hate colored contacts more than anything."

"Yeah, I noticed Delroy's contacts."

"I wasn't really feeling him, but after a few months he suddenly was being nice to me. Staying late at work with me. He even stopped wearing the contacts for a little while."

"Oh, that's how he got you."

"Yeah, he talked all this revolutionary talk. But it's so strange, I could never read him. We've been dating all this time and I swear I don't know him. I know about his family and some of his goals . . . but I don't know *him*. I feel like I know more about you than him."

Alex shook his head and thumped a beat on Affrica's leg, loving the feel of her, happy that he could touch this beautiful woman.

"I know how you feel, Affrica, I just keep dating these women who are set on changing me or proving that I'm not as handsome as I think I am."

Affrica frowned. "What?"

"I dated this woman and after a few months she started telling me I wasn't that cute. I would shrug at her and make it a nonissue. Because I actually didn't care about cuteness. I was a cop working a dangerous job and just wanted somebody soft to come home to. I stayed with her much too long."

"So she kept telling you that you were not fine. But you are."

"I should have broken up with her."

Affrica wanted to talk about Alex's looks for a moment. She looked at Alex, who looked quite uncomfortable.

"Alex, if it's a nonissue, why do you look so uncomfortable? You are an incredibly attractive man. You know that, don't you?"

"Affrica, that's not the point."

"No, Alex, I understand that, but why are you so reluctant to deal with that one fact about yourself?"

Alex was blushing, trying not to look in Affrica's eyes. He felt like a chump. "I had some issues growing up. When I was a teenager a lot of older women were always really, really nice to me." He looked at Affrica. "They would coo at me as if I were a baby. They would give me stuff."

"What stuff? You had sex with an older woman?" Affrica was intrigued.

"Yes."

"A lot?"

"A lot. Till I went to the military and got my butt kicked for being a so-called pretty boy. I didn't think

I was a pretty boy. I thought pretty boys were light skinned with curly hair. I'm far from those things."

"The new pretty boys are very dark-skinned, bald-headed men, with funny-colored eyes."

"I'm not that either."

Affrica looked at Alex's brown face. She tried to place one character about his face that stood out and made him attractive, but she couldn't.

"You're just overall gorgeous. Sorry." Affrica shrugged her shoulders. She wanted to kiss his attractive lips. "Your eyes. You have really beautiful eyes, Alex."

Alex made a face at her, then crossed his eyes and wrestled her down onto the mattress. He tickled her, till happy tears rolled down her face.

Alex looked down at her. "You are the most beautiful woman I've ever seen."

They hungrily searched each other's mouth, pulled and teased lips and ears. Affrica ran her hands along his arms, his sides, relishing the hardness of Alex, the long, firm muscles of his legs and the short, tight muscles of his stomach.

Later as she rode him, he gently scratched her back and held her full buttocks in his hands, furthering her movements, biting his lip and moaning her name. That same night after her blissful climax, she finally made him lose control and explode.

Twenty

The lobby of building 1 was packed with tenants. Chairs had been brought in, and people were having a heated question-and-answer session with Affrica.

"But where are we supposed to go while you build these new houses?"

"For those people who cannot find temporary housing we will provide you kitchenettes and large rooms around the area. We've gotten a list of clean hotels that promised to make the citizens of Irving Housing welcome. The Lafayette Hotel promised to house sixty-five families. Their rates would be changed and you would only pay a monthly fee that would not be above the rent you are paying now. If you are on assistance, we will provide payment vouchers. Also, whatever payments are accrued by you will be reimbursed."

"How will you house all these families? How can you spread us out like that?"

"Well, to be honest with you, in the long run, you and your families will be better for the sacrifice you will be making now. This is what is so important that I feel you as a whole should understand. In the long run, in the future is what matters. Right now,

I will admit to you, will be strange. You'll be leaving this place you've known. . . . some for all of their lives. But I promise you if you can get over the next few humps and bear with me, bear with the construction workers and the bureaucracy, you will live in homes. I don't understand why public housing has to be something run-down, a place falling apart. In my city, public housing will mean something else."

People were convinced. Affrica waited for questions. The people of Irving Housing were quiet. They were proud of this young woman. They respected her opinion more because she had actually lived in the houses. Mr. And Mrs. Tallie remembered Affrica running around the courtyard with her large Afro blowing in the breeze. They remembered her determined mother who was always arranging something, helping somebody. And because of that, they trusted her.

She was one of them. She ate at the same restaurants and did her nails at the same place as these people. These people did not trust August Watson. They knew he was crooked, and they really did not trust politicians.

Later on, Affrica stood talking to Ramona. The forum was finally over and even though there were some slight differences of opinion, Affrica got the people of Irving Housing to consider her idea. The ones who were opposed to the demolition were the most boisterous and visible of the large group gathered in the lobby of building 3. Delroy had stood there waiting a few seconds after the end of the meeting had been called, when he grabbed Affrica's hand swiftly and waved at the milling guests and reporters.

"Excuse me, excuse me, I have an announcement

to make. Excuse me!" He waved wildly and people stopped walking a bit.

"Mayor Bryant and I have an announcement to make!" Delroy yelled, when he couldn't get anyone's attention. Everyone stopped in their tracks and started unrolling extension cords and popping the lights back on. The people of the houses stopped also and once again gathered around the reporters and podium.

When he saw the photographers shooting and the reporters writing, he bent down dramatically. He knew he had their attention. He got down on one knee in front of a flabbergasted Affrica. She looked down at Delroy and with her eyes implored him to smile. Not wanting anyone to see, she squeezed his hand and opened her eyes wider, all the while still smiling and acting embarrassed but glad.

"Affrica Bryant! Will you marry me?" Delroy said excitedly. The buzz started. So many photographers were taking pictures that Affrica was temporarily blinded. She shook her head at Delroy with a fake plastered smile on her face.

Ramona's mouth was hanging open. She couldn't believe the audacity. *Oh no!* was her only thought. She smelled a rat. *I'm going to have to tell her soon.*

The reporters were silent as they waited for Affrica to vocalize her answer. "Yes," Affrica said slowly. Delroy slipped a ring on her finger and embraced her. He quickly kissed her passionately for the cameras. Affrica's hands remained at her sides. It took everything she had not to wipe her lips. She was so disgusted and overwhelmed that she felt like crying.

"Let's see the ring!" a reporter yelled. Another series of pictures were taken.

Affrica's mind was racing. She had said a lame yes to Delroy's proposal, and it was going to press immediately. *What am I going to do?* She was dizzy. Delroy left the podium to speak to the press personally. Ramona helped Affrica to the car. She said nothing. They had taken a limousine to Irving Housing. Ramona had instructed her secretary to make sure the diagrams and papers were returned to City Hall. The press followed Ramona and Affrica back to their car. Affrica just smiled strangely, saying she was happy, very happy, over and over again.

The driver left Delroy at Irving Housing. Jay Blow, who had just watched the entire thing unfold, tipped his head at Delroy, subtly. Delroy did the same. People from the Housing surrounded him and pounded his back harshly, filled with congratulations. He knew his plan was not taking hold. The newspapers were not going to talk about Affrica's speech or the citizens of Irving Housing. They probably wouldn't even mention how Affrica was able to convince even the loudest opponents to the housing project. She had actually got them all in agreement about a special commission from the Projects that would police the police. She had told them they should take down badge numbers of police officers, learn their names.

"It's your community! They must respect you," she had told the crowd.

Delroy could not believe they cheered her.

Delroy was so desperate, he knew the marriage proposal was the only thing he had left. He couldn't get her pregnant. She wasn't going to fall in love with him. This was the only thing he could do. Now any time she met the press, they would ask her about the wedding date, the wedding dress. Her policies and changes would be put to the side.

Delroy was alone and happy. He looked around for Affrica, who was nowhere to be found. He waited while the secretary packed, basking in his own light. He knew he would be getting a call soon from August. Delroy asked the limo driver to drop him off at the Mayoral Mansion. Affrica wasn't there, her door locked. He shrugged his shoulders and called the limo driver to come back and pick him up.

Delroy sat back on the leather seats, thinking about what he had done. He remembered the way her eyes had looked, like a trapped animal. He knew she wouldn't say no to him in public, if he played his cards right.

Affrica was upset, pacing her living room, steam rising off of her. She could barely breathe. "That no good SOB! That no good . . ." She held her head in her hands. "He has ruined my political career."

Ramona could only sit there agreeing quietly. She had prayed her friend would say no. "You're right, Affrica."

"He couldn't possibly be for real, could he be, Ramona?"

"I doubt it big time."

"Why would he ask me to marry him! Why? Why now? Why this way?" Affrica yelled in disgust. She wasn't yelling at Ramona, she was angry with herself, angry with Delroy for doing this, angry with Alex for having her heart and coming to complicate her life.

Then as Affrica got quiet, Ramona became uncomfortable. She was not used to seeing the usually positive Affrica so defeated. Ramona waited for a plan. Affrica always had a plan for something. She could stave off potential disaster in a matter of moments.

"What!" Affrica shouted and got quiet again. The doorbell rang. Delroy's incessant pressing caused the soft bells to be unpleasant, and he banged the door and yelled her name. She opened the door unhappily. He brought in the cold and more lies.

Ramona sat a moment in disbelief. What was going on? She shut her mouth with a snap, realizing she had been staring at the couple waiting for her to leave. She grabbed her coat and told Affrica to call her and didn't even look in Delroy's direction.

She jumped into her bright red Bug, trying not to get choked up on the way home. When she got home, she fell upon her bed dramatically. She sobbed into her soft pillow.

I'm such a fake. How could I know and not tell her? I have to tell her. If I don't tell her, she's going to marry Delroy. She'll be ruining her life. If I tell her, I'll be ruining my own life.

Ramona knew something. About a year ago, Ramona had been working late at the office. August did not like her working late. She always marveled at that, thinking how most bosses wanted it the other way. August had gone, after a quick phone call. He had been in the process of having his speech written by Ramona and Affrica. He had exited quickly. It was seven o'clock and he had called her, telling her he wouldn't be returning and she could lock up his office. He divulged to her the key code number.

"I'll just change it tomorrow. You got a pen?"

"I think I can remember four numbers, sir."

"Okay, 6-9-0-1. Just lock up."

"I'll lock up, sir."

Before she left, as Ramona had gone to lock the door, she thought about it and quietly slipped through the door. She tiptoed to his desk comically. She looked around the cluttered office. No matter how much she had told Watson she could tidy up for him, he had always refused. She had seen nothing spectacular on the desk. Something was lying on his chair. She almost let it pass, but what caught her attention was the fact that it was a handwritten note and it was in two different handwritings.

She read the note. At the first glance she knew Watson's chubby handwriting anywhere. It was all on a napkin. It was clearly Watson's describing something to another person. On the note Watson wrote *hve 2 mill. to italy for coke. By Wed.* The other handwriting, right under the first, *where u go to get it?*

Watson's thick script looped *Tke it out Irv Hsg budget.*

She made a quick copy of the napkin, folding the still warm paper into the small pocket of her suit jacket. She smoothed the pocket down and placed the napkin down, exactly where and how she had found it. She knew she had seen something she shouldn't have. Ramona left the office quickly. When she had gotten home, she stored the paper behind a fake wall in her closet, next to her gun.

The next day when Ramona had gone back to her desk, she found a shocking picture of herself in a ménage à trois. It was her with two men, in the worst position. It was an old picture of Ramona; she had had a few ménage à trois. She thought what adults did with their sex lives was nobody's business but theirs. The caption under the picture read *you don't talk and I won't.*

* * *

Ramona sat up on the bed, her face red and puffy. *What am I going to do? Affrica did not even have a plan.* Ramona felt a constriction in her chest as if her lungs couldn't get enough oxygen. She slowly paced the floor and finally decided to call her cousin in Florida, the only person who knew about everything. Ramona dialed Mandy's number. Ramona prayed she would pick up and not the answering machine.

"Allo." Her cousin responding.

"Mandy, it's Ramona."

"Hey, baby, what's going on?"

"Nothing," she said in a distracted voice. "The shit has hit the fan, Mandy!" Ramona broke down, sobbing into the phone. "Mandy, I messed up bad. I should have told her the minute I found that napkin and heard Delroy talking to Watson."

Her cousin talked her out of her hysteria, calmly reminding her of her job, her life, and ruining it. "Nobody is getting hurt."

"Yes, everybody is getting hurt. . . . I gotta go." She hung up the phone. She would have to figure out how to get Delroy and the entire mess gone. Ramona knew it would be a volcanic eruption if the public found out what was really happening to the police budget and the entire budget in general. Ramona resolved she would figure it out. She changed her outfit, sat at her prayer altar, lit the white candle, and whispered a chant, asking for guidance and apologizing for being a weak and selfish human only concerned about herself. She prayed Affrica would forgive her for lying to her. Ramona sat at her altar most of the evening. She ignored her telephone and deliberated with herself on a life-changing decision she was thinking about making.

* * *

"Delroy, how the hell could you embarrass me like that? What are you trying to pull?" As Affrica stared at Delroy with venom, she noticed he didn't have the zombie-looking contact lenses in his eyes.

He sat quietly, not returning her anger, but staring at her with agreement and calmness.

"What were you thinking? I mean, you had to do it in front of the press, the people. This is my career you're playing with."

"Affrica," Delroy started slowly. "Affrica, I want to sincerely apologize for doing it that way. I just wanted you to know how serious I was." He sat forward and adjusted his gray suit jacket. He looked at her solemnly. "I wanted you to know how serious I was and to show the world how much I love you."

Affrica frowned, her pretty lips twisted into a sneer. She snorted at Delroy, "Yeah, right." She placed her hands on her hips. "You don't love me, Delroy. Please!"

"No, Affrica, I am serious."

"If you're so serious, where the hell have you been the last couple of weeks? No, where the hell you been the last couple of years?"

Delroy was not expecting this much hostility. "Affrica, the past couple of years I've been here with you."

"No, you have not." She looked at him as if he were an alien. "What is this? What the hell did you think you were doing! You don't want to marry me!"

As he grabbed her hand, she resisted, but he kept pulling till it was extended to his lips. He kissed her hand, then placed his face on her hand. "I care about you so much, Affrica. I'm sorry you can't see it, but I do." He looked up at her with false sincerity. "You." He pointed up at her. "You, I love you!"

Affrica would have laughed in his face if not for the bright tears that were rolling down his cheeks. He sat up and wiped his face roughly and cleared his throat.

Affrica softened a little. The moment she did, Delroy laid it on. "You were so busy with the campaign; then with the Irving Housing project, I didn't want to disturb you to talk about us. Us was irrelevant. Because with all my heart I wanted you to win the campaign and be successful with Irving Housing." He stopped and acted pained. "I was going to stop all this momentum to sit you down and discuss our relationship."

Affrica was caught. "I wanted to talk about us for a long time, but you never seemed really interested."

"That's because I thought you didn't care." He looked at her so seriously, it was comical. "I was thinking about breaking up with you. But I felt we should talk, and finding that time has proved very challenging. Like lately, I've been here waiting and you're nowhere to be found."

"I've been busy," Affrica said softly.

I'll have her pregnant by next month, Delroy thought. He wasn't going to milk the guilt thing. He knew she would get angry with him if it seemed he was somehow blaming her for their fraudulent relationship.

Wait, am I falling for this drivel? He cannot be serious. Am I that blind that somehow I missed this man caring deeply for me? I have been working a lot; then this thing with Alex. I blame him, but I did my part to sabotage this relationship. No! Delroy is jerking my chain. I'm not that dumb, but what if he really does like me and I'm treating him like a piece of crap?

Affrica scratched her forehead roughly. She took one more look at Delroy's goofy face. She knew she had to marry him, at least ceremoniously. She could not ruin this one chance as the mayor. She needed people to take her seriously, not look at her as the mayor who caused a scandal at City Hall. The mayor who left her chief of staff to screw the chief of police. What would she look like? How would she ever find another job? She shook her head.

"Fine, Delroy, I'll do it, I'll marry you."

He jumped out of his chair and then sat back down quickly.

Twenty-one

The door knocked back at Alex's house and startled him back to the present. He took his head out of the folder and listened again. Sure enough, it was a knock. Alex stood up from the table quickly, his long legs easily going over the large pile of folders on his floor. His bones cracked as he walked. Looking at the clock, he opened the door for Patrick, who was shaking slightly from the cold.

"Yo, it's freezin' out there, man."

"Punk. You've been living here all these years and you're still acting as if this were your first winter."

"It feels like it." He stepped deeper into the house. "You're pretty chipper."

"I didn't tell you, we caught most of the guys who committed the crimes the other night." Alex still had his holster on. He usually took it off when he came in, but tonight he felt better with it on.

Patrick looked at Alex carefully. "You don't know?"

"Hey, man, get to the point."

"Africa's going to marry Delroy."

Alex felt his floor do a sharp tilt. His heart stopped beating a split second and then continued, pumping blood and adrenaline into his veins. Alex stared at Patrick. Patrick nodded sadly.

"I'm going!" Alex grabbed his coat. He quickly put on his sneakers and stood up.

He jumped into his Jeep and screeched out. Patrick locked Alex's house up and drove his own car slowly, wondering, after what he had seen and read on the news, if Alex could talk Affrica into rejecting the offer.

Alex arrived at the Mayoral Mansion quickly. He left his car and went straight through the security. They all knew him as the chief. He was almost running. By the time he was at Affrica's door he was out of breath. He knocked forcefully on the door. The knock echoed lightly in the hallway.

Affrica slowly opened the door, her face a mask. She opened the door wider and Alex saw Delroy sitting on the bed.

Delroy got up from the bed and came toward them. He kissed Affrica's cheek. "Look, your friend has come to share in our happiness." He grabbed his coat. "I'll let you two catch up." He smiled at them and left the building. When he got to his car, he checked his cell phone. He had four new messages.

Back in Affrica's room, the would-be couple argued.

"How could you say yes to him?" Alex asked. "I don't understand."

"Alex, you don't understand, I had all the press in my face, people were taking pictures of me. I had to say yes."

"Why, Affrica, why did you have to say yes? To, to Delroy?"

"Because he asked me in front of about a hundred people. Most of those people had a moving camera on my face."

"You lied to them all. You don't want to marry Delroy."

"It wouldn't be bad. We're so busy we would never see each other."

Alex couldn't believe his ears. "You're actually considering it?"

"Alex, I have to go through with this."

"No! No, you don't have to go through with it."

"I'm doing it, Alex." She folded her arms across her chest and looked at the floor. When she looked back up at him, his beautiful face was contorted in disbelief. He kept shaking his head, as if he didn't believe what he was hearing.

"And what about us?" he asked slowly.

"What *about* us?"

Alex looked as if he had been slapped. He held his hands in front of his face as in a palm-to-palm prayer. He scrutinized her with pained eyes.

Affrica wanted so much to reach out to him. She almost threw herself at his feet when she saw his eyes mist. But she knew she had to be strong. She couldn't allow a scandal to blemish her track record. To break up with Delroy and announce she was dating the police chief would be the worst type of scandal for a black woman. *Twisted people already have stereotypical sexual ideas about us. I can't let them get me that way. They will drag my entire life through the gutter if I do this. I cannot, I cannot.* Affrica shook her head, trying to convince herself that what she was doing was the right thing. Tried to convince herself that Alex had not left an impression on her.

She sighed deeply, and sat down on her bed. She sat there and stared at the picture of her grandmother, her entire body aching, her head spinning. Alex's hurt eyes kept flashing in her mind, but she held herself resolute and strong. She convinced herself that what she was doing was one of the many sacrifices black women have to make in order to achieve some rate of success in their lives. She couldn't let anybody drag her through the mud. If they wanted her perfect, that is what she would be. As long as she could be the mayor and be able to get her dream off the ground. *Alex is a big boy. He'll be fine,* she thought.

Alex was gone. She began getting her things ready for bed, pulling out her pajamas and grabbing her towel from its hook. She walked sadly to the bathroom and thought about something. She took her small boom box and set it on the toilet seat. She stared running the water for a hot bath, pouring in a little almond soap. The tape was already in there. She sat in the tub listening to the cassette Alex had made her. When the tape stopped and flipped sides, Affrica had already added hot water to her bathwater eight times. She finally stood up, her wet skin glistening. She took a quick shower to wash off any excess soap.

She quietly brought the radio back into her room and dressed in warm pajamas. She laid her head on her pillow, waiting for the luxurious smell of Alex to envelop her. Since they had made love on her bed she could smell his clean smell when she sat or lay on the bed. When she took a deep breath and the stench of Delroy was all she could find, she finally cried.

Twenty-two

Weeks after the proposal, Affrica was still attempting to return to normal life. She struggled to put Alex into the back of her mind, but she could not, as much as she wanted to. She lied to herself outright, about not giving a damn about Alex. She wanted to bury all the feelings, thinking they had only really liked each other for a few weeks and they had only made love six times. That wasn't enough time for someone to get under your skin. But when she closed her eyes, there was his beautiful face, his hair under her palms, his strong shoulders, his naked chest crushed against her breast.

On top of all the work she had to do, Delroy had enrolled them in a two-hour-a-week, relationship counseling session. She had been so flabbergasted when he told her that she just stared at him.

Affrica was in a meeting with Ramona. This was their first closed-session meeting since the proposal. Affrica had been avoiding all of Ramona's phone calls and they had only spoken business if they happened to find themselves needing something from each other. They were in the conference room and had completed six out of the ten agenda items.

"Billy said the model was done, complete with toy cars in the parking lot," Ramona said.

"I'm having some real problems with the budget. I was doing pretty well up until I got to 1996. None of my numbers are balancing."

"Really? Did you ask Max about it?"

"He said he wasn't the one who calculated the budget that I have. It couldn't be inaccurate, could it?" she asked sincerely.

"I don't know, Affrica," Ramona said stone-faced.

Affrica thought about it a moment, then let it go.

"Why haven't you been answering my phone calls, Affrica?"

Affrica looked up from her notes and sighed. "Because I know you love the happy endings and I'm sorry, but Alex and I are not going to be a happy ending."

"Why not? Why not be with the person you care about, or at least the person who doesn't disgust you?"

"Delroy doesn't disgust me."

Ramona rolled her eyes at Affrica. "Honey! What are you doing? Why on earth would you say yes to Delroy?"

"Because, Ramona, he claims to really care about me and I have to give him a fair shot."

"What! Since when do we give any loser who comes around 'a fair shot'? If we gave everybody a 'fair shot' you would have six kids. Give me a break, Affrica. Treat me like the adult that I am and tell me the truth please."

Affrica was thoughtful. She took a deep breath. "I cannot be known as the mayor who dumped one chief for the next chief." She placed her hand on

Ramona's lighter hand. "As a woman of color, you know how they stereotype us as the hot ones, as the ones always ready for sex. The press is going to drag me down."

"You don't expect me to believe this is all about the press. . . . Who cares what the press says? You will be judged by the work you did, not who you slept with."

"They will reduce it to that. Anyway, Ramona, Alex and I . . . we, we weren't going to go anyway. We didn't even know each other that well and we had sex . . . it was a physical thing."

Ramona shook her head. "Listen, Affrica, I may act like you guys, but I am an old woman. I'm forty-six years old and I have no kids and I'm not married. I live with regret day in and day out." She moved closer to Affrica, who was staring at her so intently she didn't blink. "I know what it's like. You feel like this is where you prove yourself, this is where everything you've learned in your life comes to a head. Wrong." She lifted a finger. "That's wrong. The real moments are years from now, when you're rocking Delroy's spawn, wondering what Alex is doing, what his children look like."

Affrica clenched her jaw, as her stomach lurched. She felt a sob try to make its way up her throat, and she pushed it down with all her strength. She cleared her throat and sat back, away from Ramona's gaze. "Delroy and I are going to try to build a real relationship. We're going to counseling."

Ramona quickly looked at her papers. "Okay, Affrica, forget it. Just forget it. Agenda number seven: Appointing Chantay Miller as the spokesperson for the rebuilding of Irving Housing."

"Yes, she should be appointed the head. So we'll work together on it."

* * *

Affrica knew Ramona was right, but she didn't want to bring any more negative attention to the office. Plus Delroy wasn't that bad. He was cute, he dressed nice, he seemed to really care about Affrica.

Ramona knew if she failed to convince Affrica not to marry Delroy that she was going to have to practice what she preached, tell Affrica what she knew about Delroy and the whole mayoral office. What would happen if she told would be ten times more negative than a silly affair.

Alex was not in denial. He understood without a shadow of a doubt that he was hurting. That was the only word he could think of when he thought how quickly everything had changed. One moment he was thinking how great it was that he could hold this woman and then the next minute she'd agreed to marry the next man.

That entire week Alex had to have done at least a thousand laps at the pool. He had a permanent chlorine smell and he didn't care. He cut through the water quickly, not stopping till his muscles screamed and he could no longer move. He couldn't believe it. Just like that she was gone.

He threw himself into work and finally told the police commissioner to leave him alone. The cop that Alex had refused to reinstate in the department was back. After Alex had fired him for selling drugs, he had gotten a job with the Ann Arbor Police Department. But then he had been fired by that department, too, for making a woman strip her clothes in thirty-degree weather, then making her walk home, while he followed her in his patrol car.

The commissioner had come to Alex's office to tell him, "Alex, I'm reinstating Palaski."

"Over my dead body," Alex said clearly. No way on God's green earth would Alex let that happen.

The commissioner tapped the man on the shoulder. "He's cleaned up his act."

"Cleaned up his act? He just made a woman walk naked in thirty-degree weather and you want me to let him in my department?"

Alex pointed to Palaski and said, "Listen, you little bastard, I don't know what you have over the commissioner"—Alex pointed to the older man—"but you don't have anything over me. You get the hell out of my face or I will arrest you for trespassing." His voice rising an octave. The entire police precinct was looking at the three men. Palaski looked from Alex to the police commissioner. He left the office quickly, realizing he would never work as a cop in Passion again.

The commissioner looked at Alex calmly. He smoothed back his hair, his hand trembling slightly. "Listen, boy—"

"Boy!"

"Oh, please, don't get sensitive now." The man waved it off.

"Now, you listen, why don't you come out with it?" Alex lost his temper.

"You let my man back into his uniform. He's a loyal servant of the Passion police force!"

"No, he's an idiot that gets his jollies by making people do humiliating things. He's sick, and I swear if I see his face in here again I will arrest him!"

"Well, Alex, if you're not here to see him, that won't be a problem!"

Alex came around his desk. "Are you threatening me?"

They stood eye to eye.

"You hear what you want, just have Palaski back in by tomorrow." The commissioner made a move to leave.

"You are a crooked wimp and I quit." Alex told the commissioner to get out of his office and he did.

Alex stayed in his office for two hours, and when he exited, he shook hands with his officers and left the station. *I'm done with that mess.* He spat on the ground at the foot of the precinct steps and drove out of the parking lot calmly.

I just quit the force.

"Yo, man!" You lose your job and you lose your lady in less than a month. Are you crazy? Nah, you ain't crazy, Commissioner Nelson is nuts, that mayor is nuts," Patrick said vehemently.

"She's not nuts."

"Wait, you're defending her after she leaves you for that zombie-eyed knucklehead?" Patrick grabbed a handful of popcorn and pressed PLAY on the movie. Patrick claimed that he would come over and cheer Alex up. He bought a six-pack of beer, two bags of microwave popcorn (he didn't like to share), and the movie *Commander Fighter Six*.

Alex was silent, holding in any and every emotion he had. He refused to talk about her. He was still too upset to say too much about her. Patrick didn't bring her up again. But Alex thought about her. He thought about the horrible mess that used to be his life. He couldn't even figure out where to begin. So he sat with his friend and watched *Commander Fighter Six* and didn't talk about the two life changes that had happened to him.

Alex had not been ready for Affrica's leaving him. He had felt her so deep inside him. He'd never met another woman who had so much in common with him. The fact that she was holding such a large office at such a young age. The fact that he was a police chief before he was forty. It was unheard of. Yet they both had done it. Broken all the rules, shaken up the system. But she wasn't meant to be. He had to get it through his head. Her work meant more to her than he did, and you know what? Who could blame her? They hadn't known each other long. He had been so suspicious of her and she of him. They had argued all the time and all of a sudden they expected that just because they had made love a few times it would all be okay. All the negative feelings were gone. But they were gone, for Alex. He wondered if those negative feelings were ever there. If they were just cloaks to cover up this attraction they had for each other. The irresistible draw.

He realized with a start that, with all his military and police training, nothing had prepared him for the hurt that he was currently feeling. With his gun, his accreditation, his large title, he still was a vulnerable man. And that shook Alex to his core. He did not like feeling out of control the way he was feeling. He couldn't arrest Delroy. He couldn't arrest the police commissioner. What would he do?

He buried himself into the folders he had. The sarge was keeping Alex informed on all that was going on.

The guys at his station would come by and talk with Alex. Most of them were putting pressure on the commissioner to have Alex reinstated as the police chief and they all refused to allow Palaski back into the department. Alex was proud of his men.

* * *

Deon Plant came to see Alex. He gave Alex a pound and sat on his couch.

"Chief, I'm getting word on a huge deal about to happen."

"Jay Blow is involved?"

"Yeah, man. But this one is different."

"How?"

"It looks like it's such a big deal the big boss man is coming into town."

Alex was thoughtful; he still had his guns. "Do you have a date?"

"Not exactly, just a code number."

"How about a place?"

"Just a code number."

"Give me the codes. I'll try to decipher them."

"Were gonna get them, Chief. You'll be back in a minute, runnin' things again."

They had a beer and Deon left.

Twenty-three

"Yo, we gonna make a huge grab tomorrow."

The Bloodhounds were once again in the warm laundry room. The group was listening to Jay Blow explaining the state of affairs. The young men were going to be lookouts for this, the largest crack cocaine deal ever made in Passion. It was also going to be made by the man himself. The cops that Watson had working for him didn't even know about the deal.

They had Tommy Weed guarding the door. No one crossed him. Chantay rolled her eyes at him when she saw once again the guys were having some meeting and she couldn't wash her child's clothes.

She hadn't heard anything from the mayor ever since she had that proposal.

How embarrassing for her. How can she like him? He's so greasy looking. Chantay shrugged her shoulders and went up to her sister's house.

It was a large two-bedroom apartment. All the windows of the apartment were open, cold air mixing with excruciating heat. People in the house walked around in undershirts.

"Girl, your apartment's hotter than mine. I didn't think that was possible."

"I can't wait to get the hell out of here."

"I'm saying, though, I couldn't even wash Kysha's clothes. I'm gonna have to go down the block."

"Did *Max* call you?"

"Girl, I am not a fool. After calling him three times and him not returning my calls, I am done. I'm not sweatin' anyone. I don't care if you work for the mayor or the pope."

"He was fine as hell though."

"Yeah, and he was old enough to be my father. So?"

"Older men are so sexy. Look at . . . what's his name? Darth Vader . . . Um." Erica thought about it.

"Oh, you mean James Earl Jones?"

"Yes. Oh, girl, every time I hear his voice I get goose bumps."

"He's okay. You like these old dudes, yet you marry a man five years younger than you."

"Girl, that was my mistake."

"Yeah, right, you know you love his young butt. Isn't he just now reaching his sexual peak?" Chantay whispered mischievously.

Chantay's sister patted her head. "I think they did these braids too tight. They itchin', girl."

"Did you oil your scalp after?"

"I forgot. I always forget." Erica pounded her head.

"Girl, you gonna bust your head open."

"I'll be back." Erica went to the bathroom to get her scalp oil.

Chantay surveyed the apartment. Erica did what she could, but through no fault of her own the place was run-down. There was electrical tape holding closed electrical sockets. Certain parts of her ceiling were sagging. Most of the polyurethane had peeled off her floor, leaving them dull and dusty.

Erica was a bus driver, and her husband pulled night duty at the airport cargo hanger. They worked hard, yet they could never seem to save enough to get out of the Projects. Something always came up that taxed their measly savings. The car breaking down, school uniforms, supplies.

The same went for most of the citizens of Irving Housing. Most people worked blue-collar jobs, their regular hours being much longer than eight. They all had their dreams and hopes for life. But somehow they got lost in the daily grind.

Ms. Johnson, the nurse, was so tired most of the time she could barely see. She worked at two hospitals. She had two children in day care and her husband was down South for a high-paying job building roads in New Mexico. He sent her money to help. Mr. Jiminez, with two sons, one in prison the other diagnosed with ADD, worked as a janitor in one of the large high-rise buildings across the river in Chicago. He spent $200 a month on the medication for his son.

"Mommy, mommy!" Kysha ran out of her cousin's room.

At the same time, Erica came into the room, massaging the oil deeper into her scalp. Even though it was hot in the apartment, Chantay loved visiting here. She usually spent a lot of time here.

"I can't wait till you live right upstairs from me or downstairs," Chantay said.

"I know." Erica touched her sister's knee with a greasy finger.

"Hey, watch that."

"Sorry."

"Come." Chantay beckoned her sister to sit on the floor. "I'll do it. You always put on too much."

Kysha stood watching them. "Mommy, we gonna move soon, right?"

"Yes, baby, as soon as we can."

"Good, 'cause I don't like the peepee smell."

"What peepee smell is that, sugar?"

"The peepee smell that in elevator the stairs it's nasty," she said matter-of-factly and ran back into Jamal's room.

The sisters looked at each other. "Man, it shouldn't be that way. A four-year-old understands how nasty it is to pee in someone's elevator or someone's stairs, but them people who do it can't. They want to live in a place that smells like urine."

Erica shook her head too. "It's not like they don't live here. They live here too. They have to smell that foul stench every day knowing that they contributed to the odor. I don't get it either."

"When we get our house ain't nobody gonna pee nowhere near our crib. We gonna have a backyard!" The women screamed and then burst into laughter. Both children ran out to see what all the noise was about, then realized it was adults acting stupid and went back into the room with their Leggos.

Jamal said, "We moving soon."

"No more pee smell anymore," Kysha said happily. They laughed and screamed like their mothers. They continued to play their games as their mothers contemplated a better life.

Twenty-four

It was nine in the morning. Ramona was at the office and Affrica was in a closed meeting with the Housing Department. This was her third pitch. They kept telling her that what she was trying to do was impossible, but she met alone with them, and even Ramona was left out of the critical meeting. Affrica was on her own. Before Affrica had gone into the meeting, Ramona had briefed her, and even though their friendship was a little rocky they worked well together.

She stepped out of her office. "Hold all my calls please," she told her secretary.

She went back to her desk and dialed the London number. She listened to dead air for about five seconds and then she heard an unfamiliar ring.

"Good evening."

"I guess it's evening now, huh?" Ramona said.

"Oh, I know that tinkly voice anywhere. Hello, Ramona."

"Hey, Holly. How are you?"

"Girl, I am so tired of this cold, wet weather. What is it like over there?"

"Cold, wet weather. It's doing a rain, snow thing outside."

"Michigan winters. I can't say I miss that. So what do I owe the honor of this call to?"

Ramona's heart was pounding. She took a deep breath. "Holly, you are one of Affrica's best friends."

"What, something happened to Frica! What happened?"

"No, no, nothing happened to her." She heard Holly sigh. "I have to tell you something."

"Hold on, this sounds serious." In London, Holly closed the door to her bedroom; she had a few friends staying over at her flat. "Tell me, Ramona."

"I messed up bad, Holly."

"Can't be that bad. No one died and you're not in prison."

"Yet."

"Yet? Oh no, what is going on?" Holly sat hard on her futon.

"Hold on."

Ramona opened her door quietly to see if anyone was behind it. She closed it and walked quickly back to the phone. She told Holly the entire story from beginning to end.

Holly did not make any immediate judgments, just asked questions, trying to see where things currently were. "Are you going to tell her?" she said calmly. But she was seething.

"I don't know, Holly." Ramona twisted a lock of hair painfully around her index finger.

"You must tell her and soon. If she finds out any other way and later finds out you knew, she will hate you. If you tell her now, she'll be hurt and upset, but soon she will find it in her heart to forgive, because you were honest with her." Holly felt really troubled about the current state of affairs in her friend's life. She was trying to figure out if she should call now or after. After.

"Ramona, what you've just told me doesn't even sound real. It sounds like some movie. How the hell did you get yourself caught up in this? And Affrica knows nothing?"

"She knows something is wrong. She's been deciphering the budgets, and the treasurer is giving her the runaround. He refuses to give her a straight answer on anything."

"He's in on it?"

"Yeah, I think. I don't really know who is doing what. But since he does the books he has to be in on it. I slept with him," Ramona confessed.

"Oy ve! Ramona! Why the hell did you sleep with him?"

"I think I have a problem."

"You slept with this man you suspected was helping the old mayor embezzle. You didn't tell someone who was supposed to be your friend the truth of what she thought was an honest boyfriend. You have written proof that the old mayor is stealing money from the budget and buying drugs probably and you are not getting anything from him to keep quiet. What's he got on you? Naked pictures. Were you a stripper at some point in your life?"

"Touché, Holly." Ramona was on the brink of tears. She would get no coddling from Holly. "He had a picture of me involved in a ménage à trois. He has pictures and a video. I don't know how he got it, but he did. He threatened to expose me," she whispered.

"Expose you! Hell, what is exposure when you're talking about somebody's life? I hate Delroy and I swear if I knew anything shameful about him, I would have told Frica in a second." Holly was upset. "You have to make this right, Ramona. She cannot marry Delroy. You have to quit. All those people in there who know about Watson and his crazy business need to be found and fired. Everything needs to be put on the table."

"I should quit?" That thought had not even crossed Ramona's mind. She thought somehow she would get to stay and be there with Affrica. Help her through. She told Holly.

"Are you kidding? You'll be lucky if she doesn't spit in your face. Do you realize what you've done? Do you realize the countless lives you've ruined?"

"Stop, Holly, stop." Ramona was hysterical. She sat on the floor of her office behind her desk. She was sobbing and she didn't want anyone to hear. She reached for the remote for her radio and aimed it and pressed PLAY.

"Ramona, I know you called me to hear the truth and I'm giving it to you. I am pretty disgusted with you myself. But I see you're remorseful, you're trying to find honesty in all this, and I admire you for that. But you lied to my best friend, you led her on and made this terrible joke on her, and that makes me mad."

"Holly, I am so sorry."

"I'm not the one to say sorry to, love, but if you don't tell her in the next few days, I'm going to tell her myself."

"What should I do, Holly?" She sniffed and wiped her eyes. Her eye makeup was all over her hands and her face.

"Tell her—"

"I gotta go." Ramona turned down her radio and listened—she swore she had heard somebody turn her doorknob. Her heart was beating wildly in her chest. She got up from under the desk and opened the door. Nobody was there, but when she looked down, an envelope was at her feet. She quickly picked it up and locked her office door. She sat at her desk and opened the envelope slowly. The infamous picture was staring up at her again. There was a Web address under the photograph: www.blackwhores.com. Under that it said *Password: Ramona.* She went to the Web site fearfully, her throat so dry she couldn't swallow. She thought she might just choke. When the page opened it was completely black, nothing but a place that said *Enter password.* She looked down at the password written on the picture. Her name. With shaky hands she typed the familiar letters in and inside were about twenty more dirty pictures of her, plus a streaming video. The writing said *You talk. We launch.*

They would launch this Web site if she said anything. How did they know?

Twenty-five

Delroy held the heavy leather bag firmly. He walked through the plane terminal quickly. The bag would be waiting at the baggage carousel. The deep-accented voice had told Delroy the ticket number over the phone, and he knew the flight number. Delroy had relayed his own series of numbers, the bag with the money, the money for the crack cocaine he was carrying through Chicago International. The flight number was 675 from St. Gantella, Italy, a very small village where the main business was the creating of crack cocaine for the United states. Tivo Baldichi was August Watson's supplier. He charged a good wholesale price that even with loss or theft made the difference up at the end. August used to take money out of the budget as if it were cookies in a jar. He didn't understand all of it, but he knew somehow Maxwell could make the bank statements and balance sheet not match up.

Maxwell had counseled the mayor on the way the money could be wrongly budgeted. A crooked mayor in Wisconsin had schooled him on how to open accounts in different ways. His Italian contacts had told him how he could get rid of people who didn't go along with his ideas and plans.

August was told to be sloppy and hire women who had checkered pasts—ex-strippers, women who've been in jail, single mothers who get no child support. He knew that, though women were nosy, if they were desperate to keep their jobs or position, they would go along with practically anything as long as you didn't expose them or their family to their past. So August stole the money easily, never thinking he would get caught eventually. He thought he was invincible, as he had up till then stolen so much money so sloppily he was actually waiting for someone to catch him, but no one ever did, because of Maxwell Townsend's sheer genius with numbers and money laundering, computer hacking. They would steal the money to buy drugs. Then they would siphon most of the money off, and after they sold the drugs and made more money they would put most of the money back.

This last purchase was the largest loan August had taken from the city budget. Maxwell and some hoe had managed to get enough money to buy thirty-five pounds of crack cocaine. Once August made a profit from his sale of these drugs he would give Maxwell the okay to put it back into the city's budget.

He had hacked fifteen bank computers, adding three new names into their account holder list, and Maxwell had delivered the money from the budgets legally with an account that never existed before he put it in. This was what a Yale education bought. His one weakness was the ladies. He would drop anything for a date and a chance to get lucky. Since he was handsome, he could get a date any time he wanted, so as he got older he became more discerning and learned to balance his evil genius with the pursuit of the right woman. He was married once already to a woman with moral issues and thus refused to help him in his embezzling. He knew she wouldn't say anything to anyone.

Today August was going to do his own delivering. He wanted to be in the trenches; he wanted excitement. He was very stoned, having just taken three LSD tablets. So he told Delroy to get the bags himself.

Delroy wasn't ready for August's new level of foolishness and questioned him on it. "Sir, why don't we send an officer to collect the bags?" Delroy knew a black man with a bag was likely to be stopped and frisked no matter how expensive his suit was.

"Sir, we could even send Jamie to the site to pick it up."

"No, no, I want you to pick it up. That way I can worry about you and then when I get it I could drive and give it to Jay Blow." Watson was on some of the drugs his boys sold for him. He had strange ideas that people went along with but never really understood. Though everyone was against this new thing and afraid of where it was going, they sadly had to depend on Delroy to pull Watson out of his *Mission: Impossible* mode. No matter what Delroy said about safety and about getting caught, August didn't care.

He had piled up the bags of the cocaine on his dining-room table. He told Delroy they should speak in code and have special rings when they called each other by cell phone. All the things he told them would bring more attention to them than lessen it.

Delroy's heart was beating so fast, he thought it

might just stop, and then he'd get caught with thirty-five pounds of cocaine. *Great.* It was a bright blue day as Delroy stepped out of the terminal. He had not seen the Italian man that was getting the money. Though they had never talked about meeting, Delroy was really curious as to what he might look like. But as he tried to stand around he realized he was a sitting target and left.

This is crazy, this is so foolish. Delroy had only gotten half of the money he was promised.

Luckily Delroy made it to August Watson's ranch in Meadowland Cove, a very affluent part of Passion. He parked his car deep into the garage and pulled the heavy bag out. While he was walking through the airport he couldn't let the police see that the bag was especially heavy or solid. He slammed the car door and found August on the phone. He went to the shutters and pulled them closed. Even though August's cottage was surrounded by trees and water, Delroy knew he couldn't be too careful. August had on a goosedown vest with jeans and large Timberland boots. He was talking to someone on the phone and didn't acknowledge Delroy's entrance.

Since when did he wear jeans? I've never seen this man in jeans, and why is he wearing that vest? This man has lost his mind. You never take your own product. He had to be taking drugs. He wondered if he could somehow talk August into putting some type of fund in his name. Delroy had a horrible feeling that wouldn't go away. He had to keep up this lie with Affrica.

He watched August pace the floor in front of him, chewing an unlit cigar. *What movie has he been watching?* He did not want to marry Affrica, nor did he want to stay another night with her, but all the money kept him there. He should have left with his $1.2 million, but Delroy chose to stay and steal and insert poison into his own community; he would pay the ultimate price later on. He watched his drugged boss. August had been Delroy's hero at some point in his life. August dropped LSD, snorted coke, smoked marijuana, and took a shot of Jack Daniels daily. He was operating through a veil of delusions and illusions. Before when he was mayor he only took coke and drank a lot, but since being out of office he'd been bored. Everyone was working for him and he had nothing to do. He took some acid onto his tongue and had decided to remain high every day for the past six weeks. His wife had left him after forty-three years, claiming she didn't recognize him.

August got off the phone. "We have a date and time for delivery. I want you to be my right-hand man."

Delroy thought about what August had just told him. "Sir, that doesn't make any sense. That puts both of us in danger. You would be better advised to send—"

"No . . . no, no, no! *We* are going to make the drop to Jay Blow. We're meeting him at the abandoned parking lot by the factory. At four P.M. we're bringing him six pounds and we're going to give him a forty-five percent advance and a fifty percent bonus if he can move all the units before spring."

"Sir, we're talking about six pounds of crack cocaine. That is a lot of little bottles to sell."

"That's between him and his drug addicts."

"But you realize one pound of crack cocaine leads to life imprisonment, but six pounds, sir, will mean . . ." He couldn't even finish. He imagined

himself serving six consecutive life sentences. He
had to come up with a sane plan. Maybe he
wouldn't show up to the drop. *August seems like he
wants all the glory. Maybe I'll just give it to him.*

Delroy was nervous and frustrated. He didn't like
the crazy look in August's eyes. *What happened to
him?* At some point Delroy had started to see August
as a sort of twisted father figure. Now he just wanted
to get the hell out, quickly. He knew this was a mess
and the whole thing was about to fall on his head.

August started throwing things into the black
leather bag. He was mumbling to himself.

But Delroy did not care what he was saying. He
stood up and walked away from August and started
making frantic calls. He called the airline and had
a ticket waiting at the airport. He did a large funds
transfer. He finally called Evelyn. A man answered
the phone. He thought he had the wrong number
till the man addressed him as Delroy and told him
to stop calling his *woman.* Delroy didn't even get a
chance to react.

While Delroy and August readied themselves for
the night's action, Affrica and Ramona sat in Affrica's large office, surrounded by papers. They had
drawings and laptops, so many papers Affrica felt
as if she might drown. They were discussing the preliminary steps to start moving the people out of the
infamous building 3. It would be the first building
destroyed, but the other buildings would remain
populated till they were ready to knock down the
actual structure. Also the abandoned factory, the
lot, and the park would all be demolished.

Affrica sat back in the leather chair. "This is really happening, even though building up Irving is

going to take some time, but we are there. We're so close. Now I just need to arrange a meeting with Maxwell about this messed-up budget. Housing's budget is all messed up. I understand he went to Yale, but I could not make heads or tails."

Ramona shook her head, not really interested in what Affrica had to say. She was distracted because she knew that right now was the time for her to tell Affrica the truth. She knew her life as she had known it was over, and she was preparing herself. She looked down at the yellow writing pad. She had written notes to herself. She looked at Affrica, the woman she admired and who was her close friend for the last few years.

"Affrica, I have to tell you something."

"Yeah, what's up?" Affrica did not look up from the desk.

"No, I really have to tell you something important."

Affrica looked up, not because of what she said, but how Ramona was saying it. She thought she knew what Ramona was going to tell her. "Are you pregnant, girl?" Affrica smiled wickedly.

"No," Ramona started bluntly.

Affrica's expression changed to concern.

"Affrica, I haven't been a true friend. I have to say this first, you have been the greatest friend to me. We worked so well together. I love you with all my heart. As a person and as a colleague it was never ever my intention to hurt you or keep anything away from you . . ."

Affrica stood up. "Ramona, what the hell are you talking about?" She was ready to run. Her palms were sweating. She felt her heart beating in her throat.

"I . . . I messed up, Affrica."

"Just say it, damn it!" Her voice was unsteady. "Spit it out!"

"I've been lying to you. I know something very bad about August Watson and I never told you. He's a crook, Affrica—"

"What do you mean crook? I mean he's not the trustworthiest man, but a crook? What are you talking about?"

"I'm talking about August stealing money. Cheating on the budgets. Treating the budgets as if they were his own personal bank." Ramona knew she had to keep talking. Affrica was shaking her head no. "He was and is. Delroy was in on it too."

With that, Affrica snapped her head to look at Ramona sharply. "What do you mean Delroy was in on it too?" she said slowly. Affrica's entire world was spinning. She sat down. She couldn't believe it. *Delroy?* Her Delroy was . . .

Ramona stared at Affrica. She had expected tears, grief, or something. Affrica just sat there looking dazed, as if she didn't fully comprehend what was going on. Ramona was thrown for a loop, so she decided to explain things one more time.

"Delroy is a scam artist. He used you to keep the power that August had. August was stealing money from the budget. That's why they are all in shambles. He's into some really crooked stuff. . . ."

As she continued, Affrica made no move to say or do anything.

Affrica was in her own head, thinking about Delroy. *It wasn't real? Our entire relationship. August tricked me into office so he could further his financial gain . . . I'm . . .* Her thoughts were unfocused. Then she thought about how she and Delroy had been a couple. *Right.* They had fought and got on each other's nerve, but they were a couple. *We made love.* None of it was real and she knew.

She looked at Ramona with unshielded disgust. She came around the desk, holding on to it for support. Her face was hot. The world seemed as if it were engulfed in flames. She focused on Ramona and felt as if she had finally found her. She scrutinized Ramona so openly hateful that Ramona started to weep.

"I'm so sorry! Affrica, I am so sorry!"

"You're sorry. You watched me . . . you helped me run for office, you . . . you . . ."

"I'm so sorry." Ramona got up from the chair. She couldn't stand being under Affrica's glare any longer. She faced her friend, who was no longer her friend.

"How could you do that? How could you let me make a fool out of myself?"

"Affrica you didn't make a fool—"

"I didn't . . . You watched me day in and day out dealing with Delroy and there was never a relationship to begin with! You watched me deal with August. You were supposed to be my friend. You three were really yucking it up about that young stupid mayor, huh?" She narrowed her eyes. "Were you sleeping with Delroy? Is that why you didn't tell me?"

Ramona was flabbergasted. "How can you ask me that?" But then she realized how easy it was to ask her that. Affrica just stood there staring into space. Shaking her head, Ramona wished she would say something. Yell, scream. But she just stood there blinking. Thankfully her phone rang. Affrica didn't budge. Ramona went around the desk and picked it up.

"Mayor Bryant's office."

"Ramona, it's Holly. You better have told her."

"Just now."

"Put her on the phone, now!"

Ramona placed the phone in Affrica's hand. "It's Holly." She stood a moment to see if Affrica would respond.

When Affrica heard her friend's voice on the phone, she turned her back to Ramona. Ramona left the office, but not before hearing Affrica start to weep.

"Are you all right, girl?" Holly's voice had released the flood that Affrica had dammed up. Affrica sobbed into the phone.

"Why would they do this to me?" Affrica cried.

"Listen to me, girl. They didn't care about you. They just wanted the money. They didn't care who they had to use."

"But . . . am I some kind of fool? Did they pick me because—"

"No. You're not a fool. Who would think that your man, *and* your old boss, *and* your friend would all be lying to you? You couldn't have seen it. Don't think that you are a fool."

Affrica cried silently.

"Affrica, they are gonna get theirs." Holly was doing her best to bring Affrica through the initial shock. "Don't worry about that. There is no way they are going to get away with this!"

"It hurts," Affrica said softly.

The two friends spoke for a long time. Though Holly could not remove the pain that Affrica was feeling, she helped her get a workable perspective on the situation.

Twenty-six

For the first morning in a long time Alex did not wake and immediately think of Affrica. He thought about his scar. It only itched whenever it was going to rain or something was about to go down. Alex jumped out of his bed, his bloodstream already filled with adrenaline. He didn't even want coffee. He got on the phone and his computer, and he looked at the code he had been studying the night before. He thought he got it last night but this morning he was sure he got it. He listened to Sarge as he went through the particulars of the day. *Longitude and latitude coordinates?* His military training had served him well.

"Sarge, I think I got it." But as he checked the coordinates over and over again, they were not co-ordinate anywhere remotely near Passion; all the ways he rearranged them, they came out in the Sahara, or in the middle of the Pacific, and one was the Tropic of Cancer. None it made sense.

"Sarge, forget it, I don't have anything. Keep me posted and Alex Palaski's back." He whispered, "We should keep this operation covert."

"No problem. Have Deon come by with a message."

"If I don't think of something in the near future I'll call and check to see if you guys did."

Alex went to swim. He knew there was a big drug deal about to happen, and he knew somehow Jay Blow was involved. They had one snoop at the Projects who came out with nothing. Even though that gang met in the laundry room, no matter how many times Alex had asked to get the judge's permission to put the room on surveillance or just bug it, he got rejected with the claim that the other people who used the laundry room would be bugged too and that was illegal without their expressed opinion. The judge had told Alex he would have to get the entire building to agree before they could bug the laundry room.

As Alex cut through the water like a torpedo, the entire time his mind was reeling, working overtime trying to figure out what those numbers meant. He read them over and over again to himself. The cold water and his burning muscles were exhilarating to Alex. He drove himself further, twisting and turning, swimming as if his life depended on it. His mind was clear and he waited for an answer. Waited for the hint of something to come like scent in the air. He finally rested, lying on the cold tile with his eyes closed. Tropic of Cancer was the first thing that went through his head, and he thought about it a moment.

Tropic of Cancer. It sounds so familiar. Beyond just being on the map, it's significant somehow. Alex took a quick shower and called the sarge.

"Hey, old man, does the name *Tropic of Cancer* mean anything to you?"

"Yeah, it does, it's that abandoned factory. You

think, Alex?" The man knew exactly what Alex was thinking.

"We have to be really careful about this. We can't just go in there with guns blazing. This will have to be quiet, me and you, Sarge. That's it, you're my backup. If it's where I'm thinking it will be, it's going to be hard as hell to get them, it's so isolated. They have tall grass for one mile on one side, a massive factory on the other side, a tall barbed-wire fence.

"We're going to do it." Alex added his leg holster and magnum revolver. He knew this would be it. He was done with the guns and bullets. He did not want to be a cop, though getting Jay Blow out of the drug business and out of Irving Housing would be the best thing. Jay Blow was a false supplier of nirvana. People who needed to escape their lives would go to him and he sold them the cure-all. Drug addiction. He thought people like Jamie were the scum of the earth, making money on people's weaknesses. *Isn't that what the world does? Make people think they need everything that's being sold⁻or somehow you aren't good enough if you don't own those jeans or those sneakers?* What Jamie did was no different, but the cost was a million times worse. Not just your money was lost if you bought into Jamie, your entire life was paid.

They decided not to take any of the undercover police vehicles, to bring their own cars instead. Alex brought a long-range rifle and binoculars. They drove casually to the highway around Irving Housing looking for cars, lookouts, or any of the young men who were arrested by Alex.

"I'm getting out," Alex said into his cell phone

to the sergeant. They would have to first overpower the lookouts, then catch Jamie in the exchange.

Alex crouched and began walking the path toward the abandoned factory. The fat one was the lookout here. Alex stayed crouched a moment, trying to figure out what he could do to get Little Man to fall down and not scream. If Alex got him from the back, he might fall on Alex and crush him. Alex crouched there like a ninja watching the fat back of this child. He realized he did not want to really hurt the boy even if he was running with this knucklehead. Alex would have mercy and not crack his skull as he originally thought he would.

Instead he stealthily crept up behind him, disarming him and dropping him in two quick motions. Little Man was a crying mess by the time he was handcuffed and in the pack of Alex's Jeep. Alex and Sarge then surrounded and toppled all of Jay Blow's "generals" in a matter of seconds. These were not mastermind criminals; they were all in fact regular young men in extraordinary circumstances. Poverty had dealt them a harsh hand and they needed help. Drug dealing and crime were their ways of asking for help, not prison.

Tommy Weed was the only one Alex had to rough up. He held his gun to Tommy's head and Tommy didn't flinch. He finally had to knock him in the head with the butt of the gun and even though he still managed to yell, "Five Oh, Five Oh," Alex and Sarge ran into the parking lot. They couldn't believe what they saw. They didn't hesitate.

While Alex and Sarge were tackling Jay Blow's boys, he and Watson were making the deal of the century.

Jay Blow had been wary of the plan from the beginning. When Jackson had told him where the drop was going to be, he told him to go back to Watson and tell him no and that they could do it steady, meeting periodically instead of doing the drop all at once. August had replied that if he didn't do the pickup, he wasn't going to get any more business from Watson, and August would have Jay put in jail for the rest of his life.

"August said, you be better off just doing it."

"Ai'ght, ai'ght. I'll do it. Just make sure he's clean. Make sure he ain't got nobody following him."

"Fine, we'll help with security," said the crooked cop.

"Yo, I don't trust ya'll. I'll do the security wit my boys. My generals." He looked at Jackson. He got closer. "Yo, why Watson wanna do such a big drop? Between you and me."

Jackson looked at Jay Blow sympathetically. "Boy, just do what he tells you and don't ask nothing."

Jay got to the pickup spot early. He commanded his men to disperse to the immediate area and make sure ain't no cops around. The Bloodhounds knew the lay of the land. They had searched the factory with flashlights, and had walked through the abandoned lot and seen nothing. The lot was filled with garbage. People used this place as a dumping ground for old mattresses and tires. A dead body had been found here once.

Jay had directed his men to stand in key areas so they would have the best views, but they would not be seen. His men were already complaining.

"It's cold as hell," Little Man had whined.

"Yo, Jay, I can't feel my fingers, man. Let me go to my mom's and get my gloves—"

"Shut up, ya'll! You proved to me that ya'll weren't punks. Ya'll even went to jail. This cat is the one that got ya'll out. Watson used his peeps at the courthouse to excuse ya'll and you complaining about some cold? Just get to your posts. And shut the hell up."

Mastermind, who had been quiet the whole time, stood looking at Jay.

"What's up? Get to your post, man."

Mastermind looked down. "This is stupid, man."

"I know you ain't challengin' me now."

"Yo, Jay, this is a dumb plan. We don't know jack about surveillance and guerrilla tactics. And he's about to give six pounds of crack. Yo, if you get caught . . . if we get caught with that, we are done. Life in jail."

"What are you sayin'?"

"I'm sayin' that I am out. I'm not doing this." Mastermind looked down again, brushing the ground with his large boots. His hands were deep in his pockets. He didn't feel good about challenging his friend but he knew this was a stupid deal.

"Then step off." Jay looked at Mastermind with venom in his eyes. The cap and hood he wore obscured his face. His eyes managed to convey his feelings.

The quiet rage that burned stayed with Mastermind as he made his way back home. He didn't think he would ever see Jay again.

It was quiet and still for five minutes. Then a Mercedes with its headlights off crunched its way through the tall grass and into the clearing. Watson was driving. He stopped the car as he got into the clearing.

Jay approached the car. Watson got out.

When Jay saw another figure in the car he reached for his gun, thinking *It's a setup*.

"Relax, it's just Delroy. He is not getting out of the car. You're doing business with me." Watson placed the bag on the trunk of the car. He was so stoned he could barely walk straight, Jay noticed, but he was used to dealing with people like that. He knew that they could be dangerous, but Jay just wanted to get the bag and go.

"That's for you," said Watson.

Jay stepped closer, his eyes moving from Watson to Delroy and back. The moment he put his hand on the bag, he heard Tommy Weed yelling.

Believing he was set up, Jay pulled his gun, ready to shoot Watson, but Watson was as terrified as he was. Jay spun around, waving his gun.

Watson made a dash back to the driver's seat of the car to find that Delroy had already scrambled into the driver's seat. Delroy threw the gearshift into reverse and left Watson covering his face from the rocks that the screeching car kicked up.

The bag slid off of the car into the grass at the edge of the clearing. Jay went for the bag and Watson scrambled.

Seconds later Alex and Sarge had emerged from behind the factory sprinting like cheetahs in the heat of the hunt. They saw Delroy drive away and Jay grabbing the bag. Watson staggered uncertainly into the tall grass.

Sarge went after Watson. Alex went after Jay.

Jay started to run for a precut hole in the barbed-wire fence, but he knew he would not build up enough speed to escape the blurring silhouette behind him. He changed his direction and sought cover behind a broken fridge.

Jay swung his gun around the right side of the
fridge and fired blindly. As soon as the gun appeared, Alex dove to the left, rolling toward the
fridge as he landed. He came to his feet a yard from
the fridge. He immediately pushed it and the fridge
toppled. Jay managed to dive free. Alex was in the
air before Jay hit the ground, and before Jay could
bring his gun to bear on his pursuer, Alex landed
on him.

One of Alex's knees came down on Jay's chest.
He thought he heard a crack when he landed.
Alex's other foot came down to stomp on Jay's gun-
hand. He stuck his gun in Jay's neck. The cold steel
was so shocking, Jay thought that he was cut with
a blade. In the darkness of the tall grass he
screamed and struggled under Alex's weight.

While Jay's left hand dug in the frozen dirt, his
right hand released the gun, and Alex immediately
kicked it away. At that moment Jay's left arm came
up with a handful of small pebbles that he flicked
into Alex's face.

Surprised with the sudden pain in his eyes, Alex
blindly tried to hold Jay down without shooting his
head off.

"Jay! Come on, man, don't make me shoot you!"

Jay punched Alex in the face, knocking him off
balance. Alex rolled away from Jay, while trying to
rub the dirt out of his eyes. But Jay pursued and
kicked the gun from Alex's hand. This gave away
his position, and Alex struck. First with a jabbing
side kick and then with an uppercut punch.

Jay landed on the grass ten feet away.

Alex could barely see through his stinging eyes.
He did not know where his gun was, but he remembered where he kicked Jay's gun.

Jay got to his feet and ran. He grabbed the bag

of drugs and bounded through the tall grass toward
the hole in the fence. Once he got there he slung
the bag over his shoulder and dropped to the
ground. He grabbed a small crumpled paper bag
that was resting at the side of the opening. Jay
pulled another gun from the bag. He didn't expect
to have to use it, but he was glad that he had prepared for a situation such as this. The word *genius*
shot through his thoughts. He held the gun in one
hand, and pulled open the fence with the other.

"Freeze. Put your hands in the air," Alex's voice
rang out.

"Damn!" Jay whispered. He turned his head
around to see Alex standing on top of the fallen
fridge, thirty feet away. *It's too dark,* Jay thought. *He
can't see my gun.* Jay turned his body around slowly,
then brought his gun up quickly.

The two shots were almost simultaneous.

Other officers with flashlights quickly emerged,
then came running when they heard the eerie two
shots. Both men lay on the frozen ground unmov-
ing. Sarge stood over Alex talking to him. He didn't
want to move him. He had no idea how hurt Alex
was. His heart was in his throat. *Not this one. Don't
take the good one.* He placed his hand gently on Alex's
form. He looked over at Jay Blow. His hood was
knocked off and his gun lay a few feet from his
hand. Someone had kicked it out of his hand. Jay
Blow groaned and startled the sergeant.

Watson had been captured easily enough. He had
fallen and couldn't get up. The sarge had to practically carry the handcuffed old man back out of
the tall grass.

The paramedics slowly placed a neck brace on

Alex and turned him over onto the gurney. Alex's face was drawn and his eyes were closed. They listened for his heartbeat, which was faint, and they took him to the ambulance. They were sad at this one. The paramedics had known Alex, and through their sometimes violent meetings they had become friendly. Their eyes were misty. In the warm ambulance they worked on Alex. He had a vest, they shouted, he had his vest. The men were buoyed and the second ambulance took Jay Blow to the hospital. The men who had been waiting anxiously for word shouted and went about securing the crime scene.

Affrica sat in her office sobbing. She didn't know about Alex yet. She couldn't believe what Ramona had told her. She hadn't spoken to anyone but Holly about it. Her world was over and she knew it. A veil of self-pity descended on her. *Why? Why would they do this to me? I never bothered anyone, I didn't even want to be the damn mayor. They convinced me to do it.* She was going to leave the mayor's seat. She felt that she couldn't do the job, not after such a scandal. *How could I ever show my face again? I'm a damn fool, a laughingstock.*

She heard commotion out in the hall, a few people running. She knew that people usual worked late at City Hall. She stepped out of her office, knowing her face was probably a mess, but she didn't care.

Her press secretary ran up to her. "August Watson has just been arrested for drug possession and a shoot-out happened between the police chief and another drug dealer." He ran out of the building.

"Alex," she said breathlessly. Ramona, who was packing her things when the news came down, was already in front of Affrica. "Come on. Come on, Affrica, I'll take you. Come on."

Affrica stood looking at Ramona suspiciously. She didn't think she could stand up for another blow. Ramona grabbed Affrica's purse and said her name loudly, snapping Affrica out of her trance. Affrica woke up and started toward the doors. She got into Ramona's car. She was counting. She knew she had to think of something or she would just lose her mind. The only thing she could think of was counting. Affrica felt as if her brain were going to explode. Her mind was racing. *Alex in a shoot-out. Alex in a coma. My Alex?*

But he wasn't her Alex. She had broken up the best thing she'd known, only to be engaged to a criminal. She had gone against her true emotions for political power. She felt as if she were just as bad as the rest of them.

Affrica pressed the button for the radio. They listened to the news in shocked silence. The male reporter said August was a drug addict and was attempting to deliver six pounds of crack cocaine to a petty drug dealer. Delroy had escaped from police custody somehow. They said Alex was in a coma after being shot. A cry escaped from Affrica's lips. Affrica was leaning forward toward the radio.

Ramona looked at Affrica's pain and felt nothing but remorse.

"Oh, Affrica, I am so, so sorry this had to happen. I'm so sorry. I never meant to—"

"Shut up! Shut the hell up!" Affrica shouted. She wanted to hear the radio report. She needed to know what was going on with Alex. She felt this was her only way. Ramona's mouth closed with a snap and she didn't say anything to Affrica for a very long time.

***

The press bombarded her the minute they drove up to the hospital. Everyone was talking at her at once. Foolish questions. They asked if she knew about August. Did he take drugs while she worked for him? "Where's Delroy?" they asked her. She sidestepped the questions, trying to make her way to Alex.

She greeted the officers who were in the waiting room. They were smiling, and she was relieved when they told her he was fine. She was led through a short hallway and she swallowed hard when the nurse patted her shoulder and left. She opened the door and saw the most beautiful sight she thought she'd ever seen. Alex was propped up on the bed chatting with a Latino man. Affrica looked at Alex. Both men looked up when they heard the door squeak open.

"Affrica!" Alex said happily.

She went to him. "What a mess this is, huh?" She was sitting on the bed with her head buried in his neck. Alex felt a deep sadness and relief. She began sobbing and Alex held her closely. Patrick left the room quietly. Affrica cried into Alex's shoulder for what seemed like forever, her body convulsing violently against him, causing his ribs to pound in pain. She finally lifted up her face and looked at him, her face wet, eyes red. Her teeth were chattering.

"Are you okay?" She quickly took off her coat and wiped her face. She grabbed a tissue off of the hospital nightstand.

Her life was put into prospective. While she was sitting in the car driving to the hospital with Ramona, she didn't really care anymore what the woman had done.

"Yes, I had my vest, and the bullet was lodged in it. It was centimeters from flesh." He took a deep breath. "I'll be a little sore for the next week and I just have a hard time catching my breath."

"We heard on the radio on the way here that you were in a coma and the drug dealer was dead." She looked at Alex softly.

He touched her hand. "I'm fine."

Alex had a large bruise on his ribs, which they had covered with a large Band-Aid.

"Alex, it's all a mess," she said tearfully. "Ramona was lying to me this whole time, it was all a big lie."

Alex sat back. "Yeah, I know, I heard."

"You heard? Ramona told—"

"No, Delroy was caught for a brief time and he spilled his guts. But somehow he got away. We don't even know how he got away, but he escaped from custody. When they had him, he gave numbers and names for shortened jail time. He gave up August too."

"Delroy." She was unable to cry or speak. She just sat on Alex's bed and shook her head.

Her head was down. She was so happy and so very sad all at the same time. Her beautiful face was filled with emotions. There were loud noises outside Alex's room, and she knew soon his room would be filled with people.

"I'm sorry, Affrica." He interrupted her thoughts.

"You're sorry . . ." She squeezed his hand. They were cold. She looked at him with worry in her eyes.

"I'm sorry, because I should not have let you go. I should have challenged you and whatever drove you to thinking you needed to marry him for some other reason besides love."

She leaned back on the pillow with him. "I've never felt the way that I did with you."

They held each other locked in an extended kiss. They didn't care who was watching, but the flash of a camera made them both look up to see that reporters had entered the room.

The expressions on the faces of the reporters revealed that what they just saw was a story just as unanticipated as the shooting.

Three days later

Affrica's doorbell rang and woke Alex from his nap on the couch. He heard Affrica open the door. He heard the surprise in her voice as the low-talking guest introduced himself.

"Yes, he is here. Please, come in." Affrica opened the door.

Alex sat up. *It's probably the sarge, come to pay me a visit.*

Alex rubbed the sleep out of his eyes. He did not hear the visitor enter the room.

"Hello, son," said Frank Bartholomew.

Alex stood up, shocked. "Dad? What are you doing here?"

"I'm sorry if I'm intruding," said Frank. "You're not an easy man to find. Well, yes, you are." Frank looked at Affrica.

Alex shot a frowning look at Affrica too.

She threw her hands into the air. "Hey, I didn't have anything to do with this."

Frank looked at his son. "Do you have a moment?"

"Sure. Do you want to sit out in the back?" said Alex.

"No, here is fine." Frank sat down.

"I've got something in the oven. Would you like something to drink, Mr. Bartholomew?" Affrica asked over her shoulder as she walked back to the kitchen.

Both men answered at the same time. Frank said, "Yes, please, water." Alex said, "Vodka, straight, please."

They stared at each other.

"You mother said to say hi for her," Frank began. "She had wanted to come and see you in the hospital but I assured her it was not serious."

I guess you thought that you were being practical. Why waste a trip to see your son just because he was shot? After all, he was wearing a vest. Alex's thoughts betrayed his hostile feelings.

Alex suddenly realized that he was showing his emotion on his face. He relaxed his muscles and sank into the chair.

"So, what are your plans, now that you are off of the force?" Frank seemed nervous to Alex. Alex had never seen his father fidgeting with his hands.

"I'm starting my own detective agency," Alex said without a trace of excitement.

Affrica entered the room holding a tall glass of water and a short empty glass. She handed Frank the water and tossed the other glass to Alex. "You know where the spirits are." She walked back out.

Alex stood up and walked to the liquor cabinet. They weren't big drinkers but did stock some wine for special occasions. He opened the cabinet, then stood there in silence for fourteen full seconds. He closed the cabinet, put the glass on the table, and sank back into his seat.

"Dad, I like who I am. I would love it if you accepted that I am not you. Nor do I want to be you . . . and I'm not Taylor . . . I'm Alex."

Frank stopped fidgeting and put his hands on his lap.

"But you know what? If you don't accept it, it's not really my issue anymore. I'm done with that. So you can say what you want about . . . Ah, I'll be right back." Alex left the room and returned with a tray of freshly baked cookies. "Here, try one. You don't know what you're missing, Dad. You will never know unless you wake up."

Affrica walked in with oven mitts on. "Uh, Alex, that tray is hot."

"What? Oh. Ouch!" Alex dropped the tray on the coffee table and blew on his hands. "Ouch!"

Affrica shook her head and picked up the tray. Again she left, giving Alex a frown as she exited the room.

Camelia heard the commotion and decided that she was not going to wait outside any longer. "I bet Frank didn't get even get down to business yet," she said as she walked up the two steps to Affrica's front door.

Alex saw the shadow that his mother cast across the entranceway. He poked his head out of the living room. "Mom? Mom!"

Alex looked at his father. "Why is Mom outside?"

"Because she wanted to give me privacy," Frank said.

Privacy? Privacy to do what? Alex thought. He noticed that his father's hands were fidgeting again.

Frank stood up. He faced Alex and took a deep breath. He lifted his hands and then dropped them to his sides. "I've been a monster, Alex."

Alex immediately felt hit with a wave of emotion. It caused him to lean on the inside of the doorway.

Frank wiped his forehead with his hand. His eyes were moist. "I wasted so many years. I'm sorry, son. I didn't know how to be anything else." At that moment, Frank Bartholomew was like a dam that could not hold back the sea anymore. A sound of primal sadness burst out of his mouth. Alex rushed to hold him up.

Affrica ran into the room. Alex and Frank were locked in a staggering embrace. At first she couldn't tell who was holding whom up. Then she saw Frank convulse with a deep sobbing. She touched Alex on the shoulder. He looked up at her, eyes wet.

"Please let my mother in," he said.

Affrica walked to the front doorway, confused. There was a woman standing there, looking very concerned. Affrica opened the door and the woman came in. She walked slowly toward the sound emanating from the living room. She stood there in the doorway. Affrica came to stand next to her. The two women held hands as the two men mourned lost time.

Epilogue

A year after the shoot-out and arrest of August Watson, the residents of Irving Housing Projects finally saw the construction begin for the new Irving Community Neighborhood Houses.

August's lawyers could delay the trial no longer. The judge that would be overseeing his trial was a woman well known for giving harsh sentences to corrupt officials.

After testifying in the trial that sent August to prison for life, Ramona overcame her own personal scandal and moved to Canada. She still works in politics and talks to Affrica occasionally.

Jay Blow is paralyzed from the neck down and resides at the Rickerfield Penitentiary Hospital. After months of deep depression and almost starving himself to death, he slowly started to interact with hospital staff using eye and mouth signals. He even agreed to be filmed as part of a documentary dealing with gang violence.

A homeless fugitive, Delroy made his way to New York, where he lives in a men's shelter. His new profession is washing car windows with a squeegee at red lights on Atlantic Avenue in Brooklyn.

* * *

Alex was right, Affrica thought, as she looked out at the exotic countryside. *Thailand is absolutely amazing.* She and Alex sat on the grassy hill near Hinsu's home. A farewell banquet had been arranged for their trip back to the city.

They had met many friends who then became family. It was not hard for Affrica and Alex to leave their cell phones and beepers in their suitcases. This last evening was filled with food, music, singing, and dancing. But mostly everyone had returned to their homes or fields. She and Alex would soon leave for the hotel in the city. They would stay there for the night and take the first flight out. But now it was their turn to say good-bye to the land that had hosted them.

Back to work. Affrica shook the thought from her head as a large butterfly flew circles around them. They were both wearing the loose, very lightweight, traditional Thai cotton shirts. She looked at Alex. She loved how his beard had grown out in the past few weeks. "You should keep this," she said, raking her fingers softly through his hairy chin.

"I might," Alex whispered, pressing his face into her neck. The sun was going down in a majestic display of color and light. It seemed that everything was alight with a burst of energy in the last moments of the sun's descent. Alex and Affrica both closed their eyes, each slipping a hand under the shirt of the other. They caressed each other's back. The fingers of their other hands interlaced. Their lips found each other and the warm sun kissed them both.

Own the Entire ANGELA WINTERS
Arabesque Collection Today